THE HOTEL MAN.
by
Garry Waite

All characters portrayed in this publication are fictitious; any resemblance to real persons, living or dead is purely coincidental except where real names or people have been portrayed for historical fact or dramatisation purposes.

All rights reserved. No part of this publication may be reproduced stored in a retrieval system, or transmitted in any form or by any means mechanical or photocopy, without written permission of the copyright holder.

ACKNOWLEDGEMENTS

Anton Mosimann OBE DL
for allowing us to use his name and reputation in a 'factional' way

Lydia Sweet
For background information of the Davico family

Sue Sharp - Monte Carlo Resident
for Historical and Present References

COVER CREDIT
Lynne Godfrey – Jigsaw Design

PHOTOS
Hotel Bristol Majestic Monte Carlo
(Anon)
Author's Photo: Jan Knight

ISBN: 9798563731523

Copyright © Garry Waite 2021

INTRODUCTION

In 1861, France accepted the existence of the Principality of Monaco. In exchange for the majority of its territory, France took on the responsibility of the defence of Monaco's remaining lands. In 1922, Louis II became the Prince of Monaco. While he was known to be strongly pro-French and had seen military service with Philippe Pétain, Louis II kept Monaco out of the war largely because the majority of the population of his principality was of Italian descent and was pro-Italy. In November 1942, Italian troops invaded the small neutral country and set up a puppet administration. When Italy signed an armistice with the Allies, German troops entered Monaco's borders. Monaco was home to about 300 Jews prior to the German occupation, and it was hosting an unknown number of Jewish refugees; some of them were deported to concentration camps. French troops returned to Monaco in late 1944.*

Before the war Monaco and especially Monte Carlo had been the chosen party venue for film stars, like Cary Grant, Audrey Hepburn, Marlon Brando, Alec Guinness, Bing Crosby and of course many others; even Winston Churchill used to go to gamble at the Casino. There were plenty of luxury hotels for guests to stay in, the Hermitage, The Metropole and the Hotel du Paris.

There was also the Bristol Majestic Hotel owned by my Great Uncle Mario Davico and his brother. It is said that this hotel was taken over by the Italians and the Germans, for billeting officers and for their HQ, while they occupied the Principality.

This story is 'facticious'; relying on some existing facts and imaginary fiction. It recounts the feats of many who lived and worked there during the occupations and the part some played in resistance fighting and the hiding and moving of Jews who had made, what they thought was their safe home in virtual paradise.

Most of the characters in the book are made up, although there are a few who were real and who played a part in history and based on research, are portrayed as accurately as possible within the confines of the novel.

I hope I have captured the atmosphere that existed during this time and that you will find the journey that some of our protagonists took, over a period of more than one hundred years, up until the years of the 2000's, interesting and heart warming.

Enjoy,

Garry Waite

*Thanks to ww2dbas

HOTEL BRISTOL MAJESTIC
MONTE CARLO 1925

HOTEL BRISTOL MAJESTIC COCKTAIL
BAR

PROLOGUE

Michael Nicolson adjusted his tie in the mirror, fluffed up his top silk handkerchief and did up the middle button on his very expensive pinstripe suit. He stood looking at himself for a minute or so to ensure everything was in place. His brown hair, with a premature tinge of grey on his temples, enhanced his already good looks. He had just turned forty five years of age: Here he was, in the recently opened, Royal London Majestic Hotel, the company's flagship; A five star luxury hotel in the centre of the city; two hundred rooms, with a budding Michelin starred restaurant, an eighteen hour brasserie and banqueting facilities for four hundred, plus a roof top pool and club.

After many years of hard work and some great management positions, he had been brought in on the ground floor to help design and implement the hotel for its opening in December 2004, just one month ago. Now, here he was, walking towards the door of his suite out into the hallway to start his first day as Managing Director of the hotel and the group.

His father and his uncle had worked hard to turn this old building into the exceptional hotel that Michael had helped create, design and inaugurate. His family, their work complete, had been hands on for the first month after the opening in December, but now it was time for their protégé to take the reins and make the hotel the success that everyone wanted. Head Office had moved from the Victoria Majestic to the Royal London Majestic so as Michael was on site.

"Good morning, sir" said the pretty chambermaid with her trolley.

"Good morning Maria," he said looking at her name tag. Despite recruiting most of the staff with his personnel manager from the beginning, with over two hundred staff, it was going to take some time to get to know all their names and with the transitory nature of the hotel industry he would be unlikely to complete that task. He went into the lift, meeting a room service waiter wheeling a breakfast trolley to one of the suites on that floor.

"Good morning sir," said the smartly dressed Indian waiter.

"Morning Rohan," said Michael once again using the name tag as a prompt.

The lift doors opened into the vast, elegant space of the lobby. The smell of luxury permeated throughout as the receptionists were busy booking people out and porters carrying guests' belongings on their familiar brass hotel luggage trolleys.

"Good morning Mister Nicolson," said the attractive reception manager a woman in her mid thirties. "Good morning Angela," he didn't need to see her name tag as he had been working with her pre-opening and with her blonde hair tied tightly back from her face and piercing blue eyes, she was unforgettable.

Alan Brooks, the front of house manager walked towards him and joined him on the walk to

Michael's office. "Morning sir, are we still on for the heads of department meeting at 10.00 am?"

"Yes Alan, I see no reason to change the format introduced at the end of last year with the opening team. Just because my uncle and father are not actually here, they know that we will continue as was — for the time being," he quipped.

"Can you ask someone to bring me some coffee and a *croissant*. We'll keep to the same routine for now Alan, let me have the Night Manager's report please."

CHAPTER ONE
Monte Carlo 1942

"Albert, veuillez entrer dans mon bureau, s'il vous plaît."

"Oui monsieur," said the young 'buttons*' as he followed his boss into the plush office where his father held court as Managing Director and co-proprietor of the luxurious Bristol Majestic Hotel in the principality.

"Albert, your mother and I have decided to send you back to Switzerland to live with your mother's family; it will be safer; we should never have allowed you to come back; it was my fault."

"But why sir," protested the 17 year old.

"Because I don't have to tell you there is a war on and the Italians are set to invade and take over Monaco. The German's also want Monaco; and I'm not sure which would be worst. But you will be safer there than here."

"But I thought we were a neutral state?" continued young Albert.

"Monaco is a strategic hold for both sides and while we are not at war, Mussolini is directing his forces towards us. He tried it in 1940 but was pushed back by the Germans, but since Prince Louis II has been collaborating with the Germans, the Italians want to control us.

*Buttons: a junior bell boy/porter.

It was raining in November, when the sound of tanks and overhead air support could be heard across the, normally tranquil beach side of Monte Carlo. There was no sound of guns just the trundle of metal on concrete as the war machines rolled over the peaceful coastal resort.

Albert was still there, there hadn't been time to arrange his departure, but that suited him as he didn't want to go anyway. He was looking out over the *esplanade*, when he saw the troops making their way down the long stretch of beach side road. The lead car pulled up in front of the hotel entrance and a fat, Albert naturally presumed, Italian, got out of the car and walked into the foyer. He rushed down stairs in time to see the officer and his entourage walk toward the reception. In perfect French, he asked the receptionist if he could speak to *Monsieur* Richard Nicol. Albert's father came out of his office. The Italian officer proffered his hand in a gesture of *bon homie* which the hotel director reluctantly accepted.

Presenting him with an envelope the officer said, "By order of El Duce, Benito Amilcare Andrea Mussolini, Prime Minister of Italy and leader of the Italian armed forces, I hereby take control of your hotel to establish headquarters for our work here and as a billet for my officers. I hope we will cause as little disturbance as is feasibly possible. You are very welcome to continue catering for your normal guests but we will require total facilities for us and please keep a record of all our expenses as this will be paid for by the Italian War Government."

'Fat chance of that,' thought Richard, but he had little choice.

The next few months passed peacefully, in fact it seemed a very strange experience having all these officers wandering around the hotel even though they took advantage of the staff — especially the young women — but the younger officers were good looking and almost charming, meaning that the girls were not put off: Fraternising with the enemy, however was frowned upon. They even joined in with the New Year's Eve celebrations at the hotel although it seemed incongruous to welcome in a 'Happy New Year' under the circumstances where nobody really knew what the future was to hold!

With the sudden disappearance of some of the senior porters, rumour had it that they had been arrested and deported to Germany for being part of the French resistance which had now appeared in the principality due to what seemed to be an imminent threat from the Germans, let alone the existing threat of the Italians, Albert had been promoted to second head porter. Not that startling really as there were only four left and the number of visitors had dropped considerably; after all people were not clamouring to stay at 'Mussolini's Headquarters' except of course Italian tourists.

Albert was out with his waiter friend, Pierre, for a drink in the harbour area when they were joined by a couple of friends from a neighbouring hotel. They were discussing the situation regarding the Italian occupation and the threat posed by the imminent arrival of the Germans.

Charles told Pierre and Albert that he and his friend Georges had met some interesting people who had asked them to join their political group and suggested that the boys went with them to meet their new found colleagues.

They entered a smoky bar in the backstreets of Monte Carlo frequented by the more dubious residents of the up and coming fashionable resort.

"*Bonsoir Messieurs,*" said Charles as he approached the table of a good looking couple, 'in their early thirties', thought Albert, drinking *pastis.* *"*ce sont les amis dont je vous parlais.*"

"*Bonsoir mon amis,*" replied the man extending his hand ***"*je m'appelle René et voici ma collègue, Esther.*"

"*Enchanté,*" said the boys together.

"Your friends Charles and Georges said that you may be interested in joining our little group" said René lighting up a *Gitanes* which he offered to the young men who accepted.

"Would you like a drink?" asked René indicating his *pastis.*

"A beer please," echoed the two boys. René raised his hand to the barman and said,

  *These are the friends I was telling you about
 ** I am René and this is my colleague Esther.

*"*deux pression s'il vous plaît.*"*

"So are you both French patriots despite living in Monte Carlo?"

The boys nodded in unison although at this time Albert was not admitting to his English, German and Italian heritage: But being fluent in the three languages, plus his native French, was helpful.

"You are aware," continued René taking a sip of his aniseed drink and a further drag on his *Gitanes,* which he seemed to inhale down to his boot straps, "that France and its allies, is at war with the Germans and the Italians?

Once again the boys nodded their comprehension although both would have to admit that their true understanding was limited.

"You know that the Italians are occupying the Principality at the moment but it will not be long before the Germans come in. You also probably know that the Italians tried to occupy Monaco in June 1941 after they had declared war on France. When the Germans occupied France in May 1940, they were careful to leave Monaco alone as they wanted Monaco to remain a centre for German international banking and commerce, something they first started building towards in 1933. Therefore when Mussolini and his troops declared war on France a month later and marched troops into Monaco, they were forced to retreat by the Germans."

He took a breath and another mouthful of his drink and a draw on his cigarette.

Two draught beers please

*"*Deux pastis de plus, s'il vous plaît,*"* again, beckoning the barman.

He continued, "We are not so much afraid of the Italians, as they are not warriors more followers, after all it is said that they have one forward gear on their tanks and three reverse," he smiled at his own jibe, "our problcm is the Germans. Although the Germans occupy the north of France and the Vichy army, under the control of that old fart Marshall Petain, with whom our esteemed leader Prince Louis II has had to co-operate with while taking orders from the German high command and seek out all Jews, including German and Austrian. He did this in a Royal Decree in July last year saying that all Jews had to register with the government. Many have already been deported, especially the German and Austrian Jews who came to Monaco to escape the Nazis. Those Jewish nationals of Monaco were given false papers by Louis but the others who arrived here have not been afforded that protection. Those are the ones that we have to watch out for."

The barman brought two more *pastis* and asked the boys if they wanted two more beers, they accepted.

"So?" asked Albert, "while the history lesson was welcome," he said somewhat sarcastically, "what has that got to do with us?"

René gave a knowing smile, "Esther and I work with the French resistance: A group of people that try their best to disrupt the lives of the Italians

Two more pastis please

and the Germans. As I said the Italians are pussycats compared to the Nazis but we reckon they will come here by the end of the year; we need to be prepared; so we want people from everyday walks of life to join us in helping destroy the enemy from within."

"If, and it's a big if, we decided to join you, what do you think we can do? After all, we are still kids really," said Albert with a nodding Pierre beside him.

"Don't worry, you will not be asked to shoot people or blow them up — not yet — but your work means that you are in constant touch with the enemy at your hotel; therefore you will hear things that might be of help."

"But we don't speak Italian — or German," said a forlorn Pierre.

"I speak both — and English," said a retiring Albert.

There was a silence around the table as everyone took in this information. A huge smile came over René and Esther. *"*Incroyable, quelle trouvaille*," said René, ecstatic with the news. "Then we are going to have to get you started. We will explain what we want and teach you how to get messages to us as you cannot be seen to be meeting with us or anyone outside of your existing circle of friends in case the secret police start watching us all. Do you play football?"

 "Sorry?" replied Albert.

"Join the local amateur team that meet every
Incredible, great job!

Saturday afternoon. There you will find your contact. He will liaise with you about your work. We will go into more detail later, but at the moment, *mes amis*, drink up. You are about to become part of the war effort against the forthcoming invasion of the Nazis."

"That's all well and good," said a confused Albert, "but I can't always get Saturdays off."

You can always do your best," replied René.

―⸘―

Despite his apparent dishevelled appearance René Borghini was no street fighter, he was Secretary of the Presidency of the National Council and a leading member of an intelligence network, that worked with the resistance in France and the Principality, while, his compatriot, Esther Poggio was his liaison officer. From a wealthy, well respected Catholic family, René had no need to get himself involved with the resistance, as he would have been above suspicion, but his love for France and especially his beloved Monaco, where his family were held in great standing meant his sense of duty was immense. They, and many others, were to become an important part of Albert and Pierre's life for the foreseeable future.

"*Alors ma chérie qu'est-ce que tu en penses?*" asked René to his right hand as they left the bar.

"I'm not sure, they are very young," replied his liaison officer.

"Easier to mould, and after all you are the *liaison*"

  So my dear, what do you think?

he smiled, as they walked down the lantern lit streets to go their separate ways until the next time, "you will ensure that they are kept safe — as is possible."

CHAPTER TWO
London Majestic Hotel January 2005

"So please confirm what is on this month?" asked the new MD eager to get into his stride. This was his first solo heads of department meeting since the New Year. Although his position had not changed, normally his Uncle would be at the meetings, but now that he and his a father had handed the reins to Michael, he was on his own, although he knew they would always be there if needed. He also knew that he had to pull out all the stops to make sure that this hotel was going to be the best and the busiest in London.

"Nothing much out of the ordinary until Valentines Night on the obvious date this month, but the most important date for us is a few days before that. The Fifty Eighth BAFTAS on Saturday the twelfth of February" said Gregg Wilkins, newly promoted to general manager of the hotel due to Michael's appointment as MD. "We have the whole of the top floor split into dressing rooms and make up areas and organisers suites as requested. Occupancy is 98% for five days and then drops on the thirteenth to 75% and then back to 90% for St Valentines on the Sunday."

"Alex, what banquets have we got for this lot?"

"Thursday the tenth, a welcome cocktail for all the artists and organisers followed by the inaugural dinner; not everyone will attend. There are several

'A plus' celebrities that will be staying in their suites and other hotels."

Alex Rifkin was the Banqueting Director and had worked at the Grosvenor House Hotel before joining Majestic. He had been involved with the arrangements and menu for the banquet.

"What's the menu Alex, Chef?" asked the MD. Despite holding a Michelin star in his previous post, the young chef, Pierre Dupois was fairly old school, with a dislike for fads, diets and allergies!

"In order not to offend the new wave of foodista luvvies," he said akin to spitting out bad wine, "we have had to become adventurous with the dietary restrictions: Half the *canapés* will be vegetarian to pander to their delicate natures.

For the starters there will be a choice of *Ajo Blanco,* a Spanish almond soup or a an exciting *Caraway-infused carrot salad, with celeriac and spicy aubergine dip.* Main courses will be *cauliflower Wellington* and we have to cater for some normal people so we have *breast of corn fed chicken with a wild mushroom risotto.* Dessert will be a gluten free *sticky toffee pudding or fresh fruit salad*"

"Well done chef, what more can they want?" "Not more, just different" said the anglicised Frenchman with a sarcastic smile.

"All the butlers ready Raymond?" asked his boss.

"Certainly are sir," replied the 50 year old head butler who joined the hotel from the Dorchester at its inception.

"And Angela, any problems from your side?"

"I have one receptionist off which is a bit of a pain, but the others will have to cover the best they can."

"Good — porterage alright Alan?"

"Yes sir all shifts covered and everyone on for the five main days."

"Housekeeping OK Mavis?"

"Yes sir, we are bringing in a couple of extras to see us through the three days or so of the BAFTAS, but apart from that, fine. The flowers are all arranged as are the special requirements, you know, feather pillows, silk sheets, goose down quilts, hairdressers on call and all day hot and cold running chambermaids!" said the woman who had seen it all in her 25 years as housekeeper in some of London's best hotels.

"Right, well that's good — Susan," he turned to his secretary as the others were leaving.

"Arthur Radford is waiting to see you," said Susan. Arthur Radford had been the financial director of the company since 1983 who Michael had met when he was GM of the Nice hotel. He had been with the group for the best part of 40 years and had been instrumental in the development of the hotel on the financial side, with Michael.

"Well, we have got off to a good start have we not?"

"It would appear so," said Michael, maintaining a respectful tone in front of the bespectacled sixty year old number cruncher.

"Right then, there are a few things I would like to

catch up on if you have the time?"
"Of course Arthur, fire away."
"Great, let's get down to business."

The alarm went off at 6.00 am on a cold and miserable London morning in February 1985. The twenty five year old senior trainee manager got out of his single bed at the top floor of the hotel in Battersea where he was doing his management training following his three year Management Degree (BA) course at the Swiss *Ecole Hôtelière de Lausanne* (ELH). Michael Nicolson had been public school educated and although had plans on being a barrister or something more exciting than the hotel business, he was persuaded by his family that entering the family business could well be the best thing for him. Not wishing to disappoint he accepted the challenge and although he found some of his course work slightly boring he did enjoy the practical side such as the kitchen and housekeeping. One of the highlights of his training was to be a three month *stage** at The Langham Hotel London in the restaurant and kitchen and a further three months at the Dorchester Hotel; but today was the first day in the family hotel, starting in reception in this four star premises in the up and coming area of Battersea.

This is where he met Christine. She was a twenty year old receptionist with the darkest brown eyes

*stage: a non paid placement for experience

you could imagine, auburn hair in a pony tail, very slim with a great body and pert breasts, she was indeed a delight and obviously on everybody's radar as the way everyone spoke to her and looked at her, meant she had many admirers.
"Hello," she said. "Welcome to the Victoria Majestic. I'm Christine."
"Hi, I'm Michael, pleased to meet you."
"So you are our highflying management trainee are you?
"More of a low flying hawk trying to keep my eyes open and learn as much as I can," he replied with a smile.
"Well you won't learn much from me," returning his smile "except maybe how to smile and flirt a bit."
"Not sure that will help me too much," he laughed.
"With a smile like that," she said, "it could get you anywhere, even in trouble." She was obviously in flirt mode and it was working. The days went by and Michael had immersed himself in the day to day work while constantly making notes as to where he felt improvements could be made. After a couple of weeks he suggested to Christine that they may go out for a drink after work that evening. They were both finishing at 8.00 pm having both done an extra four hours to cover. She looked at him carefully.
"It's not that you are not attractive, because you are and you are extremely likeable, but rumour has it you are part of the family that own the

group and I'm not sure it would be a good idea."
"It was just a drink," he sighed.
"Well," she replied, "if that's all you want………you had better find someone else." She laughed.
"Ok, but I don't shit where I eat."
"No," he replied "that can be a bit messy, I've stopped doing it."
"Really?" she asked sarcastically.
"Yes, I have had to change restaurants," he said. They both laughed.
"OK, you smooth talking bastard, I'll meet you outside the Prince Albert at eight after I've gone home and freshened up."
"Where do you live then?" he asked.
"Just around the corner from the pub."
"Blimey, that's a bit expensive isn't it?"
"Yes, it's not mine though. It's my Grandmother's; she lets me have a one bed apartment in her building."
"That's good for you. OK I'll see you at eight tonight." They both finished on time and Christine left the building as he went upstairs to his room to shower and change.
He arrived dead on eight, but she wasn't there. He went in and ordered a beer, she came in moments later. He stood up from the stool as she came towards him.
"You look great" he said as her hair was now flowing freely and she was wearing a pair of jeans showing off her fabulous figure and a simple stretchy top enveloping her perfect breasts and a bolero jacket over her shoulders.

"Thank you, you don't look too shabby yourself, out of a suit!"

He laughed, "Shackles of the job," he said matter-of-factly. "What would you like to drink?"

She looked at the gins on offer and said, "I'll have a Tanqueray and tonic with a slice of cucumber please."

The barman came over and Michael said, "The lady will have...." And the barman interrupted, "A Tanqueray and tonic with a slice of cucumber..."

"Obviously a regular," he said with a grin.

"Well, I told you it's just around the corner, so it's handy when I dump a bloke 'cause he's boring me, I don't have far to go" once again that smile appeared.

"On the other hand, if you are getting on very well with someone it's not far to go if you want to take him home."

"Hold it cowboy, don't get above yourself. These goods are precious," she said running her hands down her body 'Mae West'sh' "and they don't just go to anyone."

They sat nursing their drinks and chatted animatedly. They were getting on well and both appeared eager to know where this would go.

·-•⊙⩽⩾⊙·-•

Two weeks had passed since Michael had started seeing Christine. They met for drinks, pub snacks and laughed a lot. On this occasion Michael was being a bit more adventurous so they went for dinner at London's oldest restaurant, Rules, a ten minute taxi ride from Battersea. The food and

wine were going down well and they were their usual relaxed selves discussing their days and work in general, although Christine was very wary of discussing anything to do with politics within the company in case she was speaking 'to the enemy'. That withstanding they were getting on well. After dinner Christine said "would you like to come around to mine for a nightcap?"
"Uh, yes; that would be nice. What.....?"
"Don't analyse anything, just say yes or no."
"Yes, of course" said Michael hoping that this could be the evening that they would get close. They got to Christine's house and went in. There was a stairway that led up two flights of stairs until they reached the attic. She opened the door and they walked in to a stunning wood beamed, modernly furnished lounge with an American kitchen — quite unusual he thought — which led off to presumably a bedroom and bathroom. She went over and put on some music. Neil Diamond the order of the day.
"What would you like to drink?" she asked, "I have brandy, gin or vodka."
"I take it the gin is Tanqueray?"
"You must be joking darling, I can only afford that when someone else is paying" she laughed. "London Dry I'm afraid."
"That's fine," he said thanking her.
They sat on the sofa with their drinks in their hands. She turned toward him and smiling said "You really are surprisingly nice you know."
"And you," he said with just the right amount of

mickey taking, "are very observant for such a young woman."

She laughed and moved forward to kiss him. He responded and they locked together in an emotional embrace with the right amount of sexual intent. He lay back on the sofa and she crawled on top of him once again kissing him passionately. She could feel him responding as he was getting hard, so she got up and moved them into the bedroom. She was on the bed and he lay with her. They kissed more passionately, her hand found him and he moved his hands to her firm breasts and erect nipples. Before long they were naked and making their first joint venture into their sexual and intense, emotional journey.

CHAPTER THREE
Growing Up Quickly

Albert was standing at the reception desk when Umberto, the fat Italian commander was talking to one of his senior officers. He couldn't hear too much but what he could understand was that 'the Germans were persuading Louis II via Marshall Petain to deport all the German and Austrian Jews back to Germany, Austria and Poland via France.' This was not the war that the Italians wanted to be involved in; they only wanted domination not revenge. They were also concerned that the Germans were going to push through to Monaco in the near future.

Albert reported these conversations at football practice with Claude, the trainer for the under 21's local team and Albert's resistance contact. Claude took good note and passed it on to his immediate superiors.

Life went on quite normally for Albert and his pals, they just fed information, however innocuous and they were occasionally rewarded with a few Francs, but they weren't doing it for the money they felt that they were doing it for France and especially their beloved Monaco.

Being part of the so called French Resistance was not what they thought it would be. The highly romantic image of the stories that reached the principality from the mainland had excited young men and woman since the Germans rolled through France in 1940. Compared to the acts of heroism perpetuated by folklore, the boys thought that their function was pretty worthless but they enjoyed their contribution to the cause.

However, things were going to change. The news passed down the grapevine that Mussolini had been dismissed by the King of Italy in July of that year (1943) as he, the King, had reached an agreement with the Allies. This meant that Germany was on the move and in September of that year they rode into Monaco unchallenged. By then nearly all the Italian soldiers had left apart from a few that went into hiding not wishing to return to an Italy influenced by the Nazis. Albert's hotel had been emptied of the Italian occupiers only to be replaced by the Germans.

In September of 1943, the nearly nineteen year old Albert was on the porter's desk when the Mercedes Benz 770 pulled up outside of the main entrance and in walked Kurt Hauser an *Obergruppenführer* in the Waffen SS who was to take command of the Nazi operations in Monaco. The Italians had presented no real problems to the residents although Prince Louis II had been accused of collaboration with them with Marshall Petain, under pressure from the Germans to register and list the whereabouts of the Jews that had come to live in what, they thought, was the neutral safety of the principality. Under the German occupation their safety was now in grave danger. The Nazi obsession with ridding the World

literally 'Colonel Group Leader'

of Jews was not going to be tempered by the idyllic surroundings of Monte Carlo.

Kurt Hauser was a formidable figure and Albert was impressed by his stature of six feet, broad shoulders and squared chin that sat well in his black, perfectly tailored Hugo Boss designed uniform and shiny cap with the distinctive *Totenkopf* insignia.

***"Guten tag, ich würde gurne mit Herr Nicol, sprechen"* said the German, as Richard came out of his office. In customary style the officer clicked his heels raised his right arm, saying *"Heil Hitler."* Richard obviously felt that this required no arm movement in return, or in any sort of salutation.

"On instructions of Adolf Hitler, Reich Führer of Germany, I am assuming control of Monaco and its citizens and will take over your hotel as our Waffen SS Headquarters. I have been to see your Prince Louis II with my papers of authority and introduction and have his cooperation to do so.

Thank you. Please billet my senior officers and we will wish to use the facilities of the hotel and any expenses will be paid for by the Third Reich"

'I've heard that before' thought Richard and muttered under his breath *'on y va encore un fois'* — here we go again!

At football practice that weekend Claude called a few boys to remain afterwards and meet him in the dressing room.

*skull and crossbones. translated as a 'dead head'.
** Good day, I would like to speak to Mister Nicol

"OK *Mes amis,* " said the gentle giant, "as you all know by now the Germans have ensconced themselves in our beautiful country. Sadly we will not be able to drive them out until we have help from the British or the Americans —God forbid — but we have to try and make life as difficult as we can for the bastards. Our task this month is to search out the whereabouts of our Jewish friends who have made their homes here since before the war. We will hear from our sources, which include the local police, who we understand have been encourage by Prince Louis II to do their best to avoid a blood bath or a cleansing, by warning those concerned to either hide or run from here. Your jobs will be to be observant and monitor where any of these people may be. They could be friends of yours or your families and when the raids start you will have to help inform them and assist them in hiding or escaping."

*"*Putain!*"* said a jubilant Albert. "This is more like it, something constructive," as they left the meeting.

"*Oui*, and more dangerous," said his friend.

Back at the hotel, it occurred to the intrepid Albert that he was sure there were a few of the staff in the hotel who maybe of Jewish families. Sarah and Rachel Gold were sisters and chambermaids in the hotel. He went to the housekeeper's station and saw them.

"*Bonjour mes belle filles*," he said jocularly as he approached the older, Rachel, a good looking
Fuck me!

auburn haired with, what appeared to Albert as a fat arse, but attractive enough young woman in her twenties and the lovely Sarah, who he had seen around. She was a pretty blonde with a lovely body about the same age as Albert.

"What are you doing in the servant's quarters?" asked Rachel.

"*Cherie*, we are all servants in the hotel business. I have come down to see if you and your colleagues are OK. Are our German guests giving you any problems?"

"Not really," replied the girls, "In fact one of them was flirting with me the other day," said Rachel.

"I have to ask you a question, are you and your family of Jewish origin? I ask because you know that the Germans are going to start looking for Jews to send back to Germany and only God knows what that will mean. I am not prying, I am just asking because a few friends of mine are trying to keep an eye on those that might be affected."

"Do we look Jewish?" asked an offended Rachel.

"I don't know" said Albert, "I haven't really met many, but someone told me that when you started work here, your surname was Goldman and I don't have to be a Rabbi to know that that is pretty Jewish."

The girls looked at each other and with some distrust stared at the young man.

"Our family is Goldman" said Sarah, who had until now kept silent. Her sister scowled at her. "When we came from Austria, before the war started, our father decided that we would be safer if we changed our name to Gold, he said he could see what was going to happen if Hitler got into power."

"You must let me know where you live so as I can keep an eye on you" said Albert.

"Albert, that is the worst chat up line I have ever heard," laughed Rachel.

"I think he's serious," replied her younger sister.

"I am" said Albert, "do you live nearby?"

"About twenty minutes on the bus," said Sarah.

"What time are you leaving today?" asked Albert.

"Four o'clock," she said.

"I'll come with you" he said.

"That's not necessary," said Rachel defensively.

"I'd like to," protested Albert.

"No thank you." said Rachel emphatically.

"OK," said Albert walking away muttering '*gros cul*,' (fat arse).

"I heard that," she said.

Back at the porter's desk, the phone rang.

"Albert, it's Sarah, sorry about Rachel, she likes playing mother hen. She feels very responsible for me. She forgets she's only five years older than me. I would like to let you know where I live. On Friday she's not working and I am finishing at four, could we meet afterwards?"

"Yes, I'll meet you at La Fontaine just down from the hotel."

"Ok, until then."

Albert sat there nursing a beer waiting for Sarah who arrived just after four o'clock. He stood up as she sat down.

"Hi," they both said feeling a little embarrassed. Ordering her a beer, he said, "Your sister doesn't like me does she?"

"Don't worry she doesn't like anyone really. She's frightened that everyone knows that we are Jewish."

"I can't tell you very much," said Albert thinking he was like a secret agent, "but there are many people here who are trying to protect Jewish people from the Nazis and we have all vowed to keep a look out for you all. That's why I want to know where you live."

"You are very kind," said Sarah putting her hand on top of his.

"This is our address," she said writing it down on a paper serviette, "don't lose it" she implored.

"Don't worry I won't," he said smiling into her blue eyes.

"When is your day off?" he asked.

"Monday, why?

"So is mine, maybe we could go to the pictures and have a drink afterwards."

"I'll have to see, but I would have to be back before eleven, or they will send out the search dogs," they both laughed. "I'll tell you when I leave on Sunday afternoon."

"OK," they finished their drink and he walked her to the bus stop.

"À demain,"

*"*À demain*" she said as she stepped on board and blew him a kiss.

She was nearly eighteen and he was nearly nineteen.

'Could be worse' he thought as the bus trundled down the road, 'Could be worse.'

*until tomorrow

CHAPTER FOUR
Work Comes First — 1985

Michael rolled over and found the beautiful Christine, hair spread over the pillow, lying perfectly still. He leant over and kissed her forehead. Her eyes opened, "Hello," she said smiling.

"Good morning," he replied returning the smile

"Are we both starting work at four today?"

"Hmmm, yes;" she said, "what are we going to do before work?"

"Breakfast?" he asked naively.

"I'll have to work up an appetite," she said putting her hand below the sheet to find what she was looking for and was pleasantly surprised as it was obviously looking for her. Once again, they moulded into one with him making gentle strokes and passionate kisses which moving in unison seemed to go on forever, until they both climaxed and lay there holding each other.

At four o'clock they were at their stations. They smiled at each other as they prepared for their eight hour shift.

"I really enjoyed yesterday," said Michael in a whisper. "So did I," she purred. "We must do it again soon," once again with that disarming smile. They did, many times; in fact they carried on their relationship for some time. Michael by now was in his third month at the hotel and had moved from reception to Banqueting where he had been responsible, with the Banqueting Manager, for several banquets. It was the company's biggest hotel at the time but only had capacity for 150 in one room and 50 in another with dividing doors to create a 200 banquet when necessary. This meant that Michael could run one of them on his own. He likened banqueting to the theatre. In the morning you would enter the room where the night porters had finished their cleaning duties and were replaced by the banqueting porters who, like stage hands, were awaiting instructions on how to lay up the room. The assistant banqueting manager (Stage Manager?) explained the 'layout' to the staff who then placed the tables and chairs in the right places with the right amount of chairs to each table. Enter stage left the 'extra waitresses' or 'ducks' as they were affectionately known who laid the tables, polished cutlery and glasses as they went. Housekeeping would arrive (set dressers?) to place flowers in pedestals and on the tables. The wine waiters and barman further dressed the room with the bar staff preparing their section and the wine waiters ensuring the wines were prepared and ice buckets were strategically placed around the room. Prior to curtain up, the staff would gather in the banqueting suite to be briefed by the banqueting manager in charge (Theatre Director?) as he would explain the running order, the menu and the dietary requirements as requested. A fifteen minute 'fag break' and then the doors would open and in would come the guests; unaware of the amount of work and preparation that went into such a show — and why should they? They only came for the performance. After the event the guests would leave, the staff would clear away and the porters would dismantle the tables and chairs, leaving the room to be cleaned until the next event, which would be the next day; sometimes lunch and dinner in one day, especially at weekends with weddings. But Michael loved banqueting; it was also a very profitable part of the hotel business.

Christine meanwhile had been promoted to assistant head receptionist and that created an excuse for a dinner out on their next free time. On this occasion it was a Sunday, so they decided to go for Sunday lunch instead of dinner. This created an opportunity for some afternoon delight which they took advantage of. Lying there listening to some music, Michael said "I'm leaving the hotel at the end of the month."

"Oh," said Christine sounding somewhat disappointed.

"It's ok," he replied "I'm going to the Langham for three months and then after the summer to the Dorchester."

"You are a high flyer aren't you?" she said somewhat sarcastically.

"Well, that's the way the system works; it's great

experience and gets me ready for my first senior post."

"And, where will that be""

"I have no idea; anyway it's a while away at the moment."

The couple became even closer over the next six months and had fallen in love; which neither of them had really wanted, both too young and ambitious, but it was what it was.

Christmas was coming ever closer and the Dorchester was at its busiest. Once again Michael had found himself in banqueting; and with the Grand Ballroom at the Dorchester it didn't get much better. With a 500 hundred capacity for a sit down meal it proved to be a clockwork operation especially from the kitchen under the auspices of the great Anton Mosimann and Michael was in his element.

Michael received a call from his father saying that the family were gathering at Uncle Marc's house for pre Christmas drinks before everybody got too busy. As he was no longer working with Christine he was more than happy to take her as his guest, the family had met her several times over the last few months but this would be the first large family event.

"Do you really want me to go?" asked Christine nervously, "after all, I'm not one of you, I'm just an employee."

"They know who you are, and they like you, you

know that. You will have met some of them."

"If you're sure."

"Of course I am. It will be fun. Uncle Marc's house is fabulous."

Their car pulled into the long gravel drive way that led to the entrance of the six bedroom house in Wimbledon.

"Blimey," said Christine as they walked into the grand entrance hall, "this is bigger and better than the Victoria."

He laughed, "it is a bit isn't it?" They were offered champagne as they entered the main room where about sixty guests were milling around chatting and drinking while nibbling canapés that were being served by elegant waiters in black tie pirouetting around the huge room. A good looking man in his mid fifties approached the couple. Uncle Marc extended his hand to Christine and in a beautiful, educated French accent said, "*Bienvenue ma Cherie*," and kissed her on both cheeks, while turning to his nephew with a strong embrace and equal kisses, "*et toi moi grand professionnel*"

"*Merci beaucoup mon oncle préféré.*"

He laughed and turned to Christine, "He is a cheeky so-and-so, he calls me his favourite uncle — but I am his only one."

They all laughed as he beckoned, "come through, come through, come and say hello to Aunt Adele."

The kissing of cheeks and hugs once again took place while the very attractive fifty year old greeted her nephew and his girlfriend.

"Why don't you take Christine around and introduce her to the few people she may not know, ('few', thought Christine, I only know about ten') while Michael and I join my brother in the study. We have a bit of business to attend to. Please excuse us," he said to Christine as Michael smiled at her, lightly shrugging his shoulders implying he had no idea what it was about.

Michael and his Uncle went into the typical grand study in plush burgundy colours, leather Captain's chairs, a world globe on a stand, which Michael always thought housed the bar and there was a map of Europe with a few pins in it showing the company's small hotel empire. His Father got up from one of the resplendent leather chairs at the side of Marc's huge wooden desk and approached his son repeating the embraces. Proffering him a seat he asked *"Comment vas-tu mon fils.?"*

"Tres bien merci Papa,"

"How is the Dorchester? I have heard good things about your work. Have you enjoyed your year?"

"I certainly have father, I have learned so much and met some great people."

"Not least Christine?" he asked inquisitively. "Yes, she is very special."

"So what are you going to do when we send you to Nice in the South of France to take over as Senior Assistant Manager of the Nice Majestic in January?"

Michael stopped in his tracks. This had come as a bit of a shock. He was hoping to go back to the

Victoria as deputy Manager.

"I didn't realise that was your plan? I hadn't given any thought to this move."

"Michael it is very important that you take this post as it confirms your place in the group and starts you on the way to take over the company. Your uncle and I are getting older and while we have plenty of years left, we know the time will come when the share holders will want to know our intentions and they must see that our successor is ready, willing and of course able. All of which we know that you will be. However, baby steps are important, but I would like to think that by the end of the century you will be ready."

"I thank you for your confidence in me; I will have to talk to Christine."

"No Michael, you have to tell her that is what you are going to do. You can take her with you if you wish. The position comes with an apartment near the hotel and while she is very competent I do not think it wise that she works in the hotel with you. Anyway, I don't think she speaks French does she?"

"No," said Michael dejectedly.

"In that case you will have to sort your situation. You finish at the Dorchester on the second of January and will fly to Nice the following week giving you time to have a Mediterranean holiday and prepare for your new post. Now, go and enjoy the party. We will be out in a minute. Remember Michael, work always comes first."

He left the office and made a bee line for his

girlfriend. He was already in turmoil and didn't know how he was going to tell her. She smiled as he approached, "Thank God you're back, I was getting a little overwhelmed. They are all very nice, but jeez, I wish the French would stop talking to me in French and then wondering why I don't reply!"

"I have to talk to you," he said looking at her with concern.

"Why, what's wrong?"

"Nothing, but it may cause a bit of a problem. Let's go into the salon." He walked her towards the outer room which was empty and away from the crowd. They sat down.

"You're freaking me out Michael, what's wrong?"

"Nothing really my love, but things have changed." He started to explain everything and about the conversation in the study. Her eyes welled up as the realisation that she was going to lose him started to hit her. He could see she was upset. "You could come with me," he suggested.

"Oh fuck off Michael, you know that will never happen. I don't speak French, I don't want to leave my family, I am still only twenty one and I am not sure that I want to leave England. Anyway you will be working all the hours and I wouldn't be able to get a job."

"You wouldn't need to; my salary will more than keep us both."

"Oh yeh, and I'll just hang around in the house doing the washing and ironing, clean and cook for you in the hope that maybe you will pop in for dinner! Oh no, of course, I can go out for lunch 'with the girls'" she said sarcastically.

"Darling, work has to come first. We can work it out, I know we can."

"No Michael you can fucking work it out on your own."

She got up and walked out of the door back into the large lounge and lost herself in the crowd.

Michael just sat there with his head in his hands.

'What the fuck am I going to do now?'

CHAPTER FIVE
Things Are Hotting Up — 1943

The young couple sat looking at each other over their glass of wine. They had been to the cinema to see, *'Douce* a Love Story' The film set in Paris in 1887 told the story of the aristocratic Bonafé family and their seventeen year old daughter Douce who falls in love with the estate manager but knows their class difference will always keep them apart. It was as to be expected a love story, that had made Sarah cry and she leant on Albert's shoulder crying gently, he had put his arm around her to comfort her. She had looked up at him and kissed him gently on the mouth, she smelt good and despite her reddened eyes they were lovely. They had walked to the bar from the cinema and were now picking at some Camembert and drinking their wine.
"You know things are going to get worse here don't you?" said Albert putting a piece of the creamy cheese on the point of his knife and offering it to his new found friend. A little sensually she accepted the offering with her mouth.
"Are your parents making any arrangements to go away from here?"
"I don't think so, they seem to think that, especially when the Italians were here, that Prince Louis would protect immigrants."
"That may have been the case then, but with

Petain putting pressure on Louis, as he is in turn getting pressure from the Germans, things will change. I can hear a lot over the breakfast table as they talk, not expecting me to speak German. You must stay safe, I've only just found you, I don't want to lose you, but if it means leaving you or finding you arrested, deported or dead — or all three — then we have to consider the possibility."

They finished their wine and walked to the bus stop in time for the last bus.

"I wish I could come with you, but there would be no bus to come back on and I am on duty at seven tomorrow."

"That's alright," she said as she went to kiss him goodbye. "Thanks for a lovely evening," she looked at him again and this time kissed him more purposefully.

He watched her get on the bus and stood there until the bus turned the corner.

Sarah and Albert had been quite an item since first they met. They consummated their relationship in his bedroom some few weeks after they had had their first date. Life was so precarious during these difficult times and nobody knew what the future would hold, if there was to be one.

The black Mercedes rolled into the back streets of terraced houses in a suburb of Monte Carlo followed by a canvas covered army truck out of which alighted six SS soldiers. The leading officer stepped out of his leather clad limo, straightened his cap and walked towards an unimposing wooden front door. He thumped his leather glove covered fist, against the flimsy structure. "*En Nahmen de Führer öffnen!*" There was no reply so the officer indicated to his troop to break the door down. It didn't take much effort; the door collapsed inwards and the armed soldiers entered the premises. There was a great deal of shouting and screaming as people started to run out of the house. They were lined up against the wall in the street. There was an old man in his eighties, an elderly woman, a younger woman and two young children. Two soldiers were herding them along when there was the sound of rifle fire; then silence, except for the sobbing of the young woman and her children. The older man spat on the floor: a soldier lifted the butt of his weapon and smashed it with a sickening crunch on the old man's shoulder causing him to wince in pain. The old lady put her arm around him. Two soldiers came out of the building supporting a man, who had obviously been shot in the leg and threw him in the back of the wagon. The convoy drove off leaving the old lady and the younger woman to help the old man into the house followed by the weeping, frightened children.

———⋄———

The atmosphere in the bar that night was subdued as members of the 'football team' and other associates discussed the recent Nazi manoeuvre. Michel Badeaux was a forty year old carpenter who was part of the resistance and a friend of Claude Allard, the football 'coach', who was deeply upset and worried for his friend's life.

"Albert," he said looking directly at the young man, "you and Pierre must try and find out where they have taken him and what they are going to do with him. We think we know but need confirmation; get a message to me when you have something and we can meet, but you won't have much time."

The two boys left the bar.

"How are we going to do this?" asked Pierre, "especially without being caught."

"We only have to listen, Pierre."

"It's OK for you, you speak German, I don't know any."

"I have an idea" said Albert, "when they are in for breakfast let me know and I'll find an excuse to come in to the dining room and maybe we can hear something that may be of interest. The boys spent a restless night thinking that things were getting real now and that maybe they could be of use after all. The following morning, Albert was at his desk when the internal phone rang; it was Pierre,

"Most of them have arrived," said Pierre in some form of covert way.

Albert walked into the restaurant with a pile of tablecloths that he had taken from the housekeeping. He put them on the *dumbwaiter

*(dumbwaiter- form of sideboard used by waiting staff)

next to a table where half a dozen soldiers were having breakfast. *"*Was ist mist dem Verräter passiert den du gestern Erschossen hast?*"*
"We were told not to kill him. Apparently he is part of a group of so called resistance fighters and they need him for questioning."
"Well," said another, "if this lot are as effective as the ones in Paris, it shouldn't be much of a problem." They all laughed.
"But Otto," replied his colleague, "a bullet or a bomb is the same from wherever it might come."
They all nodded in agreement. "True," continued Otto, "but at least he is one less to worry about."
"Is he in the usual place?" asked a third who wasn't on the raid.
"Yes, and he's due to be executed tomorrow night."
"Will they get the information they want from him by then?"
"You know what Herr **Haupsturmführer* Weber is like, he can get blood out of a stone"
"— or piss out a Jew lover" said Otto and they all laughed; "whatever, he'll still be shot"
"*Ja Ja,*" they chorused banging the table.
Albert went over to Pierre, "They're going to execute him tomorrow night" whispered Albert, "I must get a message to Claude" Just then a firm hand gripped Pierre's shoulder. He went white as the stern face of the SS man was looking at him; Albert thought they were both going to shit

What happened to the traitor you shot yesterday?
**(Haupsturmführer – Captain)

themselves as the soldier said, in broken French, "Boy, get us some more coffee."

"Mais oui monsieur," said a relieved Pierre as Albert slipped away.

He told his colleague at the desk that he would be back in fifteen minutes. He slipped off his porter's jacket and put on a jumper and ran out of the hotel down to the bar where Claude was having his coffee and croissant.

"What is it Albert?" he said stirring another sugar into his thick black coffee. "You've been running; must be all the football training." Albert started to tell him what he had heard in the hotel dining room including the words 'usual place'.

"OK, we don't have long," mused Claude, "we'll have to sort things quickly. Can you and Pierre be here at six this evening?"

"Yes, I finish at four and Pierre is on split shift meaning, he will be off from four 'til eight."

"OK, I'll see you all here at six."

Albert ran back to work and put his jacket back on and was behind his desk with hardly anyone knowing he had been gone for twenty minutes.

―――⋆―――

That evening in a smoked filled bar, the familiar faces including Charles and Georges had been joined by half a dozen men that the boys had not seen before, although Albert was pretty sure that one of them was a local *Gendarmarie*. Auguste Gagneux was indeed a policeman. Thirty two years old and married to Sophie and with two

small children. He had been in the local police force for ten years and was now a Lieutenant. There were many of his colleagues who had been helping Jews leave Monaco by informing them of forthcoming inspections and house calls. Some had left the principality others had just gone into deep hiding: But everyone had not forgotten that the Nazis were just as interested in the Jewish sympathisers. Michel had been betrayed — or just been found out — they had to make amends.
"Some of you know Auguste," said Claude, "he will be running this show because of his knowledge of the fortress where Michel is being held."
"*Mes amis,*" started Auguste, taking out a local plan of the area and in particular the fortress part of the Prince's palace on the east side that overlooked the sea, and placed it on the table.
"This is where Michel is," said Auguste putting a cross on the site.
"There are three roads leading to and from the castle. The main one is under control at all times by the Prince's Guards. However, this track is little known and runs alongside this minor road, one of the three that go to and from the Palace. We are splitting into three groups" he said looking at his colleagues. Pointing to four of them, "you will be in charge of securing a vehicle to get us there and to escape. You four," he said pointing to a somewhat motley crew in the darker area of the bar table, "we will need your guns, knives and some explosives Didier," the bearded man nodded

as his *Gauloise* balanced on his bottom lip, "and you François will be responsible for obtaining some rope in case we have to escape in an unconventional way. It's a long way down so you'll need a big roll and we'll need some chloroform; as the local *farmacie*, that shouldn't be too difficult." François smiled and shrugged his shoulders, "that and many more helpful drugs" he said as the group laughed quietly. "If we can do this without shooting anyone that would be good," continued Auguste, "but if you have to — just don't miss. We will approach the castle under cover of dark tonight. We have no time for rehearsals, so this will be it. There are two SS guards at the entrance to the fortress. It is a tower with three floors. There is a barrack on the second floor where the billeted soldiers are. There is normally only a handful, as they need twelve for rotating shifts. There is also, normally, only one at the entrance to the holding cells of which there are three. Two of us will approach the entrance of the building from either side with a blade and the chloroform — just hope that the drug works, if not use the knife across the neck. Let's hope that won't be necessary. How long will the chloroform be in effect François?"

"The amount on each pad will last about half an hour, forty minutes"

"That should be enough," continued Auguste. Pointing to Francois and his two colleagues, Jacques and Jean he said "We will be the group that goes to the top floor having knocked out the two guards at the entrance. Didier you and your group will go to the second floor and keep an eye on the barrack room. If anyone leaves, take care of them if necessary; also lay some explosives just enough to blow up a few people and some doors as a distraction," he smiled.

Now there are two entrances as you go down the corridor," Auguste was drawing arrows and explaining as he went, "when we get here," he said pointing at a split in the corridor leading down to a service area, "François and I will go that way. You two will go that way which will take you to the cells. Jacques, you speak enough German to draw the guard's attention don't you?"

"How about, *'Komm her Arshloch damit ich dir die Kehle durchscneiden kann.'*?

"Sounds good" said Claude, "what does it mean?"

"Come here arsehole and let me cut your throat," they all laughed. "I don't think that will encourage him, although it would certainly detract him" said Auguste.

"Actually in all seriousness," continued Claude, "it may not be as stupid as it seems. If Jacques was to say, 'come here and help me', or 'who goes there?' or any other such normal questions he would probably have to know the guard's name. By saying this, the guard is bound to react immediately and position his rifle, giving you guys the time to go behind him and floor him."

There was a moments silence while they considered the suggestion before Auguste said

"You're right it's stupid, but it might well work. It will take three minutes to get from where we separate until we get into position that is when you call him. We will come behind him and hopefully he will succumb to the chloroform, if he doesn't, we will have to cut him down. The keys to the cells are on his belt, we will then release Michel and hope he is in a condition to walk, if not we will have to carry him. OK is everyone clear as to their roles?" concluded Auguste.

"Hhrrm?" said Albert inquisitively, "what about us?"

"*Ah, oui les jeunes hommes*, your responsibility is to disable the troop vehicles and the jeeps that are here," he said pointing, "around the side of the building. Cut the tyres and remove the distributor caps, can you do that?"

The four boys looked at each other, "Yes of course," they said in unison.

"Do you know what you will need?" asked Auguste.

"Yes," said Albert, "knives for the tyres, a screw driver in case we have to lever the caps off and some pliers or wire cutters, just in case."

"Excellent: And a torch?"

"Of course, sorry."

We will meet here at six o'clock tonight just as it's getting dark. *Jusqu' à plus tard mes amis."

Excitedly the boys left feeling at last they were involved in something serious.

until later my friends

CHAPTER SIX
Where Do We Go From Here?

Michael followed Christine out of the salon, but couldn't see her. He walked out to the car, she was there, sitting on the bonnet.
"You OK?" he asked stupidly.
"What do you think?" she said spitting her reply.
"I'm sorry babe, we can sort something out."
"We can't and we won't Michael, I'm sorry I reacted the way I did. I've just had such a good time this year and I thought it would only get better. Of course you must get on with your career and I must get on with my life. I'm only young and I have so many more things to do, you just caught me too young and I was too susceptible, but I have had a great time; anyway there are more fish in the sea and maybe I'll have to meet a few sharks and a couple of tiddlers but I might eventually find King Turbot along the way. Anyway you are not dead to me yet, so we still have until the beginning of January to play."
She put her arms around him and kissed his cheek, "come on, let's get back in before your family think I'm a spoilt, immature brat; that would do my future prospects no good at all." Arm in arm they walked back in where the party was in full swing. Uncle Marc had brought in a band and they were playing some good music, so the two danced together.

"You could always come to Nice in January for a few weeks before I start work," shouted Michael above the music. She looked up at him and mid dance just reached up and kissed him. "We'll see how it goes, but for now, just.....DANCE!"

The next few weeks went very quickly. Christine and Michael were making the best of a bad job. They were both working on Christmas Day but had a couple of days off before the New Year celebrations. They went out to dinner at their favourite restaurant; holding her hand he said, "Look I know all this is going to be difficult and we have no idea what is going to happen, but I really would like you to come over with me in January, we can have the apartment and it will be a few weeks before I start work. No pressure or anything, but at least if you like it, you may want to come over on holiday occasionally."

She looked at him intently; "you don't give up do you?"

"You're worth working for."

"Oh, you know how to say the right things don't you?"

"Look I leave on the fifth of January. You book your hols for any two week period before the twenty eighth of January. I'll get settled in and make the place as homely as possible and we'll just have a good time for a couple of weeks."

"OK, OK....you win. I'll speak to the boss when I get back and see if I can organise something" she said accepting the situation.

"If you can't I could pull family rank," he said smiling.

"You wouldn't you're too professional for that; anyway, I wouldn't let you."

"I was joking."

"I know you were; having said that they know we are a couple so they will put two and two together, so I'm sure I'll get it."

They left the restaurant and went back home

"Want a night cap darling?" asked Michael.

"Why not," she replied as she came out of the bedroom wearing nothing but her smile. He stopped what he was doing and went toward her.

"Maybe we could forget the night cap, I won't wear it," he joked as he held her in his arms and kissed her, at first gently and then passionately as he lifted her off the floor and walked her into the bedroom and laid her down on the bed, She took off his shirt and he kissed her all over before getting up and taking off the rest of his clothes and crawled in beside her. Once again their bodies moulded into one as they moved sensually and rhythmically in a way that had now become second nature but still held the wonderful feelings that had helped make their relationship what it was.

"Have you got everything?" asked Christine, "all your work suits, enough shirts? You are going to have to do your own laundry aren't you?"

"Well, for this month, but I trust as the apartment is right next door to the hotel, that I will get maid service and then I'll leave a good tip so as she can do my shirts, if not they will go to the laundry."

Michael checked his ticket, looked at his watch and said, "Come on then, we'd better get going." He put his arm around her and kissed her.

They got in the car and drove the forty minutes or so to Heathrow, mostly in silence. "You will call me when you get there won't you?" she asked

"Of course, I suspect there is a phone in the apartment, if not I'll go into the hotel. I have to go in and introduce myself and collect the key anyway."

They parked in the multi storey and Michael wheeled his case towards terminal three. "Don't come any further, I hate airport goodbyes" said Michael as he put his arms around her and held her tight. "I'm going to miss you."

"I'm going to miss you too, but it's only for a week or so, then I'll be over."

"I know but that would be the longest we have ever been apart"

"It will be fine," she said encouragingly; "You'll be great." She watched him walk toward the check in desk, her eyes filling with tears. 'I wonder whether I will go?' she thought. 'Or should I make this the last goodbye?'

※

Michael took a taxi from outside Nice Côte d'Azur Airport .

"*Hotel Nice Majestic s'il vous plaît,*" 'Sunshine' thought Michael as the car made its ten minute journey to the beach side hotel. The Nice Majestic was one of the company's oldest hotels having been built in the fifties in the eclectic modernist style of that era.

With only two hundred rooms it was not the company's largest, nor the most luxurious, but it was the family's personal favourite. Michael entered the Palm Court style lobby and walked over to the main reception desk.

"*Bonjour, je m'appelle....*"

"*Monsieur* Nicolson," said the male receptionist, "we have been expecting you. I believe you are staying in the penthouse next door," he continued, handing him a key. The bell boy will show you where to go and *Monsieur Le Directeur*, Éduoard de Villiers would like to see you when you have settled in. Welcome to the Nice Majestic."

"*Merci Monsieur Armand.*" said Michael observing the name tag.

The young porter came over,

"*Bonjour Monsieur, comment allez vous? Bienvenue dans nostre belle hotel*"

'I like the boy's passion about his place of work' thought Michael as they left the building and took a short walk to the apartment that was going to be his home for the next year or so.

"*Merci,*" said Michael as the boy left the apartment. He looked around, firstly at the view overlooking the sea and the promenade; the lounge was more than adequate with large leather sofas, a TV, a record player/radio cabinet and a telephone, wall lights and a large rug. 'Hmm, not bad,' thought Michael as he wandered into the bedroom with its *ensuite* bathroom to find a large double bed with side tables 'obviously ex-hotel furnishings' he thought, in fact everything he needed for the amount of time that he was likely to spend in it.

He changed into some smart casual clothes to go back to the hotel and take the opportunity to meet *Monsieur* Villiers if he was available, he would call Christine when he got back.

Monsieur Armand called through to the director's office,

*"*Monsieur* Nicolson es lá pour vous voir si vous avez un moment."

"Please go through the hall and take the second door on the right."

Michael did as he was told and tapped lightly on the door. "*Entrez*" said the voice from inside and Michael went in. "*Enchante*," both men said as they shook hands. "Welcome to the hotel," said a man in about his early forties. "You have come at the quietest time as I am sure you know and I am afraid the coldest," he smiled.

"Don't forget I have come from the UK, this is paradise compared to London.

"Yes, I remember well, I was the GM at your old hotel before I came home to France. I avoided Paris and came straight to Nice, the weather is certainly better." he smiled.

Your start date is Monday the third of February if that is convenient. He picked up the phone and said to his secretary in the other room,

*Mister Nicolson is here if you have a moment

"Please ask Alain Chastain to come in."

"Alain is the outgoing senior assistant and his job is food and beverage orientated; I know that is one of your passions so you will find the work fun and rewarding. We don't have a deputy general manager, so the senior assistant is my right hand man. Ah, Alain," said Villiers as a young man not much older than Michael came into the room. "This is Michael, as you know he will be taking over your job when you leave on the third of February."

"*Enchanté*" said both young men.

"Welcome to Nice Majestic, if you enjoy your next year as much as I have my last two, it will have been worth your trip. You have to watch this man though," said Alain jesting at his superior, "as he will make you work twenty four hours a day seven days a week."

"I thought that was normal, didn't you Michael?" said the boss with a grin.

"But of course sir." replied the new boy

"*Lécher de cul*,"* laughed Alain, "you will get on here, won't he sir?

"He certainly will." replied Villiers laughing.

"OK Michael I suggest that you and Alain spend a couple of days of that weekend on handover so as you can show Michael the ropes. Meanwhile settle in and have a break over the next couple of weeks before you start. Any local information you require, just ask the reception. *À bientôt*"

The two young men walked out of the office.

"Listen," said Alain, "I am off tomorrow, fancy going

* *Lécher de cul* ; 'arse licker'

out for lunch and I'll give you the background of the place and we can get to know each other before the work starts?"

"That would be great," said Michael as he left the hotel and walked back toward his apartment.

CHAPTER SEVEN
The Deed is Done - November 1943

It was raining as the boys got together and checked they had everything. "Everyone bring a torch?" asked Albert.

"Of course," replied Charles. The others grunted in agreement.

"OK, let's meet up with the rest." They wandered down to the bar where they were meeting. Everyone was there. "Alright," said Claude, there are two vans outside, it will be a bit cramped but we don't want a fleet of vehicles going up the road. We will hide the vans about fifty meters from the fortress and then walk the rest of the way. When we leave we are going to have to run like fuck to get back before the guards are alerted. I just hope Michel is capable of walking. Jacques and Jean you are the tallest, it will be your task to take Michel. If he is weak which is highly likely you will have to carry him between you so as his feet don't touch the ground; Everyone clear? Boys are you ready?" He looked at the group who nodded affirmatively, "Let's go."They went outside and piled into the waiting transport.

The rain was getting heavier and the sound on the roof of the van was deafening, the body heat was causing the windows to steam up and the whole place was uncomfortable but it was only a twenty minute drive to their destination. It was pitch black as they drove through the woods with only the side lights of the vehicle on and even they were covered in brown paper to avoid them being spotted. They stopped about one hundred meters from the fortress and dismounted. They went off in their separate groups, the boys making their way to the car park at the rear.

"The first thing we must do," said Albert, "is let the tyres down. If we get caught trying to remove the distributor at least they won't be able to give chase so easily.

They waited until they could see the other groups enter the building and then proceeded to let the air out of the tyres before cutting them, while Charles and Georges quietly opened the bonnets of the vehicles. Shining a torch into the engine area they found the distributor caps, removed them and cut the wires leading to them and threw them into the bushes. With thumbs up, their tasks had been performed and they walk backed toward their transport.

Claude and François made their way to the front of the building followed some distance behind by Jacques and Jean. They separated as they got near the bushes and François crawled along the ground behind the bushes until he could safely crawl alongside and toward the right hand side of the building, until they were either side of the entrance. The two guards were engaged in conversation and smoking, as, with their backs against the stone walls, the two friends slid alongside them and with a nod of agreement approached the guards and simultaneously put their arms around their necks and the pads over their mouths. Trying to cry out the Germans absorbed the chloroform very quickly and slumped to the ground quietly as the two men held them on the way down. By now their friends were beside them and they all entered the building. Quietly climbing the stairs the four designated led by Auguste, continued to the split in the walkway while Didier and his crew stayed on the second floor keeping an eye on the barrack room. They laid some explosive charges opposite to the door, which were hidden by some rubbish that had been left there. Meanwhile the other four had split into their relevant pairs and were making their way in the opposite direction to arrive at the top of the stairs on either side of the cells. At the rehearsed time Jacques' voice rang out in a loud whisper, *"Komm her Arshloch damit ich dir die Kehle durchscneiden kann.?"*

This was enough to disturb the guard's day dreaming as he removed his rifle from his shoulder and moved toward the area at the top of the stairs, by which time Francoise and Auguste were behind the soldier and with knife in one hand and the drug in the other they forced him to the ground where he collapsed in deep sleep. They removed the keys from his belt and went to the only cell that was occupied. Inside, Michel lay motionless. They approached him and François put his hand over the poor man's mouth. He had been truly beaten. His eyes were black and he was covered in blood. He groaned as he started to come around.

"Hello my friend," said Francois, "we will get you out of here. Can you walk?"

"No, my leg is broken I think."

Francois beckoned to Jacques and Jean, "You'll have to carry him."

The boys lifted him off the bunk. "I think he's too hurt to carry him over our shoulders. We'll have to support him either side around our shoulders." They got him out of the cell and gently supported him as they carried him down the way they had come in, his feet not touching the ground.

As they were making their way down, Didier who had hidden himself keeping eyes on the barrack room, was disturbed by the opening of the door and a soldier came out without a jacket and made his way to the nearby toilet. The mood in the smoked filled room was buoyant as the soldiers were drinking beer, reading or playing cards.

A sweat came over Didier as he waited for the SS man to come back. He heard his steps and secluded himself even deeper in the dark of his hiding place. The man stood by the door for a minute, put his braces back over his shoulders before going back in. Didier exhaled as the danger seemed to have passed. 'I would have dearly loved to cut his throat' thought the Frenchman as he heard his colleagues making their way towards him.

"Come, come" urged Didier, "they are moving around."

Jacques and Jean hurried past the door as quietly as they could. Auguste looked at his watch. This had taken them twenty minutes, so they would be out hopefully before the chloroform wore off. The rest of the team filed quietly out of the door, stepping over the sleeping guards. Michel wasn't a big man and his rescuers could carry him with relative ease this short distance, but now they had one hundred meters or so to carry him back to their vehicles.

The two guards at the entrance started to come around. Realising what had happened they raised the alarm with their colleagues. They all came out of the room and started asking what had happened; one rushed upstairs to see his colleague lying on the floor and the cell door open.
"Achtung, Achtung, der Gefangene is geflohen,"
He roused his colleague; "What happened?" He shouted.
"I don't know, I heard someone call me and then another one knocked me out with chloroform. Shit, the prisoner has gone."
He got up and they both went down to mix with the others.
"They can't have gone far," said the Oberscharführer.*
The squad rushed outside shining their torches then someone put on the flood lights illuminating the area. The escapees could hear the commotion as they hurried along the path towards the boys and their waiting vehicles.
"Go to the vehicles and take one of the three
*Oberscharführer: senior squad leader

roads each and follow them, they will have to be on one the routes," ordered the squad leader.

As they got to the vehicles they could see the slashed, deflated tyres, "*Die Bastarde haben die Reifen aufgeschlitzt,*" yelled one of the drivers.

"Just drive as they are," called out the leader. The men jumped into their vehicles to find they were unable to start them.

"In that case run after them," he said pointing to the roads that led from the compound.

The Frenchmen could hear the shouting as they climbed into their vans and sped off down the tracks.

"*Ils vont être très énervés,*" said Claude laughing as the vans tore down the road into the town.

"I'd be a bit pissed off too if I was the man in charge wouldn't you? He's going to have a lot of explaining to do to the Commandant."

"Yes, but" said Auguste guardedly, "it won't end with them being angry, they will come down on all of us with a typical German iron fist. We will have to work on our alibis, just in case."

"We must carry on as normal though," said Claude.

"We will meet in the bar at lunchtime then," said François.

"We are working in the morning," said Albert, "but we will come tomorrow before the evening shift."

"And I will be at the station," said Auguste, "they will undoubtedly come to us for information"

"More importantly what are we going to do with Michel?"

"We'll take him around to my brother the doctor, they'll expect us to go to the hospital," said François.

"Or not" said Auguste "I suspect they will go to all the doctors in the town in an effort to find him. Laurent has an attic which is well hidden. He will attend Michel there. But we will have to make arrangements to hide Michel more permanently as they will be looking for him."

Auguste and François took Michel to Doctor Gagneux's surgery. They carried the patient to the door and rapped gently on it. A bearded man in his early fifties opened the door. "Auguste, François what is happening? Come in, come in" said Laurent as he shook the men's free hands in a clasp of friendship.

François started to explain the situation while the Doctor examined him. "He really should be in the hospital," said the medic. "He has a fractured jaw and a damaged eye which I am pretty sure has made him blind. He has three broken fingers and I think his leg has been fractured during his questioning, to go with the unattended bullet wound he received when he was arrested.

"For questioning, read torturing," said Auguste, "what can you do?"

"I can strap up his leg and make him comfortable and then later I will make some plaster of Paris and encase it. I'll put some splints on his fingers and a strap around his head in the hope of holding his jaw. He's probably in a lot of pain so I'll give him some morphine to relieve it. God knows what I can do with his eye, I will attend to it now the best I can and look further tomorrow. Now go, they will be looking for you — or anyone they can find. *Allez, allez vite!*"

As the two resistance men parked the van, they walked towards the bar for a drink. Suddenly the streets were alive with German vehicles. Soldiers were jumping out of covered trucks spilling into the normally quiet streets. They went into Franck's bar and found Franck in his usual position behind the bar with the habitual pipe wedged between his teeth. Auguste went over to him, "Give me a bottle of red wine please Franck and we have been here for a few hours, *d'accord?*"

"*Oui, naturellement,*" replied Franck taking the cork out of the bottle and passing over two glasses.

Auguste and François sat in their usual spot and poured themselves a much needed glass of wine. They acknowledged the other handful of people in the bar.

Just then two SS men came into the bar. Silence fell as the patrons eyed the soldiers with suspicion.

"Can I help you gentlemen," said Franck. "Would you like a drink?"

"No thank you, we want information."

"Ah well, you have come to the right place," said Franck sarcastically. "What would you like to know?"

"Have you heard about the escaped convict who was sprung from his prison cell?"

Franck said, "No I haven't heard about the escaped convict who was sprung from his prison cell."

"Are you trying to be funny," said the German.

"I am sorry, I thought it was one of those jokes, *mon ami*?" said the Frenchman with a smirk.

"It is not a laughing matter *Monsieur*, we need to find him and the people who carried out this act."

"Well, I am afraid I have not heard anything and I have been here all day and my customers have not told me anything."

The two soldiers looked around the room and spotted François and Auguste in the corner of the room. They approached the two men with their hands on their Luger holsters. François suddenly laughed, a false laugh and Auguste joined in.

"What are you laughing at?" asked one of them

"A joke my friend. Are we not allowed to have a joke now?" asked Auguste.

"Where were you this evening," asked the other soldier.

"We've been here most of the evening haven't we Franck?"

The barman looked at the clock on the wall and said, "Nearly three hours yes" and as an aside to the soldiers, "they are on their second bottle but I am hoping they will buy another." He laughed.

The German's pulled out two chairs and sat opposite them putting their caps on the table.

"Your papers" the two men handed them over.

"Now what can you tell me?"

CHAPTER EIGHT
A New Chapter 1986

Michael picked up the phone in his apartment and the switchboard operator answered.

"Can you give me an outside line please?"

"*Certainment monsieur Nicolson*" said the telephonist.

Michael dialled the number of the Victoria, Alice, one of the switchboard operators, answered.

"Victoria Majestic, how can I help you?"

"Hello Alice, this is Michael Nicolson, how are you?"

"Hello sir, fine thank you. How is sunny France?"

"Not so sunny, but not cold. I suppose it's snowing there?"

"No sir, but it's bloody cold. Do you need a switchboard operator in Nice?"

"How's your French?"

"*Touché monsieur!*" she laughed, "I suppose you would like to speak to Christine?"

"Yes please," said Michael already feeling a little 'homesick'.

"Reception," came the familiar voice, "how can I help you?"

"I have a broken heart can you send someone to fix it?"

"Michael, how are you? Arrived safely obviously? How's the hotel?"

"I haven't done the tour yet, but have met the GM and the incumbent Senior Assistant and am having lunch with him tomorrow. They all seem

like decent chaps. How are you, missing me?"
"Blimey Michael you haven't been gone twenty four hours yet! But, yes I have been thinking about you. What's the apartment like?"
"You'll love it," said Michael looking out of the panoramic window overlooking the sea. "It's got everything we need."
"We? You don't give up do you?" she said laughing. "Look I have got to go, I have the hotel number what's your extension?"
"501,"
"OK, I'll call you later."
"OK, byee."
He put the phone down, 'I am glad I spoke to her, she seemed in good spirits'.
It was now early evening, 'time for a walk, I must go and find out more about the area' he thought. He wandered over to the hotel and introduced himself to the *concierge*, "Hello, I am…"
"*Monsieur Nicolson*," interrupted the head porter, "welcome, how can I help you?"
"Thank you. Have you got a street map and a recommendation for somewhere for dinner this evening?"
"*Mais oui monsieur*," offering him a town plan and circling a bistro and a more elegant dining venue on the map.
"Thank you," said Michael as he made his way out on to the street, almost colliding with a tall, elegant and very attractive, dark haired young woman in her mid twenties.
"*Excusé-moi Mademoiselle*," he said standing back

to allow her passage.

"*Pas de problem,*" she said as she and her perfume wafted by him. 'Nice has some nice scenery,' he thought as he made his way down to the promenade and took a walk past the shops and bars that aligned the road. At about seven, having enjoyed his walk, he made his way to the bistro that the *concierge* had marked on his map. On the way, he picked up a copy of the local newspaper *Nice – Matin* to take with him to *Le Petit Escargot* five minutes from the hotel, in a side street obviously popular with the local business community, with just a smattering of tourists. He sat at a corner table and ordered half-a-dozen snails, a steak and *frites* and some bread and wine. He browsed through the paper and was pleased to see that his reading ability in French had not gone below par. He soon got fed up though and his mind went back to Christine. What was going to happen with them? He took a sip of his red wine. He was still very young and so was she and he had his whole life and career ahead of him. But he did like her very much and didn't want to leave her behind but he had a feeling that if she came over that could well be the last time he would see her. Oh well, as the Spanish would say, *'que sera, sera'*

·•·◦৩✧ᧉ◦·•·

The next day, Michael had agreed to meet Alain Chastain for lunch, again at *Le Petit Escargot*, 'obviously a popular place' thought Michael as he met him at the entrance. They shook hands and went in. This time they were greeted by Marie the owner who welcomed Alain with open arms. "*Bonjour beau*" she kissed him on both cheeks and extended her hand to Michael, "This," said Alain is Michael Nicolson who is taking over from me at the beginning of February,"

"*Enchanté Michael,*" said Marie, again kissing him on both cheeks. "Come gentlemen to your table" she said leading them to a round table in the corner.

"What would you like to drink?" asked Marie

"Shall we just start with wine Michael?" asked Alain.

"Suits me," replied his colleague.

"A bottle of Chablis please Marie," as he took the proffered menu from her.

The wine arrived and they ordered their food.

"*Santé mon ami,*" said Alain raising his glass.

"*Santé,*" said Michael taking a sip of the golden liquid.

"So where are you going Alain?"

"The company's flagship hotel in Paris, as deputy General Manager; I'm looking forward to it, but the weather is better here. And where were you?"

"The hotel in Battersea and that's probably colder than Paris!"

"But you are part of the family aren't you?"

"Yes, but that makes no difference believe me, the only advantage — if it is one — is that I tend to be being pushed through. You have been here two years haven't you?" Alain nodded to confirm that, "Well it's planned for me to be here for only a year, but it may become two."

"That will be enough, it's a fairly simple hotel to run and you'll get on with De Villiers he's a decent enough man; he likes to pass on responsibility and considers himself as much as a mine host as a director, leaving the day to day running of the hotel to me, or now you!"

"You are not married are you?" asked Alain.

"No, not at the moment; I have a girl back in the UK but we're both still young and she has a lot to accomplish so it will probably fizzle out."

"Just as well; apart from the long hours which will keep you occupied, there are plenty of good looking young women around Nice that will love to meet an educated Englishman," he said laughing.

They finished their starters, Michael had *Snails* again and Alain a *French Onion Soup*. They finished their Chablis and Alain ordered a Gevrey Chambertin to go with their Steak *au poivre*.

Marie poured a little of the red wine in to Alain's glass to try and he nodded his approval, "*Merci Marie.*"

"Speaking of good looking women," continued Michael, "I bumped into one yesterday as I was leaving the hotel. She had dark hair, was my height and quite elegant. Do you know who she is?"

"I think that might have been Juliette Varon, was she wearing a suit?" Michael nodded, "yes blue if I remember"

"Yes, that's Juliette, she's the sales exec for the Le

Negresco, she's a friend of De Villiers she calls in now and again."
"What sort of friend?"
"No, nothing like that, she used to work at the hotel before she moved to Le Negresco. We work with her on a few projects; she's a bit of a 'fridge', sorry is that a word you would use in English to describe someone who is a little frigid, icy, cool?"
"I suppose you could, so not a man-eater despite the way she looks?"
Alain laughed, "I suppose if you know how to open the fridge door you would be fine."
They finished their steaks and savoured the last of the red wine. They discussed procedures in the hotel and Alain gave him as much background information as possible.
As Alain insisted on picking up the bill, Michael succumbed, "So come in on Saturday the first and we'll pack in as much as we can that weekend.
They walked slowly back to the hotel talking about the social life and things of interest to do in what was basically a seaside resort. They said their *adieus* outside the hotel and Alain said "we'll meet next week if you like. Maybe we can make a four with my girlfriend for dinner? I'm sure you'll manage to find someone by then," he smiled knowingly.
Michael went back into his apartment and looked at the view, 'I think I might enjoy being here,' he thought. Just then the phone rang, it was Christine. "I'm at home now," she said, "I left a

little earlier this evening. The hotel is quiet. So, have you settled in?"

"Sort of I have just come back from a long lunch with Alain, the assistant who is leaving. Nice guy."

"Did he fill you in on the hotel?"

"A little. We will have a change over on the weekend of the beginning of February."

"I suppose Nice is full of beautiful women?"

"If it is, I haven't seen any yet," said Michael thinking about the good looking Juliette.

"I'm sure you'll seek some out" said Christine with a little bitterness in her voice.

"Look, I have a few weeks before I start, as you know, so why don't you get a flight over?"

"I don't know Michael, I'm not sure that there is any point."

"What do you mean any point?" he said defensively. "Just treat it like a little holiday."

"I'll think about it. I'll look at flights, costs and timings and see what I come up with."

"OK, if you want me to pay for the flight, I am happy to do so."

"I can pay for my own flight," she said somewhat indignantly, "but thanks for offering. I'll call you later in the week."

"OK, take care; Love you."

"Love you too."

The phone went dead. 'Maybe she's right' he thought 'I don't suppose it will go anywhere, anyway. But it would be nice to spend some time with her before I start work in earnest'.

CHAPTER NINE
Clamping Down

"Now what do you have to say *Messieurs*?"

"I am afraid there is not much we can tell you," said François, "we have been here for some time and apart from a few friends that have come and gone, we haven't seen or heard anything."

"You *Monsieur* are a Gendarme," he said looking at Auguste, "you are in a position to let people know that we will turn this town upside down until we find the convict and the people that helped him escape."

The two soldiers stood up and put on their caps. With the customary click of their heels and raised arm and a *Heil Hitler*, they walked out of the door. The two friends let out a sigh of relief. "I think they mean business, I have a feeling they are not going to give up. We must talk to René Borghini and find out what the resistance is going to do."

The next morning there was a flurry of activity in the hotel as Albert and Pierre went about their tasks. The soldiers were assembling outside the hotel in lorries as the officers went out from the hotel to get into their waiting vehicles. This was to be the beginning of a clamp down by the enemy. Albert had heard them discuss over breakfast, that orders had come down from the North of France that they were to start rounding up Jews and deporting them. So not only were they trying to find Michel and those that rescued him, but also anyone involved with the Jewish community and any attempt to try and help them.

Albert had to get to Claude and Auguste. He went to the bar in the hope they were there. He went in to find Franck behind the bar polishing glasses with a cloth that should have been consigned to the wash some days before, with his signature 'cavalier' pipe hanging on to his teeth.

"*Bonjour Monsieur Franck*," said Albert out of politeness as he entered the dimly lit hostelry.

"*Bonjour Albert, com ça va?*"

"*Bien merci*, have you seen Claude or Auguste?"

"No, but they are coming in for a drink in about an hour."

"I'll come back," said the young man. "Tell them I have to talk to them."

"*D'accord*," said the publican as he re-lit his fading pipe.

As Albert was walking back to the hotel he saw the two men walking toward him.

"*Bonjour*," they said in unison.

"I need to talk to you," said Albert with urgency.

"Come in to the bar then," said Claude.

They took a seat in the corner, the two men ordering *Pastis* and Albert a beer.

"What news from the hotel?" asked Auguste.

"Warming up, as I expect you know, as *Gendarmerie*," continued Albert. "They are not only intent on finding Michel and those that helped him, but they are now going to start hunting down the Jews that live here."

"Yes, you are right," said Auguste, "we have been informed by the Germans and also our own Prince

Louis, under duress from Marshall Pétain, that we have to make a list of the Jewish residents that reside in the principality. Obviously this will take some time and we will do what we can to inform them — at great risk to my men I have to say — so as they can make arrangements."

"But that will not always work will it?" asked Albert.

Just then the door opened and everyone fell silent. In walked the imposing figure of René Borghini with a very attractive young woman on his arm that everyone later came to know as Madeleine Darieu, René's love. It had been assumed that Esther had been his muse, but no, she just worked with René as did Madeleine, but the latter was special. She was dark haired in her early twenties who had moved from Paris with her mother while her father remained behind.

The five of them sat in the corner drinking *Pastis* and in Albert's case, another beer.

Albert then explained what he had been listening to during breakfast and the fact that the Gestapo and SS were going full out now to quell what they saw as a dangerous situation for them and their colleagues. They had to clamp down

"Well done Albert, you have done well," said René "we are aware of the direction that the Nazis are taking and we have done some preliminary arrangements to move some of our Jewish friends and some of the resistance that are in trouble. In Cap d'Ail there is a converted trawler that from the outside looks exactly like any one of the boats that set sail each morning. However this one has been gutted inside where the storage would normally be and has been replaced by bunks. Needless to say, that people weight is greater than a shit load of fish which will mean that the vessel can only achieve some five to six nautical miles per hour. Our intention is to get as many people to Spain as we can. Switzerland is too far. But the boat can make the trip to Barcelona in two days. It won't be comfortable and it may stink a bit of fish but I think that's better than a Nazi firing squad, or a death camp like Auschwitz."

The young woman joined in, "Yes, where my father has ended up. I'm sure he would swap his mass grave for a shitty fishing boat."

The reality was not lost on the boys.

"We have also sorted two safe houses outside of Monaco around Cap d'Ail which we will have to use as stop off points. We will have to get our friends there as inconspicuously as possible. That means the healthy must make their way by bicycle. It is only — and I say only for the fit amongst us Claude," they all laughed — "about twenty kilometres, it is quieter and as we are a nation of cyclists, should not attract too much attention. However one of the first people we have to move is Michel and his immediate family. How is Michel, Auguste?"

"He has made a good recovery considering. He has lost the sight of his eye and the use of his fingers on the one hand and obviously walks with a limp. My brother did what he could under the restrictions he had. However he was questioned by the Gestapo the other day and despite having his 'secret' room, he was shitting himself. He would like to move him on as soon as possible."

"Understandable," replied René. "We will have to move fast as the Nazi's patience will wear thin and then they will start on the innocents."

"Albert, can you and the boys procure a few bicycles?"

"Yes, in the parking behind the hotel, the soldiers sometimes leave their bikes there, or outside of their normal billets. I am sure we can borrow some, better to do a few at a time otherwise it will look suspicious."

"Good," said René, "how are we going to move Michel?"

They all looked at each other, Auguste said, "I think it might be easier for me to go to my brother's house and move him, it won't seem unusual to an onlooker to see me there and any way, his house is fairly secluded, but I will need someone to meet me at the border of Monaco as I will use a police vehicle and I cannot cross over my territory."

"Good point said René. We have our contacts in Cap d'Ail where we have the houses I will arrange the *rendezvous* when we have the timings. It will be best to meet outside *Le Stade* Louis II:* from there it's only a couple of kilometres on the Avenue des Castelans to Cap d'Ail and the safe house. Let me know when Auguste."

sports stadium

"We will have to arrange transport for his family won't we?" asked a concerned Claude.

"I am afraid to move them all at once; it would be dangerous and attract attention which would not help them. They are not Jewish and are not under suspicion otherwise the Gestapo would have arrested them all before now. We can get them out at a later date, or God forbid, when this is all over, they can make their own way to Spain — or bring him back to France."

Auguste adjusted his belt and cap on his uniform and told his colleagues he was going to interview somebody and made his exit swiftly before anyone could ask him where he was going. Climbing into his state issued Citroën he made sure there was nothing obstructing the back seat and that he had some blankets to cover his cargo. He took the short drive to the outskirts of town where his brother's surgery was. They embraced as Laurent opened the door. Checking that he had not been followed, Auguste walked in and his brother led him upstairs to the secret room. Sitting in a chair was a very fragile Michel with a bandaged leg and a head wrap still.

"Bonjour, mon ami. Com ça va?" asked Auguste.

*"Je suis baisé," replied the injured man.

"Yes, they did a pretty good job on you didn't they? Did you tell them anything they wanted to know?" asked Auguste knowing the answer.

"Non, rien!"

*I'm fucked

"I didn't think so my old friend. Now we have to get you out of here. We have to get to the French Border, where there is a safe house from where we are going to take you to Spain."

"I don't want to go to Spain," said Michel protesting. "What about my family? I can't leave them behind: and what would I do?"

"About the same as you would do here — nothing! But your family will be safe and I am sure they would rather they knew that you were safe and that you will be reunited with them at a later date rather than executed in the church square. Get yourself ready we will leave in fifteen minutes."

The two brothers walked downstairs.

"Be careful Auguste, it's only a short trip but full of danger."

"I know, but what are we to do? There are many wrongs that need righting and we can only do what we can, when we can."

Laurent gave him a small bag containing some tablets, "He must take these," said the doctor, "he knows the dosages and they are written on the bottles anyway, but if he doesn't take them he will be in trouble."

The two men walked back upstairs to collect their friend. They hobbled down the stairs to the front door. Auguste checked around him and opened the door pulling the seat forward so as Michel could lie on the back seat. The patient let out a groan of pain as Auguste helped his leg inside the cramped vehicle.

"Sorry Michel, not long now and you can lie down

again. Meanwhile we'll cover you with these blankets. If we get stopped…………..well, if we get stopped we'll just have to hope for the best."

Auguste once again hugged his brother, "*Bonne chance mon frère,* be careful."

"*Merci, a bientôt,*" he said with a jocular wave of his hand, climbed into the car and started on the journey to the border.

⋯⸻⋯

Albert, Pierre, Charles and Georges made their way in darkness around to the back of the hotel where a lot of the bikes were kept for occasional use.

"*Mon Dieu,*" said Georges "there's loads of them; They are not going to miss a few are they?"

"Only the ones that don't have one when they all have to scramble," laughed Charles.

"*Ok mes amis,* let's go quickly and quietly. Meet you back at the barn."

The resistance had a small holding area which was owned by Claude's auntie and uncle where they kept horses and a few other animals. It was only twenty minutes out of town, not far from the doctor's surgery: but it was ideal for hiding most things and bicycles seemed to fit the bill. After an uneventful ride the four boys ended up at the barn to be greeted by Claude's uncle who opened the barn doors for them and they took them inside and covered them with hay and spread a tarpaulin over the top.

"We'll need a few more," said Albert, "We have a choice, we could get another four now, which would do us for a while, or we do it another day. But I think that they may find out that some are missing and might mount more security, which will make it more difficult in the future."

"But I'm knackered after that ride," protested Charles, "I don't fancy walking back and then riding here and walking back again."

Gaston, Claude's uncle, said "I can drive you back now and drive you back again later, if that helps."

The boys looked at each other.

"That would help," said Charles. "Let's go."

They bundled themselves into the big old Citroën and made their way back to town. Gaston dropped them fifty metres from the hotel and they walked down the promenade until they got to the hotel. It had just turned ten o' clock. The boys walked around the back and surveyed the situation. All was quiet so once again they picked their four bikes and got on them and started to ride out of the parking area.

"Achtung, Halt!" rang out from behind them as torches lit up their path. The boys peddled like hell, as if their lives depended on it — and it probably did.

"Arête ou je tire," shouted one of the soldiers threatening to shoot if they didn't stop. The boys kept pedalling and they were about to round the corner to freedom when a shot rang out. Charles collapsed with a jolt and his bike fell to the ground.

"Keep going," shouted Albert. "We can't stop or we will all be in the *merde!*" Charles lay on the floor with a bullet between his shoulder blades. Blood was pouring out of his young body as he jerked in nervous reaction, then with blood dribbling from his mouth he spasmed once more and for the last time.

Half a dozen soldiers got on their bikes and chased the three remaining boys, but their knowledge of the back streets was superior to the enemy's, as they were able to make their escape. Back at the hotel, two soldiers stood by Charles' body and one pushed him with his foot.

"He's dead," said one.

"*Scheiße*," said the other, "he's only a kid!"

"Yes," said his colleague, "but he was stealing German property."

"Is his death worth a fucking bike?" exclaimed his friend.

"No, but this is war. If he had had a gun pointed at you would you ask him to put it down? And if he didn't, would you wait for him to shoot you, or would you shoot first?"

"*Ja Ja,* I know but it seems such a waste of a young life."

"Kurt, we have young friends dying every day at the front. That boy is only a few years younger than us. This is a war."

"Yes, and one that I am not sure we should be fighting," said Kurt as he walked back to the hotel; ten minutes later the others came back.

"We lost the little bastards," said one.

"The advantages of having young legs," gasped the other as he tried to catch his breath.

The boys were pedalling for their lives, with tears in their eyes with the realisation that they had not only seen their first death, but that it was their friend who had died.

They got to the farm and Gaston opened the door and could see that they were all distressed.

"What happened?" asked the older man.

"They shot Charles," sobbed Georges, his close friend.

"Is he dead?" asked Gaston.

"I would think so," said Albert, "he was next to me and went down like a sack of potatoes; if he wasn't dead then the pigs would have finished him off by now. Or, he's not dead and they will question him and torture him. Either way he will die, it's best that he is dead now; it stops further pain and also stops him revealing any information."

"Jesus, Albert; is that all you can think about?" asked Georges.

"I am just being practical my friend, there is nothing we can do now except accept Gaston's kind offer to take us back to town and go our separate ways. Pierre and I will listen out for information in the morning at breakfast and see what we can find out, if anything. Now let's go."

They piled into the old car once again and made their way back.

Albert sat in the front next to Gaston just staring out of the windscreen.

'What have we let ourselves in for?' thought Albert as the rain started again and glistened on the windscreen from the oncoming headlights. 'Shit, is that soldiers?' panicked Albert, but no, the car drove by without incident. Everyone sighed with relief.

⁂

Auguste, mindful of the task he was taking on, made the ten minute journey to *Le Stade* Louis II. He approached the stadium on his right and turned just before it, drove parallel to it and at the end turned left and stopped his car on the quiet corner. A grocer's van pulled up in front of him and flashed its lights three times. Out got two men and walked toward Auguste. The *gendarme* got out of the car and greeted them warmly with strong handshakes.

"How is the patient?" asked one.

"Fragile," replied Auguste. "He took a good beating."

"Bastards," said the other. "Quick let's get him in the van. There are soldiers all over the place."

The men gently helped the injured man out of the back of the police car and shuffled him to the waiting vehicle. One got into the covered wagon and hauled Michel up while the others supported his body. He was laid out on the floor and covered with a tarpaulin and then crates of vegetables were place across the width of the van, blocking off their human cargo. Handing the men the bag that Laurent had given him Auguste said, "These are his medicines. Make sure he takes them."

Nodding their understanding the three men shook hands and went their separate ways. Auguste watched as the van turned around and disappeared down Avenue de Castalans and into the relative safety of Cap d'Ail. 'At least he would be safer there than here — God willing'.

Turning around himself, he made his way back to his station. At the next intersection there was a road block. He was waved down by two SS soldiers while three or more stood to one side holding their machine guns.

Auguste wound down his window. The soldier raised his hand in the now customary half salute, "Where are you going?" He asked.

"Back to my station," said Auguste.

"Where have you been?"

"On patrol," replied Auguste.

"Why?" continued the inquisitor.

"I would have thought that was obvious," said Auguste wishing he hadn't been quite so flippant. "It is part of our job to patrol," he said clawing back the situation, "anyway we had heard there was some commotion and it is our place to protect people and assist our German friends where we can," trying not to be sarcastic, while the words were sticking in his craw.

He waved him through the road block and Auguste, slightly sweating, made his way back to the station. Around the town there was plenty of movement of soldiers. When he entered the station, he asked his colleague what had happened in his absence.

"The SS came in asking us if we knew anything about some kids stealing their bikes." Auguste laughed, "Is that all they have to worry about?"

"I'm sorry Auguste, it's not as funny as it could be; they have killed one of the young boys."

"Shit, who was it?"

"Charles Trottier, — his family have been informed. We had to stop his father from going out with his pistol to shoot the bastards who murdered his son."

"I'm not surprised," said Auguste as he remembered the young man who was full of enthusiasm and had been looking forward to doing his bit for the resistance. So, they got some bikes, but at what cost? There would be no peace now. They were going to have to do as much as they possibly could, to help get the Jewish people to safety, as they would surely be persecuted now; as well as keeping an eye on the resistance and those that helped them — like us.

CHAPTER TEN

London Majestic Hotel March 2005
Management meeting Monday 10.00 am

"Good morning everyone," said Michael, "I trust those that were lucky enough to have the weekend off had a good time. Now it's back to post mortems. I've asked my secretary Susan to join us in her other role, as she is working with Coleen on sales and marketing who needs a volunteer, don't you Coleen?" asked Michael.

"Certainly welcome the input," replied the young woman with a hint of an Irish accent.

"Susan has been responsible for setting up our media section. She has revamped our website and our email marketing skills and will be monitoring our Trip Advisor comments and reply where necessary. So Susan, what's been the feedback for the last couple of weeks?"

The pretty, but slightly dumpy, curly-headed blonde secretary was eager to let her colleagues know that she warranted her integrated position within the marketing department.

"The main feedback at the moment is still about Valentine's night. Comments around the food and service are still positive. We did have one complaint on Trip Advisor that said they waited too long for their food, and drinks service was slow, but they enjoyed the evening. Others said that the show was good and we have had several requests for information for our Christmas and

New Year packages when they are ready."

"Well, that's promising; Bloody hell Christmas already!"

"We also got a couple of comments that will please Chef," continued Sally, "several clients mentioned that the lack of great staples like Beef and Lamb were missing from the menu in place of what could only be described as 'rabbit and hospital food' — not my comments Chef."

"I totally agree with them," said an irate Frenchman. "I would have preferred to do a classic Beef Wellington or a great Crown of Lamb, but what can you do? We are trying to cater for everyone. We can't have a menu of six choices, especially on a fixed price menu."

"Point worth noting Chef," said Michael, "it might be worth considering supplements for the other dishes over and above the fixed price menu."

"How about we charge extra for the vegetarian and soppy dishes?" said an aggrieved Chef!

"Maybe we can discuss that Chef," said Michael with a smile on his face.

"Feedback from the BAFTAS Sally?"

"As you probably know sir, those types don't usually bother to comment unless it was all shit! However we did get an email from BAFTA themselves who thanked us for the standard and quality of our hotel and they hoped that they can work with us again. I wrote back on your behalf saying what a pleasure and a privilege it had been and that we looked forward to next year. They asked us to provisionally make the same arrangements for 2006."

"Well, that's good."

"We also got a lovely email from one of the mothers of a young actor in the Harry Porter film,"

"Potter!" interjected her boss. "Harry Potter, Sally."

"Whatever," said his secretary, "I'd still rather watch when 'Harry Met Sally'," they all laughed; "anyway, it was his first red carpet and he couldn't believe his luck when he was told he was staying in one of the best hotels in London and found himself sitting next to Johnny Depp's stand- in at the dinner."

Again everyone had a laugh, "Where was Johnny Depp? Why wasn't he here?" said Michael.

"He was at the Savoy boss" said reception manager Angela.

"That's not good enough. Coleen, let's keep in touch with BAFTA make a bee line for the top dogs for next year; try and get hold of some of their agents and see what you can conjure up. Great work to you Mavis, I believe housekeeping had a result?"

"All went smoothly sir, and if the tips that the girls received from the rooms was anything to go by, then we got it right."

"Excellent," replied a satisfied MD.

Turning to Coleen again, Michael asked, "What have we got coming up Coleen?"

"Well as you know boss, the biggest event we have this year after the BAFTAS is the Jewish

Holocaust Memorial Society London Branch Dinner to mark the sixtieth anniversary of the end of World War Two in May. The actual memorial day is on the fourth and fifth of May, but that is more solemn, so the dinner on Sunday the eighth is more celebration of those that survived, rather than those who didn't."

"How many are we expecting?"

"About four hundred."

"Are they having a Kosher menu chef?"

"Mister Wilkins and I sat with the organisers last week and we decided to make it Kosher for everyone, even those that are not." said the Chef who seemed to be more understanding about that requirement, than catering for the vegetarians.

"We decided on a simple *Smoked Salmon*, followed by *Breast of Chicken in a mushroom and red wine sauce* with a *Brûléed Lemon Tart* to finish. We discussed Fillet Steak or Rack of Lamb, but cooking temperatures would cause a problem with four hundred people; and experience tells me these sort of clients tend to like their meat either over cooked or rareish and it would be a difficult ask, whereas chicken is more universally acceptable."

"Agreed," concurred their boss.

"Wines?" asked Michael directing his question at Alex, the banqueting manager.

"We will be offering Kosher red and white wines, but if anyone wants ordinary wines or even non alcoholic we will have a small selection for them."

"Wine without alcohol must be like talking to

yourself," said Michael "and in my case almost as boring."

They all laughed politely, "I'm sure that's not the case," protested Angela, reception manager, slightly blushing at her unintended, somewhat sycophantic, remark.

"You should be inside my head on a bad day," laughed Michael diffusing the embarrassment.

"Thanks everyone; any other questions?"

They all looked at each other and nodded their acceptance that the meeting was over.

Michael sat in his suite and poured himself a glass of wine. He'd had a good day, but sometimes found the late evenings on the lonely side. Having been married for some seventeen years and building a life with someone you love and then find it falling apart to the point of no return, takes its toll. They had had one child who was now at pre senior school in France and he would see her during holidays; thankfully he still got on well with his ex wife so custody and visiting rights had never been a problem. He knew he wasn't the only man in his mid forties that had found himself in this position, but it didn't help or ease the disappointment he felt. Still, he had plenty to be grateful for. Here he was as Managing Director of this hotel and soon would take over as MD of the group, something he was looking forward to. After all, his father was now eighty and his uncle seventy five and although Radford, as financial director, had been running the company on a day to day basis, his family wanted Michael to step up to the plate now. It was agreed that he would run this hotel for a year or so and then step into the position hopefully while his father and uncle were still alive. Now however, what mattered was the success of the flagship of the group.

'I would like to meet someone and share my success with them,' thought Michael as he swirled the red wine around his mouth and, with a satisfied glow, stayed in his armchair listening to his music until he drifted off into a light sleep, waking some forty minutes later and got undressed ready for his bed.

'Tomorrow is another day,' he thought as he got into the crisp white Egyptian cotton sheets and turned out the light. 'Another day...........'

CHAPTER ELEVEN
Nice Majestic

Christine got into a taxi at Nice airport and asked for the hotel. Michael was waiting outside as the car pulled up and she got out. She put her arms around him as the driver took her bags out of the car. They kissed, "Hello," she said smiling.
"Hello," he said. "It's lovely to see you."
"And you."
The driver put the bags in front of the entrance to Michael's apartments. He paid the driver and opened the door. They got into the lift and he pressed the private penthouse button. They looked at each other and he pulled her towards him and kissed her passionately. She responded. They exited the lift and he opened the door to the apartment; kissing her as he pushed her backwards into the room.
"Whoa cowboy, take a breath," she chided, "I want to look around first. There's plenty of time to study the bedroom later; and where's my glass of Champagne? after all I am in France." Suitably chastised Michael went to the fridge and opened a bottle of Bollinger and poured out two glasses.
"A lovely view Michael," said Christine as she gazed out of the balcony windows.
"It certainly is," replied Michael, his vision securely fixed on her perfectly formed rear end. She turned around seeing him studying her, "You are incorrigible," she said as she took her glass.

"Come on then show me around."
"Well, this is about it, apart from the bedroom."
"Oh come on then, let's get it out of the way," she said jokingly. They went into the room, "Obviously old hotel furniture," she smiled. She kissed him with purpose and rubbed her hand over his trousers, and undid his zip. They fell to the bed and kissed more intensely. He had missed her and he thought she must have done the same as she took control. Soon they were sharing familiar territory and movements. Their passion culminated in a mutual explosion of love and they just laid there on their backs looking at the ceiling.
"Hmm, seems like you missed me," she said as she turned her mouth towards him. He kissed her, "Certainly did!"
"God knows what you'll be like after six months, that's if I come over again."
"Well, you will won't you?" he pleaded.
"Let's just get through the next few days and see what happens, shall we? Let's just enjoy it now! I'm going to take a bath and then I presume you are taking me out for dinner."
"Of course."
She went into the bathroom, ran her bath and put in some French bubble bath. The suds filled the bath as she immersed her body into the hot water. Michael walked in with her freshly topped up glass of champagne.
"So are we going to eat in the hotel restaurant tonight?"

"No, I thought we would go to this lovely bistro that I have been to a couple of times. I'm not sure we should eat at the hotel this time around. Probably better when I have settled in."
"Ok, if you don't want people to see me,"
"You know that's not true, it's just...."
"I know, I'm only joking; I'm happy to go where ever you suggest."

They took their seats in the corner at the round table with its braid tablecloth and free standing candle. Marie came over with two *Pastis,* as an invitation from the house.
"Bonsoir Monsieur Nicolson,"
"Bonsoir Marie, c'est mon amie d'Angleterre, Christine."
"Enchante mademoiselle, bienvenue à Nice."
"Merci," said Christine shyly, hoping that that is where the conversation in French would end. Marie gave them both menus.
"How's work?" he asked as Christine took a sip of her *Pastis,*
"Shit," she exclaimed, "that's horrible what is it? It tastes like aniseed balls and I hate them too!"
"*Pastis*, and yes it is like aniseed, liquorice. Don't drink it if you don't like it."
"I won't thank you. Yuk! I never saw you drink that before."
"Well, 'when in Rome',"
"Yes but we're in France."
"Exactly, I rest my case." They both laughed.
They spent a beautiful evening together, drank

too much wine, laughed as they always did and went back to the apartment and made love until the early hours.

The ten days went by very quickly, but they had spent some quality time together without the constraints of work, or even working together.

The time had come to say goodbye and they drove silently to the airport in the taxi. "I had a lovely time," said Christine, "thank you."

"The pleasure was all mine — well, I hope not all mine."

She laughed, "No, I had my fair share." She leaned over and kissed him warmly.

"We'll keep in touch won't we?" asked Michael.

"Darling, you know how much I love you and how much I have learned from you, how much fun we have had and how proud I am of you and what you are going to become. We are both young; you are a gorgeous man inside and out and have so much to offer, as I would like to think I may have, so just let life take its course. Don't let's make any promises we can't keep. You have got to concentrate on your work; as you always told me 'work comes first', make this work for you. We'll keep in touch and yes I will come over and see you again if the situation allows me to."

"Whatever that means," said Michael somewhat despondently."

"Yes, whatever that may mean." She kissed him again as the taxi pulled up in the front of the airport.

"Just leave me at the gate, I'll be alright and like

you, I hate goodbyes,"

"But.....," started Michael, she put her finger on his lips and said, "For me," she kissed him and walked into the departure lounge. He watched her go through to check in, she turned and waved; he waved back and then got back into the taxi and started on his return journey. 'I'm going to miss her' he thought, with a tear in his eye.

It was Michael's first official day at the hotel. He and Alain had spent time together socially getting to get to know each other but this was change-over weekend. The day was spent visiting each head of department in their relevant places and getting to know them. The weekend went quickly and the two new found friends met over dinner in the hotel restaurant for the last time.

"So, what do you think?" asked Alain.

"Yes, good," replied Michael "however I feel you may have had a problem with the food and beverage and in particularly the kitchen and Roger, the Head Chef."

"Hmm, *mais oui*! He's very old school, very set in his ways and is not willing to change. Villiers likes him, but Villiers is not F&B orientated; as I said he is more front of house and numbers. As you know, Pierre Troisgras, Anton Mosimann, Roger Vergé and the Roux Brothers have taken the industry by storm, but I can't get Roger to look at the new styles. He's still intent on following the teachings of Escoffier and Pelleprat; not that I'm knocking it, after all they were the masters, but

others are changing their ways, why can't Roger?"
"Safety?" asked Michael, "if he has Villiers behind him and he has his security, do you think he's just happy to trundle on producing what he is comfortable doing?"
"Probably, however the percentages are good and we certainly have no complaints with the banqueting, but the restaurant is suffering."
"Well," continued Michael, "maybe the new broom can sweep clean?"
I wouldn't bank on it," concluded Alain.
They said their *adieus* and Alain said he would pop in the morning to say final goodbyes. "I wish you the best of luck my friend. As I am staying with the company I am sure that we will see each other again"
The following morning, Michael went into Villier's office and said, "I'm ready to go, *Monsieur Villiers.*"
"In that case, said the director, "management meeting at ten o'clock this morning."
"Perfect."
Everyone was assembled as Villiers re-introduced his new Senior Assistant Manager.
"As most of you are aware, Michael is part of the managing family and is here not only to polish his already refined experience, but to learn from all of us on how an hotel like ours functions. He will have some new ideas which we will welcome without losing the character of our small hotel."

⁕⁀⊱⊰⁀⁕

Three months into his time at the hotel much had already changed. He had been keeping in touch with Christine regularly, but had since formed a relationship with Juliette Varon. She had come into the hotel on several occasions and on her earlier visit in March was introduced to Michael. He remembered holding her hand as they extended their cheeks for the customary greetings.

"Juliette has a huge booking at Le Negresco," started Villiers, "and has asked us if we can take her overflow. I'm sure we can help, can't we Michael?"

"Depending on the dates Sir, I am sure we can help. If you would like to come into my office Juliette I am sure we can come to some arrangement."

She was indeed a good looking woman; her dark hair pulled to the back of her head, dark brown melting eyes and striking features. She sat opposite him and crossed her legs. She explained that she needed twenty rooms for the last weekend of the following month. Michael phoned the reception manager to check availability and confirmed that they were available; they agreed a price.

"You speak very good French for an Englishman," she said.

"You speak very good English for a French woman," he quipped in reply.

"My mother was English, my father French and I went to school in the UK, what's your excuse'" she smiled.

"My Father is French, my mother Italian, I was

born in France and educated in England and in Switzerland."

"And are now a highflying young hotelier?"

"Low gliding rather than highflying methinks!"

They both laughed.

"Look," he said, looking at his watch, "it's lunchtime, would you like to have lunch with me while the reception manager is drawing up the contract?"

She hesitated, "yes, OK" then followed with "that would be nice."

They sat in the restaurant overlooking the *esplanade*.

"Would you like something to drink?" he asked his guest.

"Just Perrier water for now, I may have a glass of white wine with my lunch."

The menus arrived and Michael ordered two Perrier waters and a bottle of Chablis.

"So how long……?" they both said at the same time.

"You first," she said.

"I was going to ask how long you have worked at Le Negresco and how long were you here?"

"I left here a year ago after two years. It was the right move at the right time and I am really enjoying it. We get a lot of famous people in the hotel which is always a distraction. It's smaller than this hotel, but it has a wonderful old-world feel and of course such history. We have a conference that weekend which is why we need those rooms. Maybe I could return this compliment and you can eat in our Michelin starred restaurant next week."

"That would be nice, thank you."

"And you, how long will you be here before you move on to something grander?" she said toying with her *Salade Niçoise*.

"It's meant to be a year, but I am not sure. We will have to wait and see."

The reception manager brought in the contract and Michael signed it under the reception manager's signature and Juliette signed on behalf of Le Negresco.

After lunch he walked her to the door, "It was nice to spend some personal time with you," he said as he opened the door. "Do you remember that this is where we first met, before I had even started here?"

"No." she said sympathetically.

"Oh," replied Michael somewhat forlorn.

She laughed, "of course I remember, a good looking new face on the block, how could I forget?"

Since that day they had seen each other when work schedules had permitted. Last weekend was the first time that they had had the weekend off at the same time and they spent it together at his apartment, they had gone out on the Saturday evening but Sunday he cooked at home. It was a fairly simple, but debauched, two days of food, wine and sex; all of which was close to both their hearts.

What was he going to tell Christine?

CHAPTER TWELVE
Ideology or Fanaticism

Kurt Schmidt was a twenty four year old, well educated, Aryan and unmarried; the minimum requirement for an SS soldier. He was driven, as a young man, by ideology. The 'preaching' of Hitler all made sense. He joined the Hitler youth at nineteen years of age, a year before the Second World War started; within a year he was a youth leader. Having been born just after the First World War, memories of that conflict were still fresh in the minds of his father and the family. His grandfather had been killed in action, devastating his grandmother and her children, including Kurt's father. Hitler had made great strides in the rebuilding of Germany economically and had become so charismatic that millions were now following him blindly. Kurt's father had been a great supporter of Hitler's political stance and the work that he was doing rebuilding a financially devastated country: it was natural therefore, that Kurt would take on his father's beliefs and so he joined the Hitler youth.
When the war started, Kurt was twenty and was immediately recruited by the party to join the elite SS. After training, which was minimal — belief in the Führer being more important than technical or psychological skills — he was sent to France in 1941. By 1943 when he arrived in Monaco, he had become disillusioned. He had seen so much death, most of which he considered unnecessary,

but the persecution of the Jews, by now had changed the young man's view. Even *Kristalnacht** and the Book Burning** of the mid and late 1930's had had no impression on the idealist, as, at the time, he was too young to really understand.

Now he was in Monaco, he thought he may have left the butchery behind; but this latest action by him and his colleagues made him realise that this war was being fought in different dimensions across Europe and further afield — for what? The boy that had lain dead in front of him was only eighteen or nineteen. What did he think he was going to accomplish? Was he more ideological than the young Nazi in Kurt, or just as misguided?

He slept uneasily in his billet that night, trying to understand the inbuilt hatred instilled in him by the Hitler philosophy against the Jews. Why were young people prepared to risk their lives for such a perceived hated race? These people weren't Jews they were French. Or were they? After all, Jews existed in all countries. Religion was a strange phenomenon, that and fanaticism. Maybe he was in the wrong place at the wrong time.

*Night of Broken Glass, also called the November Pogrom was a mob riot against Jews carried out by SA paramilitary (Sturmabteilung : Stormdetachment) and civilians through out Nazi Germany on 9/10 November 1938
**a campaign conducted by the German Student Union the Deutsche Studentenschaft or DSt to ceremonially burn perceived 'left wing' Jewish written books in Nazi Germany and Austria in the 1930's

What could he do to change things? Absolutely nothing!

Over breakfast that morning, Pierre told Albert to come to the dining room as there seemed to be a lot of commotion among the soldiers. 'They certainly seem animated' thought Albert as he entered the packed dining room. The general chatter amongst the soldiers implied that their orders were to conduct house to house searches looking for the boys that had stolen their bikes, members of the so called resistance and Jewish families.

Albert needed to speak to Claude or Auguste. He decided that a quick bicycle ride to the *Gendarmerie* might be the most effective. Telling his colleague that he would be going on his thirty minute break he got on his bike and rode the five minutes or so to the station.

"*Bonjour, est Auguste içi?*" he said as he entered the building

"*Un moment,*" said the officer behind the desk.

Auguste came out from his office, "*Ques que c'est tu veux,*" he said acknowledging the boy and ushering him outside.

"I am sorry to call like this," said a concerned Albert, "but I think the SS are on the move."

"What do you mean Albert?" asked Auguste.

He explained the conversations that he had overheard in the hotel that morning.

"We will have to contact René and Claude and

meet at the bar at lunchtime; you get back to the hotel and I'll see you later."

Albert got on his bike and was back at the hotel in minutes just dropping off at George's house on the way.

"*Bonjour Madame Reynard,*" said Albert as Georges' mother opened the door to the little terraced town house, "is Georges here?"

""No Albert, he is off today and has gone into the centre. He'll be back in a minute, do you wish to wait?"

"No," replied the young man politely, "can you ask him to meet me in the usual place at about two o'clock?"

"*Mais oui,*"

"*Merci,*" said Albert as he got on his bike and got back to the hotel.

At two o'clock, René, Esther, Claude and Auguste were waiting when Albert and Georges came into the bar.

"Is your information sound?" asked René as he lit a cigarette and sipped at his *pastis*.

"As reliable as can be expected from the mouths of the Germans," said Albert somewhat sarcastically.

"In that case, we will have to move quickly. Auguste you have a list of all the Jewish families here?"

"Yes, we were ordered to prepare the list for the SS. We have been informing as many as possible, that the time will come when, for their safety they may have to leave Monte Carlo."

"The two safe houses are ready and the boat has been converted. We can take 20 including the skipper at a time. So we obviously cannot sail without full complement so we need to get as many as possible into the safe houses as quickly as possible."

"I have two families that I spoke to the other day who are willing to go to Spain. Others don't fancy the boat trip and will want to cross into France and take their chances with train journeys and by road" said Auguste.

"I could start at the hotel," said Albert "we have got two sisters from a Jewish family working in there that I have not approached yet, but will do today."

That night, Sarah and Albert were in bed in his room. They had made love and were just laying holding hands.

"Sarah, we have to move you as soon as possible. The Germans are set to move in on all the Jewish families and deport them. You know what that will mean don't you? Executions, prison camp — death camps — for you and your family; I can help you get away to safety. You must go," Albert turned to kiss her young lips, "I don't want to see you go, but you have to."

She started to cry and held him closer.

"Why is this happening, we thought we were safe here? What is wrong with these people?"

"That is probably a question that people will be asking many years from now. But for the moment we have to get your family out."

"Still tearful, Sarah said, "I'm not sure my parents will be too difficult to persuade but Rachel maybe."

"Why?"

"Because she has met one of the soldiers staying in the hotel and she believes that the persecution is rubbish. Apparently he's really nice — according to her."

"*Merde*, do your parents know?"

"No, they would go mad."

"Have you spoken to Rachel?"

"Yes, but she takes no notice of me. She believes this guy is different."

"Don't we all hope that they are not all the same? I will come with you back to your house and talk to your parents. Will they listen to me? After all I'm still a kid too. Are they going to listen to me or will I have to get one of my older colleagues to talk to them?"

"We can try."

They took the short bus ride to the family home. Sarah introduced Albert as her colleague from the hotel.

"Hello Mister and Misses Gold, a pleasure to meet you."

"Hello Albert," said a suspicious father. "My daughter has spoken about you a lot, I understand that you maybe more than just colleagues."

Shyly and with a moderate embarrassment Albert managed to control the situation, "It is true

Monsieur that I am very privileged to say that Sarah and I are very good friends; and I promise that my whole intention is to keep her safe, which is why I am here today."

Albert continued to explain why, indeed, he was there and how he needed, with the help of his organisation, to get them out of Monaco and France.

"We will need to get you to our safe house first which is just outside Monte Carlo. Then you will travel to Spain by boat. Be ready tomorrow morning. Take as little as you can as you will be picked up by one of my colleagues at nine o'clock in the morning. It's a twenty minute drive across the border where I will meet you."

"What about Rachel?" asked a tearful Sarah.

"She must come as well" replied Albert.

"But she won't," said her father, "but I will talk to her tonight, she's not here at the moment, she stayed over with a friend yesterday as it's her day off today."

"She has a young man," replied her mother.

"What? Who?" asked the strict family man.

"She didn't tell me, dear."

"Sarah?"

"She should tell you *Papa*, I don't want to tell on her."

"I insist, you tell me, Sarah."

More tearful than before, the thought of losing Albert and betraying her sister was getting too much.

"He is a young German soldier," cried Sarah.

"*Oy vey,*" said her father hitting his hand on his forehead.

"*Oy vey,*" repeated the mother.

"*Sacré Bleu, quelle merde*" echoed Albert realising the cat was now out of the bag..

"Does he know she's Jewish?" cried father.

"I don't know," said Sarah still tearful.

"If he finds out, we're in trouble," said Albert trying to think on his feet. "When she gets home tonight you will have to persuade her to go with you. If she refuses there is nothing I can do; or any of us."

"What about our house?"

"Hopefully when this is all over you will be able to return. If you don't leave, it would be useless anyway. I'll leave it all with you *Monsieur* Gold and I will see you tomorrow morning. *Madame,*" said Albert politely, as he said his goodbyes and went to the front door, followed by Sarah.

"I don't want to go Albert," she said putting her arms around him, "please don't make me."

"*Cherie*, I don't want you to go, but you must, for you and your family's safety."

"What are we going to do about Rachel?"

"I'm afraid that is down to the family, it will be your responsibility. I can do no more. I will see you all tomorrow." He kissed her long and hard, "who knows we may meet again when you come back. Meanwhile stay safe, *bon chance, je t'aime.*" He blew her a kiss as he made his way back to town, with a tear in his eye.

Kurt rolled over and kissed the young woman lying next to him. This wasn't the first time that they had slept together, but it was the first time she had stayed over in his room.

"*Guten Morgen*," he said as he touched her face and ran his hand down the side of her body. He spoke little French but she spoke German as well as French so German was their language of choice.

"Hello, how are you this morning?"

"Good and you?"

"Hmm," she said, "fine, can we do that again?"

"I wish I could, but no, I have to go on duty."

"When will this all be over Kurt?"

"I don't know, if Hitler has his way it will go on until he has taken over the world. But we hear from Berlin that he is getting worried about the threat from the Soviets in the East and, since he declared war on the USA after Pearl Harbour, he is scared about the US and UK coalition. Who knows it could be over in one year or ten. I know I have had enough and can't wait to get back to Germany and take up a proper career."

What do you want to do?" said the girl as she put on her skirt.

"I wanted to be a doctor before all this *Scheiße* started. I would prefer to be healing people, rather than killing them."

"Have you ever killed anyone?" asked Rachel.

Thinking back to the other evening, he answered truthfully, "No, I haven't but I have been with colleagues who have — and I have watched executions which is even worse."

"I am sorry," she said as he straightened his belt and picked up his cap. She went over and kissed him gently.

"Have a good day and don't kill anyone," she said with a nervous smile.

"I'll try not to" he smiled, "promise."

'He looks so handsome in his uniform' she thought as he closed the door behind him. She had to wait a few minutes before sneaking out of his room. She thought back to their first meeting when they had all arrived at the hotel. The twenty odd single rooms the hotel had, were on the top floor and one day Rachel covered for the chambermaid who had her day off. She had gone into his room to take fresh towels. He was good looking and for a German, she had thought, charming and polite. They knew that their relationship was dangerous and stupid, but they were young and it was war. It could be very much worse if anyone realised that they were having a relationship. If the people at the hotel who knew she was Jewish and decided to tell, Kurt would be in as much trouble as her. That is why she had never told him 'and that's the way it must stay' she thought as she opened the door and stepped out on to the hallway and down the fire escape.

"Hello," said Rachel as she opened the door to the family home, "anyone home?" She walked into the front room to see all the family sitting around the room looking extremely serious. "Who died?" she asked sarcastically.

"We all could," replied her father in a very serious tone. "What are you doing young lady? Are you playing with all our lives? Who do you think you are? Who is this German soldier and why are you jeopardising all our lives, I just don't believe you?"

Rachel stared at her sister, "You bitch!" she exclaimed.

"Do not speak to your sister like that. I put her under pressure and made her tell me what was going on. We have a problem, the Germans are starting to round up Jews and send them to Germany to camps for extermination or just into France for execution."

"Where did you learn this rubbish from?" asked Rachel innocently.

"You mean your Nazi boyfriend hasn't told you this?" said a now very angry father.

"Of course not, who told you?"

"We had a visit from a young man who works with the resistance and they are moving us tomorrow and you have to come with us."

"Who is this young man? Albert? the one that Sarah is fucking? So, it's alright for her, but not me?"

"He's not a fucking Nazi," shouted Sarah in desperation!

"Enough, enough" said the parents. "Do not use that gutter language in front of your mother and me. These are difficult times girls and we all have to stick together."

"Well, I'm not going anywhere," stated Rachel

stubbornly.

"You will pack your necessities and be ready to go at nine in the morning," ordered her father, "that is all there is to it."

"Well, I'm not going," shouted Rachel as she stormed out of the house followed by her sister and mother;

"Rachel, come back" they shouted in unison, "please!"

But Rachel was running down the road.

"We must go after her," cried Misses Gold to her husband.

"No, if that's what she wants, let her be. As much as it hurts me, we cannot sacrifice all of us for her petulant behaviour. Sarah seems to be leaving someone she cares for, for the sake of the family and so I am afraid that is the way it must be. Now go and get your things ready. We will leave the house as it is, for our daughter and hope that your friend Albert will keep an eye on her if he can. Now let's get ready."

At nine o'clock promptly a Citroën 11 CV pulled up in front of the Gold's house. The family came out with a few bags and the driver put them in the boot.

"There are only three of you, I was told there would be four."

"Our other daughter is not coming," said Gold, "we will leave without her."

"Well, that gives more room for mother and daughter in the back and you sit up front with me, but it could be very dangerous for her when they find out."

"I know, but we cannot jeopardise Sarah and us for the doggedness of Rachel. With luck Albert will keep an eye on her and if she decides to leave, he and your colleagues may be able to help her, if not, *C'est la vie!*"

They all got in the car and made the short journey to the border. As they approached there was a German check point.

"Keep calm," said the driver. "Try and look as relaxed as possible and let me do the talking."

He wound the window down as the guard approached. The guard looked around the inside of the vehicle and Sarah smiled at him and gave a wave gesture with her right hand. He smiled back.

"Where are you going?"

"Off to Nice for a day's shopping and a birthday lunch with my niece," said the driver.

He waved them on and they drove through the barrier.

As they approached Cap d'Ail the driver took a right turn away from the beach and after a kilometre turned left and parked in front of a small house. Outside were Albert and Claude. They got out of the car and Sarah went over to Albert once again with tears in her eyes as she hugged him.

"This is Claude," said Albert to the Golds.

"*Bonjour, bonjour*" said everyone offering handshakes.

"You will stay here all day until eight this evening

when it is getting dark. You will be picked up again and taken to the harbour. Do not open the door to anyone unless they say, *Cygne Noir* (Black Swan). Make sure you have all your papers for when you get to Spain as although they will welcome you, there will be certain paperwork necessary to let you stay. I will say goodbye now and leave you with our friends who will look after you. *Bon chance y bon voyage*," said Claude shaking hands again.

Sarah gave Albert a kiss, "Goodbye, I will never forget you."

"Nor me you, *ma chérie*,"

Mister Gold came over and proffered his hand. "Thank you Albert, you are a brave young man to help us; stay safe.

"I will *monsieur, merci*."

Claude and Albert got into Claude's car and made their way back to town.

"You OK?" asked Claude as they approached the checkpoint.

"Yes, fine," replied Albert, "a mixture of adrenalin and sadness."

"I am sure," replied his mentor. "You did a good job. That's just the start *mon jeune ami*, we will have plenty to do in the next few months." They were waved through the checkpoint and continued their journey homeward, in silence. Claude was right, over the next couple of months they helped many, many people escape from the Principality.

CHAPTER THIRTEEN
Nice Majestic Christmas 1986/87

Michael's phone rang in his office: It was Villiers.
"Can you pop into my office please Michael?" asked his boss.
He knocked courteously on the door, "*Entrée*," came the reply. "Hello Michael, sit down."
Looking a little apprehensive, he somewhat concernedly asked, "Is everything alright *monsieur*?"
"Of course Michael, nothing is wrong; on the contrary, you are approaching a year with us and you may wonder why you haven't been informed as to your next move."
"I had been waiting for something but I have to say I am enjoying this job very much and feel I can still do more, so I am in no hurry to leave."
"That, therefore, is good news, as I have asked head office if you can stay with me for another year. You have been trying to change the restaurant operation and have met with a bit of resistance both from Roger and me, but I think you are right; I have spoken to Roger and he is happy to remain as executive chef to look after controls and finances, but would welcome the addition of a creative chef as his *senior sous chef*. I have spoken to your Uncle and he has agreed the move, but does not want to lose Roger as it is only a few years until his retirement and he has been with the company for many years."

"Absolutely, I totally understand. Who knows, he may even enjoy the challenge."

"Indeed, so you can look for the right person. You have the coming year to put everything into action. I wouldn't make any changes until after the New Year. Christmas and New Year's Eve is already fully booked so let's go with that and ensure we have the right team in place in time for a new look 'St Valentines'. By the way how are you getting on with our friend Juliette?"

"Huhmm, very well thank you sir," replied Michael coyly.

"She's a good girl and a friend, so I am sure you will be good to her."

"Of course sir."

"Go on then, carry on the good work."

Michael went into his office and picked up the phone, and dialled Juliette's office number. "Is that the most beautiful, sexiest PR girl in the whole of Monaco?"

"No, sorry you have the right number but the wrong person; I am the most beautiful, sexiest PR girl in the whole of France!"

They both laughed.

"Listen," said Michael, "I have some good news — or bad, depending which way you look at it."

"Yes?" said Juliette.

"You are stuck with me for at least another year. They have asked me to stay on through next year."

"That's wonderful Michael, can we celebrate?"

"Of course, I cannot think of a better excuse; *Je*

t'aime."
"*Moi aussi. Un bisou.*"
He put the phone down and smiled.

The summer of 1986 had come to an end. Michael had been seeing Juliette for a couple of months since Christine had left. They had spoken on the phone. They were distant but tried to keep up a front. One day he called Christine and asked when she was coming over again.
"Michael, I'm not sure that I can. It's not that I don't want to see you; it's just a pointless exercise at the moment. I've been promoted to Head Receptionist and you know what work load that means and you have your work. You have another six months there and then you don't even know where you will be going. As much as I love you, one of us has to be strong. We'll keep in touch by letter and cards; we will always be friends. You know that you are very special to me and I will value what we had for the rest of my life and who knows we might meet again somewhere and if the time is right.... Well you know. Keep safe my darling: and be successful. I love you."
"But Christine........" the phone went dead. She had hung up.
"Give me five minutes" she said to her colleague, "I'm going to the loo."
She sat in the cubicle and put her head in her hands and sobbed.
Michael put the phone down and looked in the mirror by the phone. His eyes welled up. She had

a very important place in his young life and he respected her strong decision. Maybe she had found someone else? Maybe not, but whatever, she was right: and with typical male bravado he thought 'that means I am free to see Juliette without guilt.'

Christmas and New Year passed into 1987 without hiccups. Both Juliette and Michael took their days off on the twenty sixth and seventh of December. The days were warm and sunny but the evenings' cold. So strolls along the beach were the norm, with lunches on the *Esplanade* and dinner at home. They also took the second and third of January off together and they were getting closer as the weeks went on. He never heard from Christine again and wasn't sure whether that upset him or whether he was relieved.

Meanwhile at work, he had advertised for a *sous* Chef with experience of modern *cuisine*. He was pleased with the response he had received from the Caterer and Hotelkeeper, but he had also contacted his colleague Anton Mosimann at the Dorchester explaining his situation and that he was looking for a young dynamic chef to take on the creative side of the kitchen.

"I have just the person for you. Do you remember Simon that was *chef de partie* in the Grill?"

"Yes, I think so" said Michael thinking back.

"Well, he wants to go back to France and is looking for a good *sous* position."

"After working with you Chef, he may find this position a little tame."   Michael explained the situation with Mosimann and the hope that the new chef would be responsible for the development of the kitchen and a creative menu.

"I'll give him a few days off to come and see you. He can only say no. I'll give you his home number and you can call him."

"Thanks Chef, I'll keep in touch."

The following week, Michael was in his office when the reception phoned through. "There is a *Monsieur* Vaillant to see you sir," said the receptionist.

Michael went out to meet his prospective Senior *Sous* Chef.

"Hello Simon, good to see you again."

"And you Mister Nicolson," said the young man extending his hand. They shook and Michael said, "Come with me." They walked into his office and sat down.

"Thanks for coming over, your trip OK?"

"Yes fine *merci*," said a somewhat nervous young Frenchman.

"How is the Dorchester, and Chef Mosimann more importantly?"

"The hotel is as busy as ever and *Monsieur* Mosimann still rules the kitchen with an iron fist! But he is as gracious as ever and you cannot help but learn from him, he is still the master. You know we have two Michelin Stars now? The first hotel restaurant outside of France to be awarded two."

"Yes, I know; quite an achievement. I have your

CV but it's pretty irrelevant in this case, as you have been working with *Monsieur* Mosimann for some years now; and before that at the Capital Hotel with Brian Turner and Richard Shepherd and they have a Michelin star as well, so I think you know what you are doing. I am going to introduce you to Roger Cheveux our Executive Chef. The reason you are here is not to usurp him, but to guide the kitchen to a new level. I have already discussed it with him and he is happy to welcome you. So I thought you could get to know him better in his kitchen and then maybe spend the day in his kitchen tomorrow. I suspect we can find you a set of whites* and then we can have lunch the following day before you go back to the UK."

"That would be good thank you," said Simon as he got up and followed Michael down to the kitchen.

"Chef Roger, this is Simon the young man I told you about."

Roger came over wiping his hands on his cloth before offering his right hand for Simon to shake.

"I thought you could get to know him a bit and then he could spend the day with you tomorrow."

"Yes of course, welcome Simon, let's get a coffee," said the steady head chef with his new young *protégé*. 'The trouble is,' thought Michael as he watched them wander off to the Chef's office, 'I have a feeling that the *sous* will be teaching the chef: Just what I want!'

*the name given to the chefs standard white uniform

CHAPTER FOURTEEN
Coming of Age

Albert's desk phone rang, *"Concierge,"* he answered.

"Albert, this is Rachel. Can I meet with you after work? I finish at two today."

"Yes, I'll meet you in Jacques' bar around the corner at two fifteen."

Albert glanced at his watch, it was nearly two fifteen. He turned to his colleague and said, **"je sors juste pour dix minutes,"*

"D'accord" replied the porter.

When he entered the bar Rachel was at a table away from the window nursing a glass of orange juice.

"Bonjour Albert," said Jacques as the young man walked in, *"Ça va bien?"* he asked.

"Oui, Merci," replied Albert as he took a seat next to Rachel as he indicated to the owner that he didn't want anything to drink.

"What's happening? Why weren't you there the other day?"

"I didn't want to go," said a tearful Rachel.

"But it is not going to be safe for you here, you do understand? What made you start seeing a bloody German, did you take leave of your senses?"

"But he's not like the rest," she said making excuses, "he doesn't agree with the war or what they are doing."

*I'm just going out for ten minutes

"That's not the point, he doesn't have a choice. Not only is this dangerous for you but for him. Anyway when push comes to shove he will have to give you up or he will be deemed a traitor; and he will be shot; you do know that don't you?"

Confused and now crying she said, "What can I do?"

"I'll have to try and get you on the next boat to Spain. I can't leave work until four then I will see my friend and will come up to your house. Be there with a small bag ready to leave. Do you have a bicycle?"

"Yes my Mother has one it's still at the house."

"In that case I will see you after six this evening."

He left her there sobbing while he returned to the hotel.

At four o' clock he left his post and went home to change. At six o'clock he went down to Franck's bar. Claude was in the corner as usual. Albert took a beer, sat next to him and told him about Rachel.

"Stupid girl, why didn't she leave with the rest? We will have to send her out with the next boat."

Just at that moment Auguste came in, "The Gestapo have just left my office," he said, talking in a low but deliberate tone, "they have arrested some of our colleagues and some Jewish families. They have been taken to the tower and will be taken to Gestapo headquarters in Nice the day after tomorrow."

"*Merde*," said Claude.

"And that's not all," continued the policeman, "amongst them" he said looking at Albert "is your friend Pierre and my brother."

"*Merde*," repeated Claude, "I am sorry Auguste, what are we going to do? I will have to make contact with René."

"They will be coming back for me when they realise that they have my brother. They haven't put two and two together, but they will. They know he has been looking after the Jews and helping hide them, let alone with what happened to Michel."

"Meanwhile I will get Rachel to the safe house," said Albert.

He left the bar and got on his bike and made his way to the Gold's house. The sun was still shining as he made the short ride. He knocked on the familiar front door. Rachel opened it with her bike by her side.

"Ready?" Just as Albert uttered the word the sound of German trucks came up the street and stopped. Soldiers jumped out of the wagon and started door to door searches. "Let's go," said Albert concernedly. She had packed a rucksack and slipped it over her shoulders. They went out on to the street and got on their bikes. "Act as calmly as you possibly can — and normally."

They started to ride down the road on the opposite side to the soldiers who were now banging on doors. Just then a soldier stepped in front of them shouting "*Halt!*"

Albert's heart started beating in his throat. The

German walked towards him and Rachel, who was on the verge of wetting herself, recognised the soldier. It was Kurt. He too had recognised her and was wondering what to do or say next. He approached them demanding papers "*Vos papiers s'il vous plaît,*"* he said letting his rifle point downwards. "Where are you going?"
"Just for a ride and a coffee on the *esplanade*" said a nervous Albert handing over his papers followed by Rachel who looked at her boyfriend not knowing whether to smile or not. Kurt looked at her, hardly acknowledging her. He read the papers and handed them back to the couple. "You both work at our hotel, yes?" They nodded. He waved them through and they cycled down the road. "That was close," said Albert wiping the sweat from his brow.
"That wasn't close," remarked Rachel, "that was Kurt."
"What?" replied a stunned Albert, "My God, we were lucky."
"I told you he was different," she said as they continued on their way.
'For now' thought Albert, 'for now.'
They pedalled up the hill to the house. "Stay here until someone comes for you; open the door to no one unless they identify themselves as 'Cygne Noir'."
She put her arms around him. "Thank you, I am sorry I have been such an idiot. I will never forget you."

*Your papers please

"Just be safe, you will be given all the help you need by the people who will come and collect you, the people who will meet you in Spain will know where you can find your family. Give Sarah my love, *bon chance*" he said as he got on his bike to make his way back.

The next morning Claude was having coffee with René in Cap d'Ail. "We are going to have to release them all *en route*" said René. See if Albert can find out anything today about their proposed movements. I will speak to our team and organise a plan. I will meet you in the bar tonight. I now have to be careful, they seem to have taken an interest in me and Madeleine as well. However we must not give up. I will see you this evening."

He left like a man that had the responsibility of his little community on his shoulders. Claude remained and took a *Coñac* with another coffee. "*Bon chance, mon ami,*" he muttered under his breath as René walked down the road.

That evening they had gathered in their usual place, now more aware, that there was a lot of activity around town, as the Germans were closing in. Albert told them that he had safely delivered the girl to the safe house and how they were nearly in trouble and that the soldier recognised Albert from the hotel.

"You'll have to be a bit more careful from now on," said René. "Have you found out anymore about the Nazi's movement of their prisoners?"

"No, I am afraid not, although I did hear some of them saying that they would be driving through the countryside rather than the coast road."

"That's what I thought," said René taking out a map. Just then Auguste walked in. Franck brought over a glass of wine for his friend.

"*Merci*," said Auguste taking a mouthful. "They are moving their cargo at twenty hundred hours tomorrow as it is getting dark. They are taking the back roads rather than the coast road."

"Yes," said René, "we have established that, and I think that they will use this road as it is fairly open and they will not expect an ambush but if they go this way," he said indicating with his finger, "they will pass by here, *Col de Chemins*. There are three roads that can be used to escape once we have made the ambush. There is a fourth that will take us straight down the hill to Nice, but I don't think we want to go to Nice, we will need to double back and go to Cap d'Ail to the safe houses. I spoke with our team and this is what we will do." René started telling them the plan and their responsibilities.

"Everyone understand what we are doing? Any questions? In that case we will meet at the *rendezvous* point at nineteen thirty hours tomorrow. *Bon chance mes amis*."

Albert got into the little Citroën 2 CV and with some hesitation drove it out of town onto the high road. He hadn't driven much as he had his bike and also didn't really need a car for where he worked and lived. But he knew where he was going and how to get there. When he got to the meeting point at *Col de Chemins* the others were waiting for him. He pulled over and parked on the grass verge. Claude came over and together they walked to the other side of the road to a clearing where the rest of the crew had gathered. René was there. "Good evening gentlemen, we are fortunate with the weather, as it is cloudy, which is hiding the moonlight and the cloud means that we will also be having showers, let's hope it holds off until we have carried out the operation. Albert, here is your pistol. Only use it if you have to. You have been practicing so I am sure you will feel confident when the moment arrives. Your job is to straddle the car across the road at twenty ten hours and lift the bonnet. Face the direction of the oncoming traffic and act as if you are trying to get it started again. Claude as agreed you and the men will split up and go either side of the road. Auguste you take your position on the corner and when you see the convoy coming, flash your torch toward me. When the convoy has passed block the road with your car and place the road side bombs in case they try to reverse out of the situation or further German vehicles come up the road. Didier you and Francois will take the grenades and hide on the side of the road. When the lead car stops for Albert, throw a grenade under the vehicle. The other trucks should have pulled up at the same time, so throw a couple under the driver's cabin. We want to avoid the main body of the trucks because of the occupants. The soldiers will normally jump out by then leaving the boys in the trees to pick them off. Get the passengers out as quickly as possible and bring them to the vehicles in the clearing and we will take them on the top road back to Cap d' Ail. Is everybody clear? OK, take your places as the convoy should be leaving the tower any time now."

Everyone scrambled to their post; Auguste drove back down the road and parked up. Albert drove his vehicle across the road as instructed, opened the bonnet and loosened a couple of spark plug cables. He tucked his weapon into the belt of his trousers at the back and made sure his leather jacket covered the bulge. He wanted to pee now as he realised he was becoming a little afraid. Everything they had done before seemed simple, but this was different; people were going to be killed, maybe one or two from the home side as well. Just then he glimpsed the flash light aimed at René who in turn flashed to the waiting ambushers. He then could hear the drone of the vehicles as they rounded the corner and the headlights shone in Albert's face. He pissed himself and as he could feel the warm urine run down his leg the skies opened and the rain started to come down. The lead Mercedes stopped in front of the 2CV; Albert gave a shrugging gesture as the headlights almost blinded him. The *Haupsturmführer* alighted followed by his driver.

They moved to the car. The dark shadows cast by the two men, with the headlights highlighting them from behind, made Albert sweat with cold fear. Thank God it was raining so they couldn't see the sweat on his brow and under his arms or the urine that had now been absorbed into the material. The two following trucks stopped; the drivers remained in their cabins. There was an almighty bang and a rush of hot air with the stench of gasoline as Albert saw the bonnet of the Mercedes fly upwards and the force of the blast propel the two men forward and against the 2Cv and nearly blew Albert off his feet. Everything seemed to be happening in slow motion. The soldier slumped down the side of the little car with blood shooting out of the top of his leg from behind as shrapnel or glass severed his femoral artery. The Captain stood up from the side of the car and took his Luger from its holster and stared at Albert. He then fell to the floor and Albert could see the hole in his neck at the top of his spine with blood pumping out of his basilar artery in time with his fading heart. There were two further explosions as the cabins of the following trucks were meticulously destroyed by well landed hand grenades. The dying screams of the drivers and co drivers were drowned out by the sound of machine gun fire as the soldiers jumped down from their trucks and started firing into the road side at an enemy they couldn't see. The men in the trees pin pointed the soldiers by the light their machine guns gave off when being fired. Claude's men picked the guards off in rapid succession as he and Jacques went to the back of the first truck Didier with François went to the back of the second truck. A silence had fallen over the night punctured only by the screams of fear from the back of the trucks. Then the sound of further machine gun fire; when Claudc ripped open the tarpaulin cover he was faced with a young soldier who was even more scared than Claude but who had managed to discharge his weapon at the prisoners and Claude could see the slain crumpled on the hard seats. The young soldier raised his gun; there was a sudden crack of a pistol which hit the young man between the eyes blowing half the back of his head off. He was forced backwards off his feet and collapsed in a heap on the floor. Jacques put his hand on Claude's shoulder while holding his pistol in his right hand, "*Ça va mon ami?*" he said as he signalled to those in the truck to get out quickly. Didier meanwhile had approached the back of the other vehicle, opened the tarpaulin covers and was greeted by machine gun fire that hit him in the chest piercing his heart and killing him instantly. He fell backwards giving François a perfect shot at the soldier in the truck. That was all it took, one shot clean through the young man's heart ripping part of his shoulder from his body as he was forced against the bulk head of the lorry and slipped unceremoniously downwards. François ushered the occupants out and pushed them toward the clearing. Albert meanwhile had made his way to the truck. He could see Claude pointing and shouting at the prisoners to move quickly. Just then one of the wounded guards lifted himself up from the ground enough to get his machine gun into position. Albert was a matter of metres away from him. He took out his weapon and aimed it at the crouching soldier. He shouted *"Attention Claude, derrière toi"* as he discharged his pistol in the direction of the soldiers head. He fired three times the jolt from the discharge causing his clasped hands to shoot upward with some force but he managed to bring them back down in quick succession allowing one of the three bullets to connect with its target rendering the soldier immobile. Claude had turned around just in time to see the final shot being fired. *"Merci mon jeune ami,"* shouted Claude with a big smile. "Go back to your car and wait for me," ordered his mentor. Albert got back to his vehicle shaking from the wet, the fear and the adrenalin pumping though his body. He threw up and stood there for seconds while the rain started to wash his vomit away from the car. That was the first time that he had killed someone, but it wouldn't be his last. Claude looked inside the truck to find young Pierre sprawled over a young woman who he had obviously tried to protect, but the bullets had gone through both of them. There was an old man dead beside her and he rather hoped that he was the girl's father and that he had lived long enough to see his child be protected by a young stranger

who had found himself in the wrong place at the wrong time. He jumped down from the vehicle to be met by François. *"Notre ami Didier c'est mort,"* he said sadly. *"Merde,"* replied Claude, "we must get him into the back of the truck." The two men lifted their fallen comrade into the back of the lorry. "Throw a couple of grenades into the back of the trucks and go and join René. I'm going with Albert and we'll see each other at the safe houses." Claude went back to join his young colleague who was tightening the cables and putting the bonnet down as Claude approached.
Claude got into the little car as Albert pointed it in the direction of the high road while Auguste had got into his car and started his journey back to Cap d'Ail.
"Are you OK?" he asked
"Yes, fine" lied Albert.
The whole event lasted less than ten minutes yet Albert seemed to be playing it back in his mind in slow motion. From the moment he heard the trucks and saw the headlights to the time he threw up seemed a lifetime ago.
"You did a fine job and you saved my life. Thank you," he placed his hand on the young man's leg in a gesture of thanks.
"You are welcome coach," he laughed nervously. "I am pleased it all went well."
"Sadly not that well as we lost our dear friend Didier," said Claude.
"Non?" said a shocked Albert. *"Quel dommage"*
"That's not all I am afraid," continued Claude,

"Pierre was killed during the rescue. He was shot along with two others just as we got to the back of the truck. I am sorry Albert, we were seconds late. I found him with his body shielding a young woman which was very brave. Sadly the bullets went straight through them both. It was very quick."

"*Très, très triste*, very sad, he repeated. "He was a good guy and very young."

"So are you *mon ami*, and you are both brave, very brave."

They drove on in virtual silence until they got to the safe houses.

René and the team were already there when they got there.

The rescued parties were sitting in stunned silence as their rescuers came into the room.

"Is everyone OK?" asked René. They all nodded.

"Thank you all very much," muttered a frightened Doctor Gagneux, Auguste's brother.

"You are safe now," continued Claude, "but we now have to get you ready to leave France. People will be here tomorrow with papers for you, which will get you to Spain where you will be met by fellow resistance fighters who will take care of you. Meanwhile sleep well and open the doors to no one until someone says, "*Signe Noir*"

Just then the door opened and in walked Auguste, he went over to his brother who stood up and put out his arms in an emotional reunion; they embraced. *"Mon cher frère, merci,"* said Laurent has he hugged his brother.

"I'll see you tomorrow," said Auguste. Sleep well and get your strength."

"*Alez, alez mes amis nous devons y aller*" said René, "we must go now."

They all said their *adieus* and left to reunite at Franck's bar.

By ten o'clock they were seated at a table with some bread and cheese and red wine. René raised his glass, "to our lost friends and those that we still have," said an emotional René. They all raised their glasses, "and" continued their leader, "to our brave young soldier who sadly lost one of his friends today." They all looked at Albert; "Yes well done Albert," said Auguste, "You did a good job."

They had started to relax and enjoy themselves for a job well done when the doors opened and in walked four Gestapo in plain clothes. "*Heil hitler*," they chorused lifting their arms in the now familiar half salute. The bar was fairly busy and the officers separated, going to each table demanding papers. The lead officer went over to René's table. "Papers," he said looking at them intently. "I don't suppose any of you know anything about a group of renegades that ambushed a convoy of the Führer's soldiers escorting traitors and criminals to Nice do you?" They all shook their heads. "Ah, *Monsieur* Borghini, I have recently heard a lot about you. You are the secretary to the national Council of Monaco; such an important position and one that seems out of place in a back street bar in Monte Carlo."

"I wasn't always a politician, I was born and bred in the Principality and thankfully have many local friends with whom I am very happy to break bread and drink wine" said a cool René.

"What are you all celebrating?" he enquired. "What you consider to be a successful operation?"

"No Herr Vogel," said Auguste with his back to the inquisitor, "if you read my papers," he said handing them to him, "you will see that today is my birthday and I am celebrating with my friends. That is still allowed is it not?"

"Ah, Lieutenant Gagneux I didn't see you there. Happy Birthday," he said sarcastically. "You do know that your brother was in that convoy of traitors do you not?"

"I am aware that you had arrested my brother on trumped up charges that would have no credence in a proper court of law. But please accept that my brother is neither a traitor nor a criminal he is a loyal patriot of France and a servant to the people of Monaco: and *Monsieur* he is in your custody and therefore I expect you to look after him."

The Gestapo officer handed his papers back. "Make no mistake *Monsieur Le Lieutenant*, when we find your brother, we will look after him and all the enemies of the third *Reich* that we can find as well. Have a good evening; until the next time. *Heil Hitler*," he turned on his heels and left with his colleagues.

"*Bon Anniversaire* Auguste," they chanted as they were left alone. "You didn't say," said René as they all raised their glasses.

"I was waiting for the right moment," smiled Auguste "and I think that was it!" Franck brought over another bottle of Mâcon and raised his glass to his colleagues.

"You made no friends there Auguste," he said sucking on his pipe.

"It's a bit late for that," sighed the policeman, "*C'est la vie!*"

"Auguste," said René getting back to business "will you see Didier's and Pierre's families?"

"No," said Claude, "I will see them, he was my close friend."

"And I will see Pierre's parents," said Albert "he was my friend."

"Very well," concluded René. "For now let us relax and enjoy, as things are going to get a lot more dangerous in the months to come. *"*Bon chance et voici à notre avenir* »

As Albert went into the hotel to tell his colleague that he was only in to pick up something and would be back at four o'clock to start his shift, when a German soldier approached the desk.

"Can I help you sir?" asked Albert's colleague.

"No. it's OK, I need to speak to this young man," he said putting his hand on Albert's shoulder.

Albert turned to see the now recognisable face of Kurt.

"Hello," said Albert in German, "how can I help you?"

good luck and here's to our future

"Ah, you speak German. What is your name?" he asked as he moved Albert away from the desk.

"Albert," replied the young man, "and yes I do."

"Well Albert, I am Kurt Schmidt; you may have heard of me?" he said looking for a change in Albert's expression.

"I am not sure that I do," replied a stone-faced Albert, "you all look much alike in those smart uniforms."

"Didn't this 'smart uniform' stop you the other day in the company of a young woman with whom you were riding into town to have coffee?"

"Ah yes, that was you was it? As I say, you all look very much alike."

"Albert, let's cut the crap; you know that Rachel told you about me and I believe that you may have taken her away from me for reasons I can only imagine. I just need to know that she is alright."

"I don't really know what you are talking about," said a wary Albert.

"I think you do," replied Kurt, "but please trust me when I say I have no ulterior motive, only to know she is safe. I am sure you know that my life is on the line as well and I would not be talking to you if I couldn't trust you. If Rachel could trust you then so can I."

"I believe that she may have gone on holiday," Albert replied weakly.

"Where would she have gone?"

"I'm not sure" said Albert now feeling unsure and uncomfortable.

"Albert, the war will be over soon God willing and I may one day want to find my old girlfriend, so any help you can give me would be appreciated."

"You must think I was born yesterday," replied Albert angrily.

"If you were born yesterday, then we must have been born at the same time. I promise I am not trying to catch you out. I know what is going on here in Monaco and I also know we won't be here forever and that one day, I maybe riding out of town when I get stopped by the resistance and may be afforded the same safe passage as I gave you and Rachel." He clicked his heels and walked away.

'Maybe Rachel was right,' thought Albert as Kurt walked dejectedly away, 'maybe he is different.'

Albert got on his bike and peddled to Pierre's family home.

His father opened the door and saw the sadness in Albert's eyes.

"Come in my boy," said the father; "I take it you have some bad news for us?"

Pierre's mother came up behind her husband with tears in her eyes.

"I am sorry," said Albert. "Pierre was killed last night. As you know he was on his way to Nice where he would have probably been shot anyway," said Albert matter-of-factly, "but this way he died a hero. He was in the back of the truck on the convoy when the resistance tried to liberate the prisoners. Sadly an over patriotic German soldier, not much older than us, tried to die fighting and took some of his hostages with him. Pierre was found by one of the resistance fighters, draped across the body of a young woman whom he seemed to have tried to protect from the gunfire that ensued. He was my friend," continued Albert, "and it was a pleasure to be considered his, I wish I could be as brave as my friend was in the face of death."

Pierre's mother was sobbing, his father embraced Albert and said, "He valued your friendship Albert and reluctantly told me what he was getting into, much against my wishes, but he felt he could make a difference and said 'if Albert can do it – so can I.' He was right. Thank you Albert."

Pierre's mother came over and hugged him, "please God say he didn't die in vain," she cried.

"From his point of view and mine I hope he didn't," said the mature young man, "but when we look back on this in sixty years, will anyone be able to truthfully say that?"

He left the house some ten years older than he was yesterday, got on his bike and returned to start his shift as if nothing had happened.

But it had, his life had changed forever.

CHAPTER FIFTEEN
I Do — 1988

"Do you Michael Albert Nicolson take Juliette Marie Város to be your lawfully wedded wife to love and...................?"

Michael got out of bed first. He went into the kitchen and came back with a bottle of Bollinger. He walked over and kissed her on the forehead. "Good morning,"

"Shit, what time is it?"

"Nine fifteen, you don't think I'd offer you Champagne before nine do you?"

"Michael, you've got to be fucking joking, I've got to go to work."

"Umm, if you remember you are not working today:"

"Aren't I?"

"No, we both have a day off!"

She stretched, revealing her perfect breasts above the sheets. "So what's the shampoo about?"

"Well, Easter has come and gone, the summer fast approacheth, I have been asked to stay on for another year, we are on track for a Michelin star, the hotel is doing well and has reached its highest occupancy and turnover ever -— and we have known each other for two years next month and been together for two years in May; and I am getting fed up referring to you as Miss Valón so I thought Misses Valón-Nicolson sounded pretty cool: What do you think?"

"You're crazy," said Juliette, "why would I marry you? There's so many more men out there that I haven't even met yet! Why would I tie myself down to a struggling hotel manager" she paused — "alright may be a struggling hotel manager that will eventually become the owner of a multi-million pound empire. Hmm, when you look it that way, it almost sounds appealing!" She laughed. "On one condition, when you have had enough, you will feel free to call it a day."

"Well that's pretty cold and calculated," he stopped mid flow.

"It's not Michael it's realistic. You are twenty six, I am twenty seven. We both have careers and a lot of new adventures to follow, but, at this moment in time, I can't think of a nicer way to spend my life. So, if that is some sort of cack-handed way of asking me to marry you — you can forget the bended knee — I accept."

"He leaned forward and kissed her offering her a glass of bubbles.

"In that case, let's go for lunch."

"After we have built up an appetite," she said as she pulled him towards her and kissed him passionately on the lips and rolled him on to the bed.

―・⋅◦⟨⟩◦⋅・―

"And do you Juliette Marie Valón take Michael Albert Nicolson to be your lawfully wedded husband, to love and to ....?"

She awoke to find a glass of champagne dangled in front of her lips. 'What the hell? What time is

it? I'll be late for work".
"You are not working today, remember? We both have the day off."
"So what's with the shampoo?" she asked.
"Well," replied Michael, "Easter has come and gone……………"
'He's asking me to marry him. God is that what I want? I was just having fun; do I need that responsibility or commitment? It's true I haven't been with anyone since Michael and don't have any desire to, so what the hell'
"On one condition, when you have had enough, you will feel free to call it a day."
She pulled him towards her and they made early morning love, washed down with a bottle of champagne. 'If only marriage would always be this good.'

"I now pronounce you Man and Wife; you may kiss the bride." said the vicar and they duly obliged. It was a small ceremony at the Baptist church on the corner of Rue Vernier in Nice. Michael's father and Uncle came with their wives, Juliette's family were there as was, the General Manager of the Negresco, some of Juliette's closest friends and a couple of Michael's senior colleagues at the Hotel including De Villiers. It was a beautiful day on Saturday June the fourth when they stepped out into the French sunshine bathing the streets. The company Rolls Royce had been decorated for the occasion and the short journey to the hotel didn't take long enough. They held hands and looked at each other. "I am very happy *Monsieur* Nicolson,"

"*Moi aussi Madame Valón-Nicolson,*" he said smiling. They kissed and the car pulled up outside the hotel where the staff had created a 'guard of honour'.

The company, or his father and uncle to be precise, had gifted them the reception at the hotel and Juliette's boss had gifted them a suite at the Negresco. With Simon now the Head Chef, Roger still executive, more involved with budgets and control, the food had taken on a different level and guests were to experience an amazing wedding lunch.

They were treated to a flow of *Perrier Jouet Grand Brut* as *amuse-bouche* were passed around the glorious banqueting suite by waiters and waitresses in long white aprons and red braces, creating a modern twist on an old favourite. The menu of a *Chilled Consomme with Caviar,* followed by *Lobster Tails with Black Pasta* and a main course of *Warm Fillets of Turbot with Truffles* all washed down with a *Puligny Montrachet Premier Cru* was appreciated by all the thirty six guests. No more than Michael, who was pleased that his new chef had hit the heights with his Mosimann inspired banquet which terminated with a French classic dessert, **Oeufs à la Neige avec Sauce Vanille* served with a *Chateau Coutet Barsac* as the dessert wine.

*Fluffy light meringue – snow eggs – with a vanilla custard — just sounds so much better in French

De Villiers was at the top table and acted as master of ceremonies, as well as Michael's best man. "*Mesdames et Messieurs*, Ladies and Gentlemen, if I may indulge before the main speeches, I would like to thank our Chefs for a spectacular luncheon which shows why we will get our first Michelin Star this year and to Michael who pushed me to adapt to the changing culinary world: I am so glad I did."

"So may I ask you to take wine with our Chefs, our Head Chef Simon Vaillant and our Executive Chef, Roger Cheveux." The two proud men walked into the room to a standing ovation and raised glasses to the guests. "and if you thought that the meal was Mosimann inspired it is not surprising, as Simon worked with the great chef at the Dorchester Hotel in London before being persuaded to join us — and also it could be that, unknown to Michael, someone has flown over especially for today, the master that is Anton Mosimann." Mosimann came in to a tumultuous round of applause and walked up to Michael, who was on his feet and hugged him, "Congratulations *mon ami*, be happy....and this must be the beautiful Juliette," he said as he put her hand to his lips, "*Enchanté Madame*."

"The pleasure is ours *Monsieur* Mosimann,"

"Anton, please," he said with a smile.

"Thank you for coming Chef what a wonderful surprise," said an emotional Michael.

"When Simon told me you were getting married here, I spoke to your father and *Monsieur* de

Villiers to ask if I may intrude. They were pleased to invite me and I am pleased to be here. You have a good kitchen brigade Michael and an excellent front of house team you should be proud of all their and your, achievements."

"I am Chef, thank you."

"I must leave now, I am going back to London to prepare my new venture. You and Juliette must come over for the opening of my Dining Club in October if you can find the time; you can stay with me and Katrin."

"Thank you Chef it would be an honour."

Mosimann walked over to shake hands with Michael's family and shook De Villiers' hand before exiting with his colleagues back to the kitchen to, once again, a huge round of applause. Michael sat down again, he held Juliette's hand.

"Well," she said, "that was a lovely surprise, amazing. Did you know anything about it?"

"Nothing, nothing at all, incredible; What an end to a perfect day."

"It's not ended yet," she said with a cheeky grin. The speeches continued with Juliette's father amusing the crowd and duly embarrassing his daughter and de Villiers did a great job as best man considering he only had known Michael for a couple of years. He felt sure he had obtained background information from other family members and friends.

They left the reception and were driven to the Hotel Negresco where they were taken to a honeymoon suite with flowers and champagne waiting for them. They made love for the first time as a married couple which had not lost any of its passion. The next morning they were leaving for their honeymoon to Martinique, paid for by the bride's family. Married life was given a good start. "Here's to the rest of our lives," said Michael as they raised their champagne glasses in the first class section of their Air France 747. "However long that maybe," said Juliette and put her head on his shoulder.

The phone in Michael's apartment rang; *"Oui, bonjour,"* he said.
"*Monsieur* Nicolson, we have a problem, *Monsieur* de Villiers has been taken to hospital"
"*Merde*, what's happened?"
"It was a heart attack."
"Is he OK?"
"Well, the ambulance has taken him to the University Hospital where he is stable."
"Why didn't you call earlier?"
"Because we had to establish what had happened" continued Valerie, De Villier's secretary.
"I'll be right over,"
He woke Juliette, "it's De Villiers, he has had a heart attack."
"Shit, is he OK?"
"Stable apparently. I'm going in."
"OK *cherie*, let me know what's happening. I have a meeting at one o'clock, but I'm free most of the day."

Michael straightened his tie and slipped on his jacket, "OK," he said planting a kiss, "I'll talk to you later."

When he walked into the hotel the atmosphere was palpable. Greeting the staff he made his way to Valerie's office. "Hello Michael," said a tearful Valerie.

"What happened?" said Michael concernedly.

"We had our normal nine o'clock catch up and we were going through pending correspondence, when all of a sudden he grabbed his chest and let out the most awful roar and fell forward still moaning; I can tell you I was shit scared. I called the concierge to call the ambulance. I sat him upright and loosened his tie. He was holding his chest and sweating profusely. 'I'm going to die,' he cried. Thankfully an ambulance arrived in a little over five minutes. They put him on oxygen and monitored his heart and when they were happy they took him out to the ambulance."

"Have you informed all the staff?"

"No, just you and of course, the concierge."

"Well that will be as good as informing all the staff — it would have gone around the hotel all ready. Call the heads of department and get them in here for eleven o'clock and meanwhile you bring me up to date with what's pending from his side and that which needs to be sorted straightaway."

Michael's coffee arrived, "How is *Monsieur* de Villiers?" asked the waitress.

"We don't know Marie, but he appears to be stable. Please let your colleagues know. I will

update everyone as soon as I know something."
Valerie came into Michael's office, "are you going to move into *Monsieur* de Villiers' office?"
"I don't think so Valerie, we will wait and see how long he will be off work. Is the meeting arranged?"
"Yes, everyone will be here at eleven."
"OK, thanks."
Michael sat for a minute contemplating the situation. He was concerned for De Villiers, he had got to know him and like him, over his time there and while he was happy to hold the reins, he knew he would be happier when his boss was back. He picked up the phone and called his Uncle to let him know what had happened.
"Is he OK?" he asked.
"As well as can be expected apparently," replied his nephew
"I assume you have taken control of the hotel?" asked Uncle Marc.
"Yes sir, of course."
"*Bon chance*, and if there is anything you need or the De Villiers' family, you must let us know."
"I will do, thank you *mon oncle*."
He put the phone down and dialled the Paris Majestic.
"*Bonjour Hotel Majestic Paris, Claudette parle comment puis-je vous aider?*"
"Claudette can I speak to Alain Chastain it's Michael Nicolson."
"*Certainement Monsieur s'il vous plaît.*"
"*Bonjour Michael, comme ça va?*"
"I am fine my friend, I am just calling to let you

know De Villiers has had a heart attack and is in hospital. He's OK but under observation."

"Thank you for letting me know, please give him my regards when you speak to him. Does this mean you are in the hot seat?"

"Yes, it would seem to be."

"You'll be fine Michael; you have been there long enough for it to be a pushover. *Bon chance mon ami, et merci. Au revoir.*"

Michael sat there as the department heads came into his office, perching on available chairs, window sills and anything else they could find. 'Maybe we should have gone into De Villiers' office' thought Michael.

"Good morning everyone, I am sure by now you have heard the news. As you know I will be standing in for *Monsieur* de Villiers until his return. Just to confirm that everything will carry on as normal and feel free to come to me with any problems you may have and also to inform me of anything I may have missed at such short notice. Right, let's get down to business. An update from each department please................"

Michael had been running the hotel with no problem since De Villiers hospitalisation in August. He had been in intensive care for some weeks but was now out of the woods and had returned home. It was now mid October and plans were underway for the Christmas period. Michael phoned De Villiers' home and *Madame* de Villiers answered the phone. She asked Michael how he was getting on and he told her all was well, but wanted to know whether his boss was ready to accept visitors. She asked her husband, who told her he would love to see his deputy.

Michael drove to the De Villiers' villa just outside of the town on the hill side. He was greeted by *Madame* who took him through into the lounge where the man of the house sat stoically upright in his chair.

"Bonjour monsieur, comment allez vous?" said Michael.

"Not too bad under the circumstances thank you," replied the man, who had lost a lot of weight. "At one stage I felt that I had been hit by a bus but now I feel that there is a little man here," he said pointing to his heart, "who seems to be pedalling a generator to keep my heart working. They put a pacemaker in to keep me going."

"You always seemed so fit," said Michael concernedly.

"Come on Michael, I was overweight and smoked. I don't recommend this as a way to get healthy, but I haven't had a cigarette since the attack, have lost twelve kilos and that alone has made me feel better. Anyway, more important things, how is the hotel?"

"Well, the staff all asked me to pass on their best wishes for a full recovery, I think they have had enough of me now and want you back!"

"I doubt that," said De Villiers with a smile.

"My uncle said that if you need anything you only have to ask and Alain Chastain sends his best wishes for a speedy recovery."

"All very kind; thank them all, but how is business?"

"Well, we have had a good summer with one hundred percent occupancy and the restaurant was full every night and there was even a waiting list at weekends as the locals are booking weeks in advance now."

"That's good Michael and that's down to you; if you hadn't have woken me up about our food and beverage operation, we would still be serving nineteen sixties food."

"Thank you sir, I am pleased that Simon worked out and that he and Roger are working well together. The good news is, it has been confirmed that we will have our Michelin star in the new Michelin Guide when it comes out in January."

"That is great news. Well done. I feel very happy that the hotel is in such good hands. I hope to get back before Christmas; the doctors say I am recovering well, so I am confident that I will be back."

"Just make sure you rest and recover fully *Monsieur*, I will keep you informed of our progress." He got up and shook De Villiers hand.

"*A bientôt,*" said Michael,

"*A bientôt*" said De Villiers as his right hand man walked towards the door and said his goodbyes to *Madame* de Villiers. "If you need anything, please do not hesitate to call me."

"Thank you Michael," she said as she let him out of the front door, "I will."

That evening Michael and Juliette were having dinner in the restaurant.

"How is he?" asked Juliette.

"He seems OK, a little shaky perhaps but that's to be expected. He says he will be back at the beginning of December."

"Do you know what you are doing next year yet?"

"No, I haven't even thought about it really. I have already been here longer than I anticipated, but I am enjoying it and meeting and marrying you is one of the best things that has happened to me."

"Ahhh, how sweet, *merci mon Cherie*, the feeling is mutual."

"What if I have to move, will you be happy to go?"

"Depends where it is as to whether I would be happy, but I married you for better or worse, I just hope it isn't worse," she laughed.

"Well, once again," said Michael raising his glass, "here's to the future, whatever it may bring."

CHAPTER SIXTEEN
March 1944

It had been an eventful few months since their first major operation freeing the prisoners and disrupting the German's attempts to find those involved. Apart from the sad loss of young Pierre and the seasoned Didier, the team had managed to keep out of trouble. Except that is, Auguste who had been arrested and questioned by the Gestapo regarding his doctor brother, Laurent. Strangely Auguste had been released but the Germans were keeping an eye on him and that had curtailed his movements to the point that René had suggested that he severed contact with the group until further notice. This had also meant that the team had lost their eyes and ears within the Gendarmerie. But Albert had suggested that any information Auguste had could be left for him at the concierge desk at the hotel, as Auguste and his team often called into the hotel on and off duty. This practice was working well and the team were still getting information that helped them in their quest. Auguste would call in and on the basis of checking papers, which they regularly did, would surreptitiously slip an envelope to Albert. Later that day Albert would go down to the bar with Claude and check the contents. On one particular occasion the contents of Auguste's envelope told the team that:

'There is a group of tourists numbering twenty

adults and ten children that would like to see more of the principality by boat trips if that can be arranged. They are coming in by bus next Friday and will be here for the weekend. One of their party will come into the hotel when they arrive, to arrange details.'

This of course was coded; even the days of the week were reversed to confuse anyone intercepting the note. Sunday was Sunday, but Monday was Saturday, Tuesday was Friday etcetera. So they would be arriving next Tuesday and this was Thursday. They had four or five days to prepare.

"This means they obviously live here and Auguste knows who they are and it's his way of letting us know that we have to arrange their transportation to Spain," said Claude. "We have to get them to the safe houses by next Monday. Albert can you get a note back to Auguste without any of us showing our faces?"

"Yes, I will send one of the *buttons* on his bike. No one will be watching him."

Claude wrote a note and put it in an envelope and gave it to Albert, who got on his bike and went back to the hotel.

Once back at his desk, he called over to Dom the *buttons* and told him to go to the *gendarmerie* and hand this note in for Auguste. As the young man walked out of the door, the familiar figure of Kurt Schmidt approached the desk.

"Do you not think that I know what is going on?" he said to Albert.

"I am sorry I don't know what you are talking about," replied a now confident Albert.
"Listen Albert, I couldn't give a damn at the moment, the war will not last much longer. The Americans and the British are sure to be planning an attack by sea. I think Hitler is in disarray and the war may soon be over, Thank God! I only have two concerns; one is to get out of this alive and the other to find Rachel."
"I can't help you with either I'm afraid," said Albert making himself busy with papers on his desk.
"Albert, you know I could make life very difficult for you and your friends don't you?"
"And I you Sir, and I you." he smiled full of confidence.
"Just a word that she is Ok would suffice Albert, nothing else." A despondent Kurt walked away. Albert watched him, thinking that maybe Rachel was right after all. He would make a point of finding out if she was OK, but would check with Claude that he could give him any information.

Albert and his colleagues had now managed to help over sixty men, women, and children, mostly Jewish with the odd resistance fighter, from the clutch of the Nazis. The Germans had intensified controls at the border crossings into Spain as they were aware that this was where the French Jews were making their dash for safety. Nearly all of the fleeing families that René and his group had organised were via the boats that they used sailing to Barcelona, something the Nazis had not yet fathomed out. Nearly all of them had got to Spain safely including Sarah and later Rachel and although the team had no knowledge of where they were, they were aware that they had arrived safely, something he may tell Kurt if ever he needed a favour in return.

However things were about to turn sour as, at the end of May, Auguste was arrested for the third time but this time there was no escape. He had been betrayed by his bitter ex wife. There had been a raid on a train near Nice where some members of the resistance had been detained and questioned and two Jewish families who decided to make the journey on their own volition. Marie Cèleste Gagneux had left her husband in 1943 where rumour had it he was having an affair with a young woman from Nice: While it was not unusual for a Frenchman, of whatever background, to have a mistress, most wives were accepting of it, but when the relationship took over from Auguste's marriage, Marie gave him an ultimatum. She left him and moved out of the Principality and moved to Nice. When the Germans arrested all the people in that carriage, believing that everyone there had something to do with the Jewish families and was aiding there escape, Marie had to find a bargaining tool to avoid prison or worse execution, at the renowned L'Ariane in Nice; so she gave up her husband saying that he was indeed a member of the resistance in Monte Carlo and a Lieutenant in the

Gendarmes. However, this did not get her released; telling her that until they could corroborate her story she would remain in custody.

The Gestapo arrived at the gendarmerie at ten in the morning on a bright sunny day. Four officers in plain clothes went in to the station and arrested the officer in his office and to the distress of his colleagues, he was marched out to the waiting car.

To make matters even worse, at the same time two Jewish families that Claude had helped hide in Monte Carlo had been arrested by the Gestapo. Claude had put them in a boardinghouse that was run by sympathetic non-Jews. The owner of the property had been warning Claude about the youngest daughter and the man she was seeing. Catherine was pretty, but not very bright, and contrary to everyone's protestations she was going out with a young local non-Jew. The boy was well known and quite a charming young man but it didn't take long for him to learn the family's true identity. Being ambitious and believing that he would be rewarded, he decided to take the Gestapo along with him on his next visit. After all, it was a pure business deal, with so much paid to him per head that they captured.

Luck was on the side of Catherine's older sister however; she returned home after it was all over. Claude had arranged for her to go to one of the safe houses in Cap d'Ail. Her elder brother had been captured not that long ago while he was attempting to cross the Spanish border near Andorra. She was now all on her own and she was only eighteen.

With the things that were going on René convened a meeting in the usual place but even this was now getting dangerous. Franck had said that the Gestapo had been in on a few occasions of late, looking for information.

"This will be our last meeting here *mes amis* we will have to find another venue. Meanwhile we have heard that the Allied forces landed in Normandy on June the sixth and rumour has it that it will not be long before they reach Paris in which case the war may not last much longer. However, with the arrest of Auguste, even though I know he will not say anything under torture, they have seen us all together, and last month the Gestapo was sniffing around Le Hotel du Gare where Madeleine was staying and where I go when in Monte Carlo. They were also watching her apartment in Nice. We were due to meet at the hotel as someone had entered her place in Nice and got some change of clothes for her and I was taking them to her. She wasn't there when I got there, so I left her stuff and hung around for a while but the Gestapo came, arrested me and took me for questioning. They asked me if I knew of Madeleine's activities. Of course I said that I had no idea, we were just lovers. They asked me where she was and I said I believed that she had gone away to visit her parents; eventually they let me go and apologised; as a respected member of the Government, they said they should have known better. I accepted their apology and left pretty quickly. But they are looking for Madeleine; I have managed to get her away with some friends who live in L'Abadie in Les Basse Alpes in the hills above Nice where she will have to stay until the end of the war. If she is found, she will be shot. So you understand that this maybe one of the last times we are together. Claude you must slowly wind down and take no more risks — any of you. We have done everything we can. It is sad about Auguste and I would have loved to have got him out but now is not the time. That young girl and her family that was betrayed by that local boy, know who you are Claude and all our covers have been seriously compromised. When this is all over we will meet again, *si Dieu le veut, bon chance mes amis" after much hand shaking and embracing 'the boss' left, sadly never to be seen again.

Albert was at his desk when Kurt walked by. "Herr Schmidt," called Albert softly. The soldier walked towards him.
"I have news on that package that you wanted delivered, apparently it arrived safely and was, I believe, collected by the family. If I hear anymore I will let you know."
"Thank you Albert, thank you very much."
"You are welcome *monsieur*, but I want to know if you can help me?"
*God willing, good luck my friends.

Kurt looked around the foyer to check that no one was in proximity, "If I can," he said quietly.

"I need to know the location and situation of a friend of mine, a Lieutenant in the Gendarmerie?"

"*Mein Gott* Albert, I can't tell you that!"

Albert just looked at the young soldier with knowing eyes. He didn't move his eyes until Kurt said, "He is at L'Ariane in Nice along with many other prisoners. To my knowledge there have been no executions or deportations in which case I have to assume that there has been no change in their situation."

"Thank you," replied Albert.

On Monday July the second 1944 the streets of Monte Carlo were alive with the sound of German trucks and of the Gestapo's Mercedes limousines of the officers. Some went in the direction of Monaco, others remained in Monte Carlo itself. One such group drove to Claude's house. He was dragged out of the house and was beaten by the Gestapo's rifle butts before being thrown into the back of the truck. His wife was also taken. Further into Monaco, a group arrived at the house of the Secretary to the National Council of Monaco, René Borghini. Treated with slightly more respect he was arrested and put in the back of the Mercedes under guard. On the seventh of July, Esther Poggio, who was René's current liaison officer and 'mailbox' known as *'La Marquise'* was also arrested. They were all taken to L'Ariane.

The news was relayed to a shocked Albert whose

knees he could feel crumbling beneath him. His friends, mentors and comrades had been taken from him. Was he going to be next? Suddenly the seriousness of his situation was hitting him. Still only nineteen years of age he had seen and experienced, more than most young men of his age. It still excited him, but now his fear was palpable. Also they still had ten people in safe houses in Cap d'Ail who had to be moved. He contacted the last of the remaining group, Jacques and François and they met at Franck's. The three of them sat nursing a glass of wine trying to think what they could do.

"René and Claude are under so much guard anything we do would be futile — and suicide," said young Albert, now far older than his years. "But we do have to move the people we have. François and I can get them to the harbour but can you organise the boat Jacques? Can we schedule it for next Friday? I think we have to clear everything before the end of this month. From what I understand, the Allies will reach Paris soon in which case it could all be over."

The three men left the bar to carry out their tasks.

Later that evening Albert was at the concierge's desk when Kurt came over.

"I am sorry to hear about your friends," said Kurt.

"Where are they?" asked Albert.

"In the same place as the others were taken, L'Ariane" replied the German, "there will not be a lot of hope I am afraid. Albert, with the impending

end to this *Scheiße* some of us are being sent to the Eastern front to fight the Russians. It's not that I am a coward, but I can't cope with this anymore. I have to get away. Can you help me?"
"You've got to be fucking joking! Is this some sort of a trap? Do you think I'm an idiot?"
"On the contrary Albert, I think you are an intelligent, sharp, brave and honourable young man; and I am asking for your help. I will happily pay whatever I have got."
"I don't know, I will have to check the situation. Now go!"
'What the fuck am I going to do now? He's a bloody Nazi and I am going to ask his enemy to help him? They'll think I'm nuts.'
"You're nuts," said Jacques. "Why should we help him? He's a German Nazi bastard."
"He isn't the same as the others," protested Albert, "he has known a lot of what was going on and never said a thing; and he has helped me with information which otherwise we wouldn't have received. He's willing to pay, and God knows we need the funds. With paying all the double agents and for arms and stuff, least of all what we owe the skipper of the vessel, we have nothing left have we? With the rest of the team gone we have one last chance. Let's put him on the next — and last — boat out!"
"Be it on your head Albert, but I think you are mad."
"We can't get him any papers; he speaks no French, English or Spanish, he doesn't look

Jewish so he will probably be arrested when he gets to Spain, but at least that would be better than the Eastern front."

"Ok, you need to get him to the boat by six o'clock on Friday."

"Will do."

Later, Albert slipped a note under Kurt's door. *'The package that you wanted is at my desk. Please be there between eight and ten tomorrow'*

At eight twenty, Kurt was there. There were clients going and coming so it was a few minutes before they could talk. Eventually there was a break. Albert took Kurt to one side.

"I am doing this against my better judgement," said Albert, "I only trust you because of Sarah and Rachel and even that could be a pointless act. The only people that might help you and I mean might, when you get to Barcelona, could also be the ones that have you arrested and maybe shot! Spain may still be neutral but no one knows what they will do with an SS soldier. It's your choice."

"I have nothing to lose except my life," said a resolute Kurt, "but anything is better than continuing this madness — especially on the Eastern front."

"Be here," said Albert giving him a small part of a map showing the harbour. "I will meet you there at six on Friday; and bring the money."

"I will and thank you" replied the grateful enemy.

Albert, his colleagues and the boat, were ready for

Kurt when he got there fifteen minutes before six. Slightly apprehensive the team loaded Kurt on to the vessel. Kurt turned and handed Albert an envelope. "We will never meet again Albert, but I can only thank you and your friends for this; all of you are heroes, I don't know what to say but if I ever manage to see the girls I will tell them what a brave man you are and I only wish I had your courage and conviction. But if I did, then I probably wouldn't be here." He opened his arms for an embrace, Albert refused saying, "just get on the boat, keep your mouth shut and I wish you *bon voyage*" — and as a last word — "if you do meet them, give them my love, especially Sarah."

Kurt raised his hand as he got in the boat, this time as a gesture of friendship, not a Nazi salute. Albert watched as the boat sailed away into the setting sun.

The next morning at the hotel all hell was breaking lose. *Obergruppenführer* Kurt Hauser approached Albert's desk. "Young man, I believe you were acquainted with Kurt Schmidt."

"I'm sorry," replied Albert.

"Please do not act any more stupid than you already are," said an irate officer.

"Who is this Schmidt?" asked Albert with bravado.

"I assume you are well aware, as he has been seen speaking to you."

"Herr Hauser, I speak to all your officers and soldiers because that is still my job as a concierge, but also, you all look the same in uniform, so how can I help you?" said an unflappable Albert.

"We fear he has deserted, which I am sure you know would be subject to execution when he is caught. As will anyone known to have helped him. So if you wish to help your friend — and yourselves — I suggest you let me know where he is, before it is too late."

"My dear *Obergruppenführer* I have very few friends, most of them have disappeared or died, but I can assure you, with all due respect, none would be members of Herr *Obergruppenführer*'s army. Now if you will excuse me, I have to get on dealing with paying customers" said Albert as he turned away hoping the officer didn't notice the nervous damp sweat patches under his armpits.

Tuesday, fifteenth of August 1944 was a very dark day in the history of Monaco, Monte Carlo, France and the resistance. René, Claude, Esther and those that had been arrested on the train and those arrested from the family home and, dear Auguste, including his wife, and ten more were shot at L'Ariane at six in the evening. The part that the resistance was to play in the life and survival of the Monégasques and their Jewish guests had come to an end. The roll call of the numbers of people helped and saved ran into nearly one hundred. The losses incurred by the volunteer resistance had reached twenty, plus the local population: Police officers, shopkeepers, priests, doctors, children and many more who had put their lives, their country and their families before surrender or compliance added another fifteen to the total.

But it wasn't over yet.

CHAPTER SEVENTEEN
London Majestic April 2005

Michael's mobile phone rang on his desk. It was Maggie, his fifteen year old daughter with Juliette.
"Hello Daddy," said the sweet voice that always made Michael swell up with pride, "how are you?"
"Alright my precious, how are you?"
"Fine thanks Daddy, how's the new hotel?"
"Good darling, thank you; and school with you?"
"Yes fine. Listen Daddy the reason for phoning is Mummy and I am in London and wanted to call in and see you. Would that be OK?"
"Of course, ask Mummy if she would like lunch today and we can meet here. Say two o'clock?"
"I'm sure she would love to. OK, see you then."
He sat there for a few minutes and poured himself another coffee from the highly polished silverware. It always upset him a bit when his little girl called him. He loved hearing from her, but it always made him sad that he had missed so much of her in between years. He and Juliette had separated in 1995, five years after Maggie was born. They still remained husband and wife and their relationship continued, be it a little fractured. It was nobody's fault, work had got in the way of love, which in the Hotel Industry was not unusual. After the good work that Michael had done at the Nice Majestic he was promoted to General Manager of the Paris Majestic in 1993. It was a lot bigger than the Nice Majestic and at the

time was the flagship of the group. He reported directly to the Managing Director, in this case, his Uncle Marc. It was his idea to bring Michael in. It was time, as he had been in Nice since 1986 a lot longer than was anticipated, but with Michael getting married the family thought that he should stay there until they had settled in as a married couple. But the move to Paris was short lived for Juliette. A new baby, no family or friends proved difficult for a career girl. It was her choice to get pregnant, but both of them were over the moon when Margaret (Maggie) Marie Nicolson Varón was born and she had become the centre of their world but, the almost family motto, 'Work Comes First' was always uppermost in his head. Also a contributing factor to Juliette's decision was the 'bloody weather'. 'Why's it so cold and wet?' she would ask herself, 'it's nearly as bad as England'
'Why don't they have an hotel in the Caribbean?'
So in 1995 they sat down and she had told Michael that she wanted to go back to Nice. It did not come as a shock to Michael but he did try and persuade her to stay. On an inspection trip to Paris, Juliette secured a position as Assistant Director of Marketing at the *Georges Cinq* hotel part of the Trust House Forte group. But after a couple of years of nurseries and child carers, Juliette was getting more unhappy to leave a five year old for the length of time she needed to with a job of that responsibility. Anyway she was going to start junior school and Juliette wanted to be with her when she came home from school. So

she went back to Nice. It had worked out well. Michael would go to Nice every other weekend when he could. They had bought an apartment in Nice before they left for Paris, so as they had a bolt hole. Juliette was near her mother which enabled her to go back to the Negresco where she was welcomed with open arms. But when Michael had to return to Britain the distance was longer and time spent together as a family was less. Juliette came over as much as possible and Michael went back to Nice for holidays and longer breaks, but the weekend trips were no more. There was no animosity and both remained great friends, not just for Maggie's sake, but for their own peace of mind and friendship. The subsequent divorce did nothing to destroy that friendship, but it did give both of them the freedom to pursue other relationships although he didn't think she had and he certainly was too busy at the moment.

Michael had done his rounds and was working on future budgets when his secretary phoned through to say Juliette was at reception. He left his office and went along the short corridor to the foyer. Juliette looked as fabulous as ever and Maggie ran towards him and gave him a big hug. "I swear you grow an inch every month when I'm not looking. You're nearly as tall as me."
She laughed and cheekily lifted her dress above the knee and said, "That's 'cause I've got mummy's legs!"

"Maggie, behave yourself," said Juliette laughing.
"It's true though isn't it?" said Michael as he approached Juliette and embraced her and kissed her on both cheeks. "How are you?" he asked.
"Good thank you and you?"
"Better for seeing you two; come on, let's go and get some lunch."
He walked them through to the cocktail bar and ordered a couple of glasses of Champagne and a Shirley Temple for Maggie. The restaurant manager approached and gave them the menus.
"Chef's specials today are a *Tartare of Diver Caught Scallops and Salmon* to start and a **Tranche of Turbot with Asparagus and Hollandaise Sauce* for main course."
Michael looked at his family and asked,
"Would everyone like that?" They all nodded in agreement,
"We will all take the *tartare* and the turbot please Carl; and a bottle of Puligny Montrachet."
"Certainly sir, thank you," said Carl as he walked back toward the kitchen.
They chatted, much the same as they did on the first lunch date in Nice, with less sexual tension and an addition of a beautiful young lady of which they were both extremely proud. They discussed family and friends in Nice, how the hotel was going and how Le Negresco was doing. Juliette was now Marketing Director and was very happy.
"And what about school?" asked a concerned father.

*Tranche: on the bone fillet from the large flat fish

"She is doing very well," interjected Juliette. "She has taken her *Brevet and passed with flying colours."

"*Bravo ma chérie,* what good news."

"Which brings us to a family decision" continued Juliette, "we have been discussing Maggie's next move.

She wants to come to the UK to complete her studies and to take her A Levels then go on to further education here or maybe somewhere else. English is really her second language. I know we are all bi lingual but the last couple of years she has spent a lot of time with my mother who spoke to her mainly in English, but she is still very French."

"Well, that hasn't done either of us any harm" said Michael.

"No but we were educated all over the place she has only been in France and she wants to absorb more and broaden her horizons. It is her wish; I have had no influence on her. I will hate it, being separated from her, but she wants to do it."

"But how and where?" asked a perturbed Dad.

"Well, she would have to board for obvious reasons. She can come over to France for her holidays and half terms and you would have to have her for *exeats and be with her for special school functions and meetings."

*Brevet: an exam taken in Le College around fifteen years of age similar to GCSE O levels. Allowing students to progress to Le Lycée to take their Baccalauréat the equivalent of 'A' levels enabling them to go on to university

**Exeats; weekends off from boarding school.

"Obviously I will pop over for weekends where possible."

"Where do you want to go? And what do you want to do after?" he asked his daughter.

"I want to go to Cheltenham Ladies College to take my A Levels and then go to *Les Roches in Switzerland"

"You want to come in to this stupid business?" asked her father.

"Well someone has to take over from you when you retire Daddy."

He looked at his wife and burst out laughing. "Whatever you and Mummy decide is fine by me my precious, as long as you are happy."

Juliette placed her hand on his. "Thank you Michael, this will mean a lot to her."

"Whatever makes you both happy; that will make me happy"

"Thank you Daddy," said a happy little girl as she came around the table to give him a kiss. "I won't let you down — promise."

"You couldn't my darling, don't worry we will both be behind you all the way."

They finished their lunch and walked to the exit.

"I still love you, you know" said Juliette giving him a hug and a kiss on the lips.

"*Moi ausi ma Chérie*," returning the hug and kiss.

"And you too precious, look after Mummy and let me know what happens. Speak soon," he said giving her a big hug. She turned as she got into the black cab, "Bye Daddy and thank you," and

*Les Roches: Top Swiss hotel management school

blew him a kiss.

He watched them get in to their cab and drive away. His heart still had a place for Juliette, but would it ever be enough to get them back together?

CHAPTER EIGHTEEN
Hotel Nice Majestic - January 1989

Christmas and New Year had come and gone. The hotel had never performed so well and the relief General Manager was proving to be a success, not only on the business side, but from a PR point of view together with the backing of his staff and customers. The only sad thing about the holiday period was that De Villiers was not able to return to his post. His heart had rejected the pacemaker and he suffered a relapse. He had been in hospital over the festivities but had now returned home. Michael dialled the De Villiers home number.
"*Bonjour, Suzanne de Villiers,*" said the worried voice at the end of the line.
"Hello Suzanne, it's Michael."
"Hello Michael, how are you?"
"I am fine thank you, how is Édouard?"
"Not good I'm afraid He is quite weak and there are complications."
"I am so sorry Suzanne, but tell him not to worry about the hotel, I am keeping his seat warm."
"I think that maybe a problem Michael, I am not sure that he will be fit to return, not for a very long time."
"*Sacre bleu*, Suzanne he's only in his forties."
"I know Michael, but his father died of a heart attack at fifty so there is family history. The only way he can survive is to relax. He has stopped smoking lost many kilos and is trying to relax and he is reading, but he is frustrated and bored. He

hasn't got anything to get his teeth into and it's made him become irritable; infact, *il y a une douleur dans le putain de cul"
"I am sorry to hear that."
"I don't mean he's demanding, it's just that he hates being idle and he worries more about that, than getting better. He hates letting people down and he has developed a *camaraderie* with his team and he feels he has let them down."
"That is ridiculous Suzanne, he is very much loved by all his team and all they wish him is a speedy recovery. We can wait. I will stay here until he returns."
"Michael, I have phoned Marc Nicol and told him that for the time being he must consider relieving Édouard of his post."
"No Suzanne, what will he do?"
"Perhaps live," came the poignant response.
There was a silence while Michael absorbed her comment.
"He doesn't know yet Michael so I would be pleased if you would not say anything to him. I have enough to cope with at the moment. Believe me Michael, the thought of having the man I love around me twenty four hours a day does not thrill me, but it would thrill me less if I didn't."
"I understand, we will keep in touch, *un câlin,"
and he put the phone down.
'Looks like I am stuck here for a while' thought Michael, 'neither one thing nor the other'. The phone on his desk rang, he picked it up.

*a pain in the fucking arse   ** un câlin: a hug

"*Oui, allo,*"
"*Monsieur* Michael I have Marc Nicol on the phone" said Yvette, the secretary who it now seems would be his for the time being.

"*Allo, Bonjour, Suzanne de Villiers,*" said the woman at the end of the phone.
"*Bonjour Suzanne c'est moi Marc, comme ça va?*"
"*Allo* Marc, I am coping; thank you."
"And how is Édouard?"
"Tired and miserable, but almost doing as he is told."
Marc laughed, "That's something then. Can I speak to him?"
Of course," she walked into the lounge. "It's Marc, *mon cherie,*"
"*Allo Chef, comme ça va?*"
"I'm alright old friend, but how are you?"
"I feel about as useful as a **cautère sur une jambes de bois,*"
Both men laughed.
"Are you in pain, *mon ami?*"
"Only when I laugh," said Édouard.
"At least you have not lost your sense of humour my friend. Suzanne tells me that the prognosis is not brilliant and that you will need a lot of recovery time. I want you to take as long as you need. So we will continue to pay your full salary for the next six months and then look at the situation after that. Is that OK?"
"More than generous Marc, I can't thank you

*As useful as a poultice on a wooden leg

enough."

"Also, I know that Michael is holding the fort, but I would like him to officially take over as General Manager if you agree and then we will move him when you are fit to return. What do you think?"

"I cannot thank you enough and Michael is a natural, he will be excellent and very popular."

"I know, he is an exceptional young man and a bonus to our family business, as are you my friend and to think he wanted to be a lawyer! He wanted to join the dark side. Take care of yourself and if you need anything you only have to call."

"Thank you Marc *au revoir*."

"*Allo mon oncle,*" said Michael as he was connected.

"Michael, how are you?"

"Very well sir, thank you."

"Congratulations on your success, the hotel has been very busy and surpassed our expectations. You must be very satisfied?"

"It is a team effort as you know sir, so I am happy for all of us, especially our kitchen. You know we have our Michelin star this year?"

"We are all well aware young man and it is mostly down to your vision and determination."

"Thank you sir."

"Have you spoken to De Villiers?"

"Yes, of course we keep in contact; it is very sad."

"Yes," replied Marc, "he has been with us a while. However the chances of him returning in the near future are unlikely. So we wish to actively make you General Manager of the hotel. De Villiers is taking a paid leave of absence and when he returns we will place you elsewhere. We do have a plan Michael so now, this is part of it. It means staying there a little longer, but I am sure your beautiful wife will be happy to keep you close.

"She may well indeed, thank you sir, I will not let you down."

"I know that Michael and I wouldn't have suggested it if I thought you would. Give my fondest to Juliette and we will speak soon. *Bon chance*."

He put the phone down and despite knowing that his life had been more or less planned for him, taking on the management of one of the company's best loved hotels was indeed an honour especially at only twenty six years of age.

He called Juliette, "I think we should go out to somewhere special for dinner tonight when you finish work, what do you think?"

"What are we celebrating?"

"Do I need to be celebrating anything to take my beautiful wife out for dinner?"

"No, but you usually do!" she laughed

"I'll see you at home later. *Baisers*."

He called in his now permanent secretary, Yvette; "Yvette can you please draft a letter saying that in *Monsieur* De Villiers absence and continuing illness, the Majestic Hotel Group has confirmed that Michael Nicolson, acting General Manger, will

*kisses

be assuming the post of General Manager of the Nice Majestic Hotel as of today's date."

"Certainly *Monsieur*, congratulations, you will be brilliant."

"That's very kind but it seems a little bit like, 'The King is Dead — Long live the King!' Sorry, that wasn't a good turn of phrase."

"I know what you mean sir, and so would *Monsieur* De Villiers."

"Thank you Yvette, I am going to be relying on you for many things; I hope you are up to it?"

"Of course *Monsieur*, whatever you need."

"I suppose, firstly, it's best to convene a heads of department meeting and I suppose I had better move into *Monsieur* De Villiers office as there is more room."

"It is not just *Monsieur* De Villiers office *Monsieur* Michael, it is the General Manager's office. I will make the moves now and schedule the meeting for five this afternoon."

"Thank you Yvette, you are very kind."

"*Mesdames et Messieurs*, thank you for coming. Sorry about the inconvenient hour but I needed to talk to you before Yvette sent out the memo. *Monsieur* De Villiers may not be coming back for a very long time or, maybe not at all; sadly he is not well. The company has therefore asked me to take on the permanent post of General Manager. As I am sure you are aware it will not change our working relationship and I will still be relying on you all for your help and support."

The team applauded their new 'official' boss.
"You know you can rely on that sir," said the restaurant manager Carl Joubert, seconded by the Chef, Roger.
"Thank you, in that case, let's continue to try and make this the best hotel in Nice."
They got up from their seats and went back to their posts.
"That went well, *Monsieur*," said Yvette as she put the furniture back in place.
"Yes, I think so. Let's see what the future holds shall we? "
His phone rang, it was Uncle Marc.
"*Allo*, Michael.
"*Allo Monsieur*.
"I am sending you a new senior assistant manager. He is one of our hot new finds. He joins us from the Hermitage in Monte Carlo where he was assistant Food and Beverage Manager. It's a big jump, but he is enthusiastic and has a passion for F&B not unlike you. So he will learn from you and you will guide him. He will be with you on Saturday. Ease him in over the weekend and have him start on Monday."
"Certainly *Monsieur* and thank you."
"*De rien*, speak later."
There was a knock at his door.
"*Entrez*,"
In walked his beautiful wife. "Hello darling, what's happening? Why the sudden desire to celebrate?"
"I thought we were meeting at home?"
"I couldn't wait."

"I'll tell you at home while we change for dinner. Yvette," he called through to his secretary's office, "I am going out for dinner with my wife. I'll see you tomorrow."

"*Certainment Monsieur, profite de ta nuit.*"*

They got back to the apartment and both undressed to shower. They didn't get too far in getting ready, as the excitement of the day took over. After telling Juliette the news, showering and opening a bottle of Champagne, they fell onto the bed and made love.

"Michael?"

"*Oui.*"

"What would you say if I said I would like to think about having a baby?"

"Blimey, I hadn't thought. I wasn't sure that you would be interested yet?"

"Well, with the news that you are going to be here for some time and we are a little more secure, this could well be the time. What do you think?"

He leaned over to her and kissed her. "If that is what you want I am totally up for it. It will be very good looking, very clever, bilingual and a mould of us!"

They laughed. "So," he asked, "do you want to start now or would you rather have dinner?"

"I'd rather have dinner," she smiled. "Anyway I have to stop taking the pill. It will take time to work itself out of my system. But I am happy to start trying after dinner — until whenever.

They held each other for a while until Juliette said

Certainly sir, enjoy your evening.

"Who have I got to fuck to get dinner tonight?"
"You have already had an advantage," laughed Michael, "Come on then, the only thing to beat that is some *Foie Gras* with a glass of Sauterne."

CHAPTER NINETEEN
September 1944

The murders of René, Claude, August and Esther at L'Ariane had a profound negative effect on their colleagues as well as Monaco and Monte Carlo in general. It coincided with the Allies landing on the beaches of the Côte d' Azur, the French Riviera. This was just under three hours from the Principality and optimism was high that the Allies would soon liberate the conclave. Now, a couple of weeks later, the German residents were indeed nervous. There was a lot of action in the hotel as the unwanted guests started to pack up their belongings to leave the hotel, obviously having received orders to evacuate. News reached the remaining resistance fighters in Monte Carlo that the German departure was imminent and that apart from the road transport that they had a lot of the soldiers were due to depart by train. But it was a pointless move as they would be going straight into the hands of the Allies. Albert called a meeting with the last few stalwarts, in Franck's bar.

"I was thinking Didier that we should plant explosives on the tracks somewhere between here and Nice. What do you think?"

"Honestly Albert, I don't think the risk is worth the reward. They will be driving straight into the waiting Allies so they will get nowhere. Also, in my opinion, we are not Nazis and killing people for the sake of it now the war is coming to an end seems somehow un Christian and immoral."

"I agree," said François, "as much as I would love to kill the bastards for what they did to our friends I suppose we have to be benevolent and accept that the average soldier was nothing to do with it and like most in the military were just following orders dished out by a bloke in an office drinking Champagne — or in their case probably beer and schnapps! I am sure most of them would be looking forward to getting back to their families even if they face prison camps first."

"I suppose you are right and I bow to your maturity; I suppose I wanted one last chance. In which case my esteemed friends, shall we drink to freedom?"

They raised their glasses and in unison with everyone in the bar shouted, * *"à la liberté et à la paix."*

On the first of the month the troops started moving out and by the third, there was not a German in sight. That is apart from four young soldiers who approached Albert in the hotel, before the mass exodus. They couldn't have been any older than Albert, but their ashen-faces made Albert think that they were very scared.

"How can I help you gentleman?" said Albert, "Don't you think that you should be running off with your tails between your legs like your friends?"

"Albert" said Hans a twenty something young man

*To freedom and peace

"some of us know what you have been doing this last year and how you have helped so many people, not least our friend Kurt. We don't want to go back, is there anything you can do for us?"

Albert looked at them intently, then said, "I don't know what you are talking about, *mes amis*, I am afraid I can't help you in anyway."

"We can pay," said Hans.

"You would never be able to pay enough for what you have done to our community my friend, I think you will have to take your punishment from the Allies when you meet them."

The boys walked away and Albert watched as the dejected soldiers, whose lives were now precarious, huddled in a corner obviously feeling the worse was about to happen.

Hans walked back to Albert. "I have some information that may be of use to you if you can help us."

"What would that be?" asked Albert.

"You promise you will help us if we tell you?"

"Depends, you will have to trust me as to what it is worth," said Albert playing 'hard ball'.

The boys looked at each other and nodded their approval for their friend to make the deal.

"The last of us will be leaving on the third. There are plans to plant explosives in the hotel and cause as much damage as possible as we leave."

"Why'" questioned Albert, "what for? We have done nothing but be civil to you under the most difficult circumstances Why would you want to do that?"

"Not us Albert: The powers that are!"

"I don't know how I can help, honestly." He thought a bit more and then thought if what he was about to do would turn around and bite him in the arse — and his colleagues.

He scribbled a note on a piece of paper.

"Go down to this port tomorrow evening at six and ask for this man. It goes without saying that you need to go without uniform. Take as little as you can carry. He gave them a small map as he had done with Kurt and a note from him to Jules, the skipper of the ship. "Take money and I cannot guarantee that he can or will help you."

"Thank you Albert." Hans took out some money and handed it to him.

"Save it for Jules at the boat. No amount of money you give to me will compensate the families of those lives your people destroyed" said Albert in a last ditch attempt to make them work for this favour.

Hans offered his hand, "Thank you Albert, I am sorry, we will never forget you."

Albert reluctantly took his hand, something that he had never done with Kurt and held on to it while he stared at him and asked, "Do you know where the explosives will be planted?"

"I am afraid not, it has nothing to do with us. But if we hear more we will tell you."

Albert went into his father's office.

"What is it Albert?" asked Richard.

"I have reason to believe that the Germans will try and blow up the hotel when they leave."

"Why? For what reason? Bastards! We have looked after the Nazi scum since they got here. What the fuck is wrong with these people?

"That we may never know" said Albert, "but I think we should let the *'pompiers' know and make sure all the staff leave the building at the same time as the Germans."

*"*Tu as raison mon fils,*" said his Father. "I'll let your Uncle know what's happening."

The next day at eight o'clock in the morning there was a max exodus by the Gestapo and SS. The staff followed fairly quickly on the pretence of 'waving goodbye'. As the vehicles left, the fire department arrived along with the Gendarmes. There was not time to look for the explosives and anyway that would be like looking for the proverbial needle in a haystack. They did not have access to bomb disposal experts and even the bravest of young men, including Albert, were not going to go into a potential fire bomb. All they could do was wait.

The Gendarmes had blocked that part of the *esplanade*, diverting what little traffic there was, up into the hills. All of a sudden, even though they were waiting for something, there was an horrific bang from the corner of the building. Windows were blown out; flames spurted from the open space. The stench of gunpowder filled the air and the heat was felt by the staff hiding on the

*Fire department   ** You are right my son

beach a safe distance from the hotel; there was another explosion on the other side of the building. From Albert's point of view, the first one was near the kitchen, probably a store room area accessible to the public; and the second in or near the laundry room. The fire department started in earnest as they rolled out their hoses and started swamping the fires with water. Just as they approached the building from either side there was another explosion that blew the glass of the entrance doors out onto the street followed by a fireball that spilled on to the *esplanade* taking two firemen with it. The tops of trees were burning and the smell of carbon and sulphur permeated the atmosphere. The birds, especially the seagulls, had scattered and there was an eerie silence broken only by the crackling of the wood and combustibles in the hotel. The ambulances had already arrived anticipating injuries and they had their first. The two men were rolling around on the road in an attempt to put out the flames that were engulfing their uniforms. Their colleagues rushed over and covered them with fire blankets as the medics brought stretchers over. After a minute or so, the two men got up and although, seemingly OK, they were made to get in the ambulance which left rapidly for the hospital.

Albert and his uncle watched helplessly as the hotel was being consumed by fire. He looked over to Richard and could see the tears running down his face as he watched his beloved hotel burn. The efforts of the firemen were not in vain and after about an hour the fire was under control. Apart from the two firemen there were no injuries, mainly down to Albert and Richard's decision to get all the staff out at the same time. Maybe the four young Germans may have deserved their passage out of France after all.

Two days later the familiar sounds of army tanks were heard as the Allies arrived in the Principality. There was the expected cheering and waving of British and American flags as well as those of France and Monaco's as the convoy drove through the town. The bars were filled with locals singing and dancing in the streets. Their occupation, including the Italians, was a matter of a couple of years, but France had been under German occupation for more than four years. The third of September 1944 would be cemented in history as *le jour de libération de* Monaco. Monaco's Liberation Day, despite the fact that the Allies did not arrive until the sixth.

Prince Rainier III of Monaco (in waiting) joined the French army and was involved in the liberation of Alsace. His father did not die until May 1949 when Rainier became ruler of the Principality.

But, on the seventh of September, Richard and Albert, together with Albert's Uncle Antoine, who had come to comfort his brother and to see the damage, stood in the foyer of the blackened burnt out reception of the hotel in silence.

"We can rebuild," said Albert breaking the silence.

"With what son?" asked his father, "insurance

companies do not pay out on war damage."
"Technically, is this war damage? After all, we never were bombed, this is arson isn't it?"
"It would be a very fine line," said Antoine "and I doubt that our insurers would take that view."
"Worth asking isn't it?" said a determined Albert. "Would the banks lend us the money to rebuild it?"
"I suppose they might, depending on the cost," said Richard.
"In that case shouldn't we start? We still have to pay the staff until the end of the month, let's get everyone in and clean up the mess and see what we are facing."
"Are you putting yourself up as project manager young Albert?" asked Antoine.
"Why not, I'm younger than you two old men and I have decided that I want to be in this business — permanently — so what better way to start than rebuilding from scratch and cementing my career" said a triumphant Albert.
Well, you had better get started," said his father. "Your uncle and I will sort out the finances."
With the help of Richard's secretary and the few heads of department that were hanging around waiting for instructions as to their next move, Albert got notices to all the staff to meet at the hotel on the following Monday.
Ten o'clock on that day all but a handful of staff appeared at the hotel.
"Right everyone," said an empowered Albert, "we have a small task in front of us. Each of you go to

your areas in the hotel and with your head of department compile a list of damage and if anything has survived; damage, apart that is, from smoke and smell which is probably throughout the hotel. If we want to get our jobs back, this is where we start. Are you all agreed?"

There was a wave of almost enthusiastic response.

"So my friends and peers, if this is what you want, then in the words of Alexandre Dumas and D'Artagnan. * *'Un pour tous et tous pour un'.*"

A cheer ran out from the assembled crowd as they all joined in the rallying call. Would the phoenix rise from the ashes? They would have to wait and see.

All for one and one for all.

CHAPTER TWENTY
Hotel Nice Majestic - February 1990

De Villiers had not returned. Michael was still General Manager and the hotel had gone from strength to strength.

Robert Jourdain, Michael's deputy, had been at the hotel for just a year. He was only a few years younger than Michael, so they got on well. He was indeed a passionate food and beverage man and had taken control of that department. He had made changes within the hotel, especially room service, which had become the talk of the town. Mainly because of the acquisition of some state of the art, room service trolleys which replaced trays and old fashioned hotel trolleys. These new trolleys, from the dumb waiter family, which is what they were often called, were designed by Robert. They were like a full works station with a heated compartment not unlike a hostess trolley, but more elaborate. That meant that room service waiters could go into a suite with everything they needed to supply a full restaurant service without the need to keep going back to the service kitchens. They were nick-named Jourdain's Chariots. In French a *'chariot'* is a 'trolley' so it was more amusing for English speakers hearing it in French. But when Uncle Marc visited the hotel he liked the name and the product so asked Robert to order one for him for his house. Subsequently they were adopted as the company's standard room service equipment for all the hotels.

Michael had visited De Villiers over the last year at his home but over Christmas he had taken him a personal gift a gold Mont Blanc fountain pen engraved with his initials. The staff had collected for him and had presented him with a hamper of some of his favourite foods and wines. He seemed very touched with it all. "The pen is wonderful Michael, you should have not spent so much money, but I am very touched thank you."

"You are welcome, Sir," replied Michael graciously.

"Édouard please Michael."

"How are you feeling?"

"I am fine now and want to get back to work. Your family have been very good to me. They kept me on full salary for six months and then half salary until the end of this year. I can't complain but I need to get back on my horse."

"The doctors won't let him yet," interrupted Suzanne, "and if they could see the contents of this hamper, they would confiscate it. Look," she said lifting a bottle out of the basket, "Chateau Latour, Chateau Lafite, Chateau d'Yquem, Foie Gras amongst other delicacies including truffles; and" she exclaimed "a bottle of Chivas Regal. Is the staff trying to kill him?" she laughed.

"He's not meant to eat it all at once Suzanne, just a couple of treats a week" said Michael.

"Well, let us share a bottle of Latour while you are here Michael, that way she can't complain about me over indulging if I only have a couple of small glasses."

Suzanne opened a bottle and brought in three crystal glasses.

"1980 as well," said an excited connoisseur. "*Magnifique*," as he swilled the dark red liquid around his mouth before swallowing. "*Superb*," he proclaimed.

"Well," said Michael raising his glass, "to a *Joyeux Noël* and a healthy and prosperous new year to you both. *Santé*."

They discussed how the hotel was going and he asked after Juliette. "She must be ready to give birth soon."

"Anytime now," Michael said looking at his watch. "I had better go, I left her in bed this morning and I want to make sure she's OK. She's getting a bit fed up now, the novelty of being pregnant has worn off and the prospect of birth is taking over."

They all laughed. Michael said his goodbyes and Suzanne let him out. "Thank you for coming Michael, it always cheers him up when he sees you; he is very fond of you."

"And me him, Suzanne. Look after him, drip feed him the goody box." They kissed and he left. 'He didn't look that grand', thought Michael as he got into his car.

The following morning, Michael was meeting with Robert, Chefs Roger and Simon and Carl, when his mobile rang.

"OK, I'll be there in a second. Excuse me

gentlemen we will have to reschedule, babies wait for no man!"

"Good luck sir," they said in unison as he made a dash for his apartment.

When he got in Juliette was ready with her overnight bag and had put on her overcoat. "My waters have broken," she said somewhat frightened, reality now kicking in.

"You'll be fine," said Michael putting his arm around her and picking up her bag:

"That's easy for you to say."

"I love you" he said.

"Well we'll see if I love you when this is all over" she said half laughing.

Travelling a little over the speed limit it didn't take long to get to the University hospital where she was taken to her room.

"Don't leave me yet Michael."

"I won't my darling," he said holding her hands. She hadn't been in bed for an hour when the pain kicked in.

A doctor was by her side in minutes. "When did your contractions start?"

"I am not sure, because I had a sharp pain and then my waters burst and this is the first…Ahhh," she screamed mid conversation "the first real pain, I've had."

The doctor checked her cervix, "It's dilating so it may not be too long; the midwives will keep an eye on you now, but I won't be far away."

"Thank you doctor," said Michael.

"Oh Jesus, here we go," said Juliette as she let

out another gasp.

The nurse suggested she got up and walked around as that would help the baby move.

Michael went out to get some sandwiches, "Here," he said offering her a roast beef one. "you may need the carbs later."

"Thanks," she said sarcastically.

An hour later it started in earnest. She was moved to the birthing room and Michael was given a hospital gown and mask and told to be quiet, sit at her bedside and hold her hand. The next half an hour would be indelibly printed on Michael's mind. Expletives in French and English that he didn't know his precious wife even knew; well he did, but not delivered with such venom.

"Breathe deeply and push," said an inexperienced father. "Fuck off Michael, I'm going to kill you when this is all over" said an inexperienced mother.

"Push," said an experienced midwife.

"I am fucking pushing," yelled a woman in pain.

Further toing an froing of swear words, insults and anger as the baby's head appeared and Michael just stood there totally enthralled. His beautiful wife was yelling "you bastard" at him as he watched her normally perfect body distorting, bleeding and performing nature's wonders. With one final push, Michael's darling daughter, the most precious thing he would ever have, along with his darling wife, came into the world.

The midwife placed Margaret (Maggie) Marie Nicolson Varón on to her breasts. Both Juliette and Michael were crying; Michael through sheer disbelief and Juliette probably through pain, fear and pleasure as she held her little girl.

"She's beautiful," said Michael.

"She is isn't she? But that must be what every new parent says. But she will be."

"She certainly will if she takes after her mother," commented a husband trying to gain back some brownie points.

"We'll keep you in for a day or so, to clean you up and just to make sure you are alright" said the doctor.

"If you are OK," said Michael, "I'll come back later after you have had some rest."

"Are you going back to the hotel?" she said somewhat surprised.

"Well, I've done my bit, it's all down to you now," he said laughing and leaning over to kiss her. "Well done, you are amazing."

"Yes, and you" she said "are a shit!"

"Well, you know that — 'Work Comes First'" they said together.

"You might have to rethink that motto now you have other responsibilities," she said pointedly whilst waving him out of the door.

But he probably would never change; it was inbred in him through years of the family business.

CHAPTER TWENTY ONE
1945 — From the Ashes

Work had started on the rebuilding of the hotel soon after Albert had motivated the staff at the end of September 1944. The war continued but this no longer really affected Monaco as the fighting had moved to Germany, as the Allies closed in on Hitler and his armies. Although, in March of 1945 nobody in the Principality was to know that Hitler would be dead in April of that year and that the war in Europe would effectively be over in May. Albert's only desire was to get the family's hotel open again. His father and uncle had obtained finance to start work. The insurance company, as expected, were not to pay out, although they did come to an agreement on loss of profits and certain furnishings caused by fire damage. Their bank had agreed a short term loan at very low interest rates to get the project under way with a more long term mortgage when works were completed. Albert discussed with the family about using one of the era's best loved architects and designers, Charles-Édouard Jeanneret, known as *Le Corbusier*. Born in Switzerland but obtaining French citizenship in 1930, *Le Corbusier* was recognised as the 'father' of modern architecture. Albert sat in on the meetings and wanted input into the style but also in the practicality of the workings of what was to be a modern hotel. Architects, while creative in design, often were unable to incorporate the things that hoteliers need to operate efficiently.

Sufficient power points, access for wide loads, sufficient parking and storage and many other things. The young, budding hotelier was sure that he could contribute a great deal and in fairness, *Le Corbusier* allowed this young enthusiast plenty of rope. One thing he wanted to incorporate was a service kitchen on every floor level, serviced directly from the main kitchens, to provide top quality room service to every room. Something that until then, had not really been done; in fact had only been introduced in to hotels in 1930 starting with the Waldorf Hotel in New York; so it had not caught on in Europe until much later and even then it was pretty basic; but Albert wanted to make it better. Together they redesigned the reception area, which had been totally destroyed in the blast. The whole concept was in the 'modernist' style which would hold the hotel's design in good stead for years to come. Albert also felt that some form of automatic, electronic system would soon be available to aid accounting and reservations, so he wanted to ensure that there were plenty of power points in reception and at the concierge desk.

September 1945 and World War II was over. The Japanese had surrendered and a wave of relief swept through Europe. No more so than in France and even more so for Monaco and Monte Carlo, especially those in the tourist industry that were going to have to claw their way back to get near to their pre-war popularity: And Albert Nicol was going to be the one that did it for his family. Still a very young man, just approaching twenty four, he had already made his mark; both as a strong warrior, a brave soul and a determined young busincss man. So the same month, The Bristol Majestic re-opened its doors with its new, if not very original moniker, The New Bristol Majestic Hotel. There was fanfare and publicity as Prince Louis II and Crown Prince Rainier III attended the opening along with invited guests from pre-war days including such luminaries as Sinatra, a young Peter Lawford and many others.

Guests were treated to a champagne reception, music and dancing and a buffet to beat all buffets with lobsters, oysters and more. The band master called for attention so as he could introduce the owners, Richard and Antoine Nicol to the stage.

"Your Royal Highnesses, Distinguished Guests, old friends, our wonderful new ones and our staff. We are very pleased to be here with you today. After the ravages of the last few years I am sure we are all happy to be here at all and we keep a place in our hearts for those that are not with us today. After the explosions that devastated our little hotel, my brother and I were prepared to walk away as the cost and heartache to re-open was too much for us old people, as my son told me we were; so he decided that he would take on the task of rebuilding our family business. He retained the services of *Monsieur* Charles-

Édouard Jeanneret, *Le Corbusier*" he raised an arm toward the architect who acknowledged him to a round of applause, "and together they worked tirelessly to make this one of the premier hotels in Monte Carlo. My son's ambition, foresight, bravery — and most of us know of that for other reasons — and determination means he has earned his place at the family's table. Your Highnesses, Ladies and Gentlemen and distinguished guests may I introduce you, as a proud father, to my son and Antoine's nephew, Albert Nicol our new operations manager of the New Bristol Majestic Hotel of Monte Carlo.

There was a tremendous round of applause and hooting from the staff, as a reluctant young man was dragged on stage by some of his fellow staff members and peers. An embarrassed Albert stood at the microphone looking out at the assembled guests.

*"*Je dois faire pipi*" said Albert to gusts of laughter. "I was not expecting this; my family told me nothing of this new position nor that they were they going to bring me up on stage. What can I say? I fell into this business as a sixteen year old because I had no idea what I wanted to do. My family tried to send me back to Switzerland when the Italians came, and I didn't go and then when the Germans arrived, I certainly didn't want to go anyway. I learned so much in those few years: The importance of family, friends and country. I was fortunate to be

I want to pee!

involved with some wonderful, brave and courageous people who I miss to this day. They taught me about friendship, loyalty and family and I feel that I am a better man for it. I thank them and most of us know who they are. When I stood in front of our fire ravaged hotel I could hear the voices of René, Auguste and Claude saying, 'You can do it boy! Make your mark, be brave, be courageous be truthful and you can do anything you want to'. I can only thank my family and our staff that has worked so hard to get this hotel opened — and we made it.

I may still be very young, but I am sure there are a lot of young men who feel that the war, despite our short involvement, made them mature far more quickly than they normally would have. Even doing this, for this last year, I hope has given me a mature head on my shoulders. It was another learning experience. As for being, what is that you called me?" he said looking at his father, "operations manager? I am just a 'buttons' in a new suit and with a new ambition of which all of you," he said, spreading his arms around the room to the staff, "will be part of. Our future will be good, there are challenges but there is hope. Please raise your glasses to the New Bristol Majestic Hotel, the Nicol family and their proud staff. *A votre santé"*

"Sante," confirmed the crowd. There was a round of applause as the proud young man left the stage to start the next chapter of his life.

CHAPTER TWENTY TWO
It Started with a Dream

Richard and Antoine Nicol watched with pride as their protégé walked away from the platform.

"Who would have thought *mon frère* that one day one of our offspring would be following in our footsteps," said Richard.

"My younger son Marc has said he wants to follow his brother into the business as well" said Richard. "He's nearly eighteen now so when he's finished school, the hotel should be open so maybe we can find him a management training plan."

"*Absolument*," concurred Antoine "Maybe we can start a dynasty." They laughed at the thought, but you never know.

The France of 1900 that Richard Nicol was born into was a far cry from the post war France that he and his younger brother Antoine, now find themselves. The Prussian-French war had finished in 1870 with the death of Napoleon III. The result was the Third Republic, whose intention was to reinstate Royalty, but none of those involved could decide who they thought would be the right family. So, the Third Republic governed until the fall of France to Germany in 1940. Harsh reparations made by the Prussians meant the loss of Alsace and Lorraine. Having said all this, the French were coming to terms with a Republic as opposed to a Monarchy, meaning that France would remain a Republic for the foreseeable future.

The most important political party of the early 20th century in France was the Radical Party, founded in 1901 as the "Republican, Radical and Radical-Socialist Party". It was classically liberal in political orientation and opposed the monarchists and clerical elements on the one hand, and the Socialists on the other.

Like most wars, the Prussian-French war separated the country in as much as the provinces felt annexed from the cities and major cultures. The improvement in rural farming and the industrial revolution towards the end of the nineteenth century had meant that the unification of France and French pride were being restored.

Richard and Antoine's parents were farmers just outside of Montpelier in the Languedoc. In the 1890's they started to grow vines to start wine production. Phylloxera* devastated the wine growing areas of Europe in the mid nineteenth century. Richard's father had taken advice when he started and was told to graft his vines with the American rootstock that had not been susceptible to the blight. He also imported vines from Spain which had not been affected by the disease. *Garnacha* and *Granache* were the same grapes and with the addition of the rootstock already in place, meant that their vineyard would thrive.

*a blight that affected vines in Europe destroying production

By the end of the century, they had stopped selling their grapes to co-operatives and started selling their own wines. With the increase in agriculture and building work, workers all over France were looking for cheap red wine to drink. Languedoc – Rousillon was the area of choice. The climate allowed for vast production of economical red wine.

They soon were successful and demand had increased. Antoine and Richard had obviously been brought up in wine country and were soon learning about its production and the marketing of the product. The onset of the First World War, when Richard was only fourteen, saw an increase in demand for drinkable, cheap wine as the government had replaced water with a quarter litre of wine per man, for the troops on the front line. By 1915 that had doubled to a half litre and by 1916 three quarters of a litre and the government were supplying troops with some 12 million hectolitres a year, thanks mainly to Languedoc and Rousillon as their production was so high. The Nicols were soon supplying a million litres a year and thanks to the wine lake that had appeared in Rousillon sales increased all over the province as the lake got smaller. While the wines supplied to the army made no money the continued supply to workers and industry made a healthy profit for the Nicols and their family. At the end of the War the demand for cheap wine diminished as the French had acquired a taste for what had now become the National drink and with that, the palate of the everyday man was looking for something better. Richard had become very *au fait* with wines by now at the tender age of eighteen. He had been loading up the horse and cart with barrels and flagons of the family's product and would go around the local area selling to hostelries, bars and small farms and businesses. Young Antoine helped in grape picking and was soon involved with production, even at sixteen. The brothers enjoyed their new challenge and they focused all their energy into their parent's business.

One day when they were all in the *cave, tasting the 1918 vintage, Richard said, "*Papa*, we should look to use another grape."

"Why my son?"

"Because the French palate is changing and Europe is looking toward finer wines. We can't do much here in Languedoc, we will never be Latour, but we can add depth to our wines; such as *Dureza* and *Mondeuse*** which we could blend with the Cabernet Franc."

His father looked at him with pride. "You have certainly been studying my son, please follow up your theory, I am right behind you."

"So am I my brother," said Antoine, "let's go."

·•(✧∽✧)•·

By the time that Richard celebrated his twenty first birthday they were about to harvest their first Languedoc *Dureza*; A more full bodied wine than

*Cave: bodega, production and bottling area
**off spring of these grapes, created the Shiraz we know

their usual offering. By the time he was twenty four, Richard was in charge of sales and marketing and Antoine, production. Their product had become popular and demand increased; Albert Nicol and Sons, of Languedoc, had made a name for themselves. Alongside the still popular *Vin Ordinaire* the family had branched out to include the ever popular *Vin Rosé*.

By the early nineteen twenties they had established a route along the coast which meant buying a delivery van at a cost of 4000 francs, which frightened his father to death: But it worked.

They had also developed their Cabernet Franc blended with *Dureza* which had become very popular. Richard was supplying some of the best places locally and on the 350 kilometre route to Nice and even to Monte Carlo. Post war business was booming and they had bought another delivery van and also now had two driver/salesmen. One day when Richard went into Monte Carlo to one of his clients he sat with the owner of the Bristol Hotel; a 150 room hotel on the *esplanade*. Giovanni was a Monégasque of Italian descent with a Swiss wife and a beautiful daughter Carolina. Giovanni had had the hotel since 1905. It was a well respected hotel; comfortable, efficient, profitable, but lacked personality and style.

Over a glass of the *Albert Nicol et Fils Dureza* Languedoc 1922 Giovanni talked about the problems that they had had after the war and despite their previous success they had lost money. They didn't want to sell, but he was tired and he needed to retire but wanted to hold on to an income to provide for his family.

"Let me think about it Giovanni, it could interest us. I will see you next week. *Au revoir mon ami,*" said Richard as he got back into his car.

When he got home, he sat with his mother, father and Antoine to relate his conversation.

"What on earth are you thinking about Richard?" asked a frustrated father. "We don't have the necessary money to take on any sort of financial arrangement."

"I know *Papa*, but we are doing well and the banks are desperate to lend money. We could borrow some money against the winery to buy into the hotel."

"It is a risk my son,"

"I know, but I think it could be a worthwhile one?"

"Looking at his wife, Albert asked, "What do you think *ma chérie*,?

"His instinct was right with the wines Albert, who knows maybe he has the energy and willpower to make it work."

"With our money?"

"No Albert with OUR money. Richard has doubled our profits. It's nearly as much his, as it is ours."

"What about the winery?" asked Albert.

"I will still be involved, but Antoine can take over some of the sales; we have our salesmen/drivers.

"Ok," replied the nervous patriarch, "speak to your man and see what the deal is — but I'm not promising anything."

"I understand *Papa*, but we will make it work, I promise."

"Yes, yes, I know!"

Giovanni and Richard shook hands. The young entrepreneur had negotiated a 1.3 million franc loan against the winery. He paid Giovanni one million for 35% of the hotel. Two hundred thousand he kept for operation expenses and the other hundred he passed to his father to ensure that they could buy another truck and employee if necessary as well as another vintner/viticulturist* to assist Antoine. Richard formed a company with Giovanni. *Societe Anonyme Monégasque (Société des Hotels Majestic)* and the hotel was renamed The Bristol Majestic.

Giovanni would receive 25% of the profits plus an annual salary. The beautiful Carolina remained as public relations and sales, but with a new found enthusiasm.

Plans were drawn up for refurbishment of the hotel and the creation of a new image.

A local young hotel manager was recruited under the guidance of a part time Giovanni and a non resident Richard. The dream was coming to fruition. The Nicols were going to be a dynamic force to be reckoned with.

* Viticulturist: wine maker

CHAPTER TWENTY THREE
Life Goes On 1924

The hotel was doing well. So was Richard, it was inevitable that he would become more involved with the day to day running and Giovanni less. The young manager was still there, but he became more like Richard's assistant, although Richard valued input from the young man's limited experience. It was still more than his, but he was a natural business and salesman. It was also inevitable that he would fall for Carolina and vice versa. She was very attractive, strong, highly intelligent and exceptionally good at her job. She had taken to her new responsibilities with renewed vigour, and business in the hotel, had increased on her watch. Their relationship started simply; a drink after work over a meeting; business lunch with clients and a quiet coffee afterwards, together, plus general day to day contact; but nothing had happened yet.
"Are you free tonight after work?" asked Richard.
"I could be, what do you have in mind?"
"I thought dinner outside of the hotel somewhere would be nice. What do you think?"
"Why not?"
"Exactly, I'll meet you here at seven thirty."
"OK, *a bientôt*," replied an eager Carolina.
They had a quiet supper in a local bistro near to the hotel, *Le Petit Escargot*.
Raymond was the owner, in his late fifties, but his

daughter Marie, in her twenties, did the donkey work while *Papa* played mine host, drank too much, talked a lot and laughed even more.

"This is nice, I haven't been here before," said Carolina.

"Really? and you know this area better than me."

"Daddy and I tended to eat in the hotel."

"I understand," said Richard ordering a bottle of the *Albert Nicol y Fils Cabernet* 1922.

"We have that wine don't we," said Carolina studying the label.

"Yes, it's one of ours, that is how I met Raymond and of course your father. I used to sell them wines.

"Of course, I forgot my father used to tell me of the handsome young 'wine man' that used to call in each week. He never managed to introduce me to you."

"Well, we managed it ourselves didn't we?"

"We certainly did and it has been worth waiting for."

It didn't take too long to cement their relationship and after a couple of months Carolina asked if they could meet after work that evening.

"Of course," said Richard, "is there a problem?"

"Not really, I just have something to discuss.

They met in Jacques' bar around the corner. Settling down with a glass of wine, he asked, "What's the problem?"

"Richard, I am pregnant."

Silence fell between them. He looked into her tearful eyes. "I'm sorry," she said, "I thought we had been so careful."

"I know, don't be upset *mon petit choux**. I think it's rather nice: If you want it to be."

"What do you mean?" she asked on the verge of full blown tears.

"Well, it has come about quicker than I had thought possible, but if you feel the same about me as I do about you, why don't we get married?"

"No Richard, I can't do that to you; I'll think of something."

"I don't want you to think of anything, just us." He leaned over and kissed her gently. They went home and made love until the early hours.

"You'll have to ask my father," she said.

"Is he likely to refuse?" he asked concernedly.

"I doubt it," she said "on the contrary, I think he will be rather pleased that business has turned into a family affair."

After telling their families, who had mixed feelings concerning their children's impetuousness, it was greeted in typically French/Italian family traditions.

"We must have a huge reception" said Giovanni over a 'newly formed family' lunch at the hotel.

Albert was more concerned despite the fact that he would not be paying — well, only through his son's shareholding in the hotel.

"Daddy," interjected Carolina, "the war has not been over that long and there are still a lot of struggling people in this world and Richard and

My little cabbage: or my honey bun a term of endearment

I" she said holding his hand over the table, "think it would be nicer to just have family and a few friends."

"If that is alright with all of you," said Richard looking around the table. "I know it is a lot sooner than you all thought either of us should get married, but we have had been together quietly over the last few months and under the circumstances we think it is best for everyone if we have a quiet and quick wedding."

There was a stunned silence as both families looked at the couple.

Giovanni started hesitantly, "Does this mean......"

"Yes Daddy, I'm sorry, but I am pregnant. Actually, I am not sorry, I am very happy. We both are."

Giovanni got up from the table in disappointment.

"Sit down!" ordered Carla his wife.

"But....." appealed Giovanni.

"Sit down please, *mon chère*," repeated the cool, calm and collected mother. "What's done is done; they are both happy and Richard is an honourable young man and our daughter is not stupid; careless maybe, but stupid no! So, if Albert, Katherine, Richard and our daughter are happy with the arrangement, then so are we; aren't we?"

He sat down overruled: "Whatever you say, *ma chérie*." He raised his glass, "to two of my favourite people;" and as an aside to Richard, he said audibly and with a smile "and if you make her unhappy I will kill you." Richard stood up and extended his arms to his business partner and father-in-law, to the applause of the family table. Everyone kissed and hugged. Albert stood and said, *"Vive les mariées"**

The champagne bottles were popped, glasses were filled by the Maître D' and Carolina and Richard kissed in front of a smiling family; the next generation of the Nicols secured.

*long live the bride and groom.

CHAPTER TWENTY FOUR
Hotel Nice Majestic - February 1993

Three years had passed. The hotel was doing well. Sadly, De Villiers had passed away in 1991. The rejection of his pacemaker and a further attack meant that at the very young age of forty eight, life had taken its toll and a much loved member of the Nicol family business had gone. He was even younger than his father; as to be expected, Suzanne was devastated. Michael and Juliette, the management and some of the staff of every major hotel in Nice, as well as local businessmen and dignitaries and as many of the staff as was possible, of the Majestic, attended the funeral: The Majestic held the wake and both Michael's father and uncle attended.

Suzanne had asked Michael to say a few words; Marc also asked if he could say something on behalf of the company and the family.

"Ladies and Gentlemen, distinguished guests, on behalf of our company and our family of which Édouard de Villers was a very important part, it is with pride and a touch of sadness that I welcome you to his hotel; a place where he made his mark, endeared himself to the local community and his staff and guests. He was taken from us far too young but in his short time with us and here on earth, his contribution was palpable. Our thoughts and love are with Suzanne and she knows that if there is ever anything we can do as a family and a company she only has to ask. I ask you to raise your glasses to the life of our friend and colleague, Ëdouard." The crowd responded; Michael took the floor.

"Friends and family, Suzanne has asked me to say a few words on her behalf. I hardly feel qualified; I have only known Édouard for five years. Three years longer than I thought I would be here, and although for the last few years we have not physically worked together, I have valued his counsel and his and Suzanne's friendship. He was an hotelier through and through. He was a personality, a *bon viveur* and a true professional whose main priority was the satisfaction of his guests and the welfare of his staff; probably even above profitability, but that he achieved anyway, because of his commitment to his clients and team. I have enjoyed my time here and that which I was privileged to share with *Monsieur* de Villiers and I hope one day I will be as good a mentor to my team, as he was to his."

He raised his glass to the assembled crowd,

'Que Dieu bénisse le patron repose en paix'"

The crowd raised their glasses in silence.

Suzanne approached Michael and put her arms around him, "*Merci mon chère*"

"It was my sad pleasure, Suzanne. As my uncle said, if you ever need anything……"

⁂

Michael was fast asleep at six in the morning when he felt the bed move as an excited three year old jumped on him.

"God bless the boss, may he rest in peace'.

"Morning Daddy," said Maggie as she and Juliette looked down on him.

"Hello family, what time is it?"

"Six thirty," replied his wife to a sleepy husband.

"For why do I deserve this rude awakening?"

"Because today is Maggie's first day at nursery school and she wanted both of us to take her this morning, if you can."

"Of course," he said cuddling his baby, "I wouldn't miss it for the world."

Over breakfast Michael commented, "Where have the last few years gone? I can't believe she's three. I have enough problems realising I have been here for this length of time especially as I didn't expect to be here more than a couple of years."

"You don't regret it do you?"

"Regret what? I don't regret anything; Maggie, you, the hotel; nothing!"

"I'm glad of that. Anyway now I can go back to more full time work."

"Do you need to, after all we don't need the money?" said Michael knowing he was about to get hammered.

"Michael, you aren't the only one with a career!"

"I know that darling, but I just thought that you would be happier looking after Maggie and spending time at home."

"There are times when I think you are really in touch with me and your feminine side and then other times I think you can be an absolute wanker!" said an irate Juliette. "I love you both and of course I want to spend time with Maggie and you, but I have a life outside, the same as you do. My mind and my brain need stimulation Michael and it doesn't revolve around washing and dressing Maggie, washing clothes and preparing food for her or even you."

"Sorry darling, I didn't mean to upset you. It's just that it was your idea to have a baby and I just thought……."

"Don't you fucking dare, Michael, don't you fucking dare" shrieked Juliette. "It was a mutual decision and I wouldn't change anything, but I need to get out and do what I want as well."

He walked over to her and put his arms around her, "I'm sorry my love," he stuttered.

"Fuck off Michael, I'm angry. Go to work, I'll take Maggie to nursery." She stormed out of the bedroom.

'Jesus' thought Michael 'what am I meant to do or say?'

In later years, he was to wonder whether this was the beginning of the breakdown of their relationship; even if they had thought it would have lasted forever.

His phone rang, it was Uncle Marc, *"Allo, mon fils, com ça va?"*

"Fine uncle, how are you?"

"Tres bien, merci. I'm calling because Michael, I think you have been where you have been for too long now; and we know what a great job you have done, but we need you to progress further and your father and I want to move you — to Paris."

There was a silence.

"What do you think?" asked his boss.

"This is a bit of a shock sir," replied an ever loyal employee. "I'm not sure what to say: I am happy here, my family is here, I have established roots here, both with the community and the team."

"I know Michael, but progress is in the hands of advancement. We want you to take the job as General Manger of the Paris Majestic. Arthur Radford is leaving the GM post to join us at head office as Financial Director and Chastain will come back to your hotel as General Manager and you will go to Paris at the end of June. He deserves it, you have made it one of our leading properties and he is looking forward to it and you deserve the promotion."

"And my feelings?" said a dejected Michael.

"It's a big promotion Michael; one that is necessary for your further advancement."

"And what about my family?" continued Michael.

"Well, they will of course go with you and there is a penthouse suite near to the Champs Élysées that goes with the job."

There was an embarrassing pause before Michael said, "I will have to discuss it with Juliette."

"Of course" said Marc, "but don't forget *mon fils,* that work comes first!"

He put the phone down and thought 'the shit's going to hit the fan!'

It had been a few days since their argument and he felt that things had got back to normal. Juliette could be very volatile at times but usually came back down without injury to either party. He did accept, to himself, that he probably didn't say the right things at the right time.

"What?" asked Juliette forcefully. "You didn't consult me?"

"There has been no decision yet on my part, my love."

"It's academic isn't it? When the family say go — you go, after all, 'It's work that comes first!'"

"It's also our lives and our future Juliette. Most people would love to go to Paris. It's a five star hotel, it is the company's flagship and I am meant to be the Heir Apparent so I have to earn that position and if that means moving where they want me to, what can I say? It comes with a penthouse by the Champs Élysées and the hotel is close to the Georges Cinq. It was my family's third property opened in 1963 but bought in 1960 the year I was born. Think of the restaurants, the schools, the fashions, the party life," continued Michael trying to convince himself.

"And think of the rain, the cold, the traffic not to mention the bloody Parisians!" said an angry Juliette.

"Will you just consider the move? Why don't we go to Paris for the weekend and see how you feel after that?"

Juliette carried on wiping the surface in the kitchen for the third time.

"I'll think about it."

"That's all I ask darling," said Michael somewhat

relieved that she was at least prepared to think about it.

Back in his office he phoned Alain Chastain.

"*Bonjour mon ami, ça va?*" asked Michael

"*Très bien merci et tu?*"enquired his colleague.

"Yes not bad, thanks."

"To what do I owe this honour of a phone call from the soon to be director of The Paris Majestic?"

"You have been told?" asked Michael somewhat surprised as he hadn't yet confirmed the move.

"Of course and your move here means I get to go back to Nice as GM, something I am looking forward to. You certainly did a great job there Michael, I am going to have to be pretty sharp to maintain your work."

"Therein lays the problem," continued Michael, "I am having problems persuading Juliette to accept the post. She doesn't really want to leave Nice and I don't think she really wants Maggie educated in Paris."

"Why not?" asked Alain, "It's a beautiful city, full of art, great restaurants, fashion houses and much more, including great schools; I would have thought it would be right up Juliette's alley."

"Well, that's what I thought. Look I was thinking of coming up in the next few weeks for a weekend, or mid week depending on your availability. Thought we could do the tourist bit and show her the city."

"No problem, I'll have a word with the boss, but it won't be a problem, we are fairly full, but if you make it the first part of the week it would be better than the weekends. Also, make it before the weekend of the ninth of April as that is Easter weekend and you know what that will be like. 'Paris in the Spring' and all that."

"Well it would have to be earlier rather than later as I have to let the family know quickly although they have just assumed that I will be there when I am told."

"Well, I hope you do friend because that will affect my move and I really want to take over Nice."

"I know Alain, I don't think it will affect you to be honest, as they would put you here anyway and send me somewhere else. If we had a place in Siberia I'd end up there for disobedience!"

Alain laughed, "they wouldn't do that to the company's protégé,"

"Don't bank on it! I'll call you in a day or so. Thanks Alain."

"No problem, I look forward to seeing you."

·•◦◯◇◯◦•·

The Air France 727 landed at Orly Airport at two thirty in the afternoon. Michael and Juliette picked up their shared bag from the carousel and made their way to the exit. They had left Maggie with Juliette's mother and Michael was hoping that not only would this trip cement their lives, a sort of second honeymoon, but also to cement his status within the company and persuade her that the move would be good for them. They got into a taxi and prepared themselves for the usual dodgem ride up the Champs Élysées; the sun was shining, 'thank God', thought Michael, as they made the short journey to the Paris Majestic, with the marvellous Arc de Triomphe in view and within spitting distance of the Georges Cinq Hotel. As soon as the taxi pulled up, doormen in their fine livery had the doors open and collected the case from the boot. The elegant entrance doors opened inward as they were taken to the reception desk.

"I believe we have a reservation," said Michael, "under the name of Nicolson."

"*Oui monsieur,*" confirmed the head receptionist. "One moment please." He picked up his phone and pressed a couple of buttons, "*Monsieur Chastain? Monsieur Nicolson *est arrive et est à la a recepción.*"

Alain came into reception, handshakes and embraces were carried out as usual. "Welcome both of you," said Alain. "It's lovely to see you. Come, come....." he motioned them to the lift preceded by one of the concierge with their case. They went to the top floor which opened up to a small corridor with the two top hotel suites one on either side. He opened the door and they walked into the elegant suite with balcony overlooking the Arc de Triomphe, a dining area and a sumptuous lounge area leading to a huge queen sized four poster bed with a marble and glass bathroom with a double Jacuzzi bath and walk in shower. In the centre of the coffee table a huge display of flowers and a welcome bottle of Dom Perignon.

*has arrived and is at reception

"You shouldn't have gone to this trouble," said Michael.

"It's beautiful Alain," said Juliette. "Thank you."

"Nothing is too much for the new director of The Paris Majestic. If you don't mind and I haven't been too presumptuous, I have arranged dinner in the hotel restaurant this evening if that is OK with you and then you have the rest of your days to explore."

"That would be very nice, wouldn't it darling?" said Michael looking at his wife for confirmation that they might be getting off to a good start.

"Of course Alain, that would be wonderful, thank you."

"Good, I am bringing my girlfriend — or as she says 'fiancée'— although I haven't asked her yet. She's English. Are they all pushy like that Michael?"

Don't ask me my friend I am married to a 'Franglais'. They have the best of both worlds."

"And the worst," said his wife. They laughed. 'I'm glad she said it' thought Michael.

Alain left and Juliette walked over to her husband.

"Don't think that all this bullshit is going to make me a walkover Mister Nicolson, I'm not easily persuaded. But while we are here we should make use of the Jacuzzi and the four poster before dinner don't you think?"

"I'll open the DP then shall I?"

"Hmmm," she said as she opened her coat and put it on the chair then unclipped her dress which dropped to the floor revealing her black lingerie, "what a good idea."

She walked into the bathroom removing her bra and knickers as she went.

Very unprofessionally, but ominously, the cork shot out of the bottle, as Michael poured two glasses and followed her, ice bucket *et al*.

Alain and his guest were already in the cocktail bar when Michael and Juliette walked in.

"Ah, the honeymooners I presume," said Alain.

"Yes thank you very much for the suite Alain."

"No problem my friend, you would do the same for me."

"I don't know about that," he said seriously, "I would have to check that it came within the company's rules and guidelines about entertaining and gifting to members of management."

Alain's face dropped, "I'm kidding my friend," continued Michael, "It was very much appreciated as was the DP:"

"I'm glad, I thought I was going to be reported," everyone laughed. "This is Belinda," said Alain introducing his very attractive blonde companion.

Hugs and typical French *baisers*, preceded Alain's further invitation to another bottle of champagne. "Don't worry Michael, this is on my personal account." Michael laughed, "I'm not worried my friend; cheers *a votre santé*."

Over a perfect dinner Michael commented, "This really is very good,"

"Yes, we are aiming for two stars next year. It'll probably come under your watch and you'll get the credit," said Alain smiling.

"I promise you I will mention you in dispatches," said Michael. "So how have you enjoyed the hotel?"

"Put it this way, I shall be sad to leave, but the promotion is welcome as will be the extra salary and I must admit it will be nice to have winter sunshine. Paris is beautiful though, especially in the spring and summer. You will love it Juliette, but I am sure you have been here many times."

"I have been a few times, but not enough to know it well."

"Why don't you girls go out for lunch tomorrow and Belinda can show you around some of the fabulous shops."

"Yes, that would be a good idea," said Belinda: "That's if Juliette would like to."

"Yes that would be nice, thank you. I'm sure the men will be doing some sort of business together."

"Yes," said Alain, "it will give us time to go around the hotel and for Michael to get the feel of the place."

Dinner over, the friends said their goodnights. "It's a lovely evening and it is 'Paris in the Spring' would you like to go for a walk?" asked Michael.

"Why not," she said linking her arm through his. "Let's play tourists."

It was a warm sunny end of March morning as Juliette and Michael were sitting out on their balcony having breakfast overlooking the Champs Élysées and the Arc de Triomphe, with the Eiffel Tower in the background.

"It's a beautiful city isn't it?" said Juliette.

"Despite the Parisians?" quipped Michael.

"I don't know yet, I haven't seen any," came the quick response.

"Well, you will have a chance today as you wander around the streets of Paris, bumping into them." He smiled.

"You're meant to be persuading me to move here, not putting me off."

"I want you to do what you want to do. It will only work if you give it a go."

"Hmm, we'll see. You're meeting with Alain for a hotel tour at ten and I'm meeting Belinda at eleven. Can we dine out tonight?"

"Yes, of course I'll ask Alain for a recommendation."

After their breakfast, Michael went to meet Alain and Juliette took a bath. Luxuriating in the bubbles she thought 'maybe it won't be so bad. And anyway, we have to for Michael's career.'

Michael met Alan in his office where he was introduced to outgoing General Manager Arthur Radford.

"How are you Michael? Pleased to meet you; your family talk very highly of you and reckon that you will take the success that I and young Alain here, have made of the hotel, to another level."

"I don't know about that Sir," replied Michael humbly, "I would be happy to continue with its upward trajectory — unless of course I will be able to lay claim for your two stars later this year!"

"*Touché* young man. You will get on here I am sure. Now let Alain show you around. We can't introduce you as the new GM as I understand that you have not been confirmed as yet."

"I have been informed Sir, but the company have allowed me to make up my own mind. Hence the reason I am here with my wife, to persuade her to come with me."

"I am sure she will, Michael; she can only love Paris as we all do. I have taken the liberty to speak to the General Manager of the Georges Cinq who I believe is looking for an assistant Marketing Director; and given your wife's remarkable career and success in Nice I told him about her and he said he would love to meet her," he said handing him a card.

"Thank you sir, very kind of you; I will get her to contact him."

"Fine, in that case you boys have a wander around and if you don't mind we could all meet for a light lunch at one o'clock in the Brasserie?"

"That would be fine, thank you very much," said Michael.

"Right," said Alain, "let's start in reception." Alain was telling those that they met, that Michael, the General Manager of their Nice hotel was on a weekend break and wanted to look around the hotel.

Juliette and Belinda had taken a five minute taxi ride that morning to Galleries La Fayette to soak in some tourist atmosphere and also to get a bit of shopping therapy. They came out of Jean Paul Gaultier and Thierry Mugler fashion shops with a couple of very expensive dresses each, that would please their respective partners. Especially the Gaultier that Juliette had bought with dinner that night in mind.

"Michael is going to love that dress," said an enthusiastic Belinda.

"He'd better, especially for what it cost!" said Juliette, feeling content with herself.

"Let's go up to the roof terrace and have a glass of wine," said Belinda, "shopping is such thirsty work."

They laughed as they got into the lift. The girls spent the next hour or so, talking about their lives, their loves and their situation over a few glasses of wine and a plate of *Jambon de Bayonne.

"So this is an investigatory trip to see if you want to move to Paris?"

"I don't really want to move to Paris, but you marry for better or for worse and I suppose as he is the major bread winner, I have to follow."

"You'll love it here, I promise you. I do."

"So, how do you feel about moving to Nice? Will you find it a bit boring after the city life?"

"I don't think so. It's a new challenge for Alain

*A cured ham from the ancient port city of Bayonne in South West France close to the Basque country

and like you, I want to go where he does. I can always come up here every now and then if I feel the need. I go back to London every couple of months to see family, it won't be much different."
"I suppose I can always take a long weekend to see my mother in Nice and get some sunshine," said Juliette.
"It's not all grey and rain here," defended Belinda, "but I get your point."

"So, how did you get on with Belinda?" said Michael as he came out of the shower.
"She's quite sweet; and she really seems to love Alain; she's looking forward to the move," said Juliette from the bedroom.
"And you? How do you feel about making the move?"
"To be honest Michael, I haven't really made a decision. But I am aware that this is very important to you and that will of course influence any decision I do make," she said as she appeared from the dressing room in the Gaultier dress that she had bought to impress.
"You look absolutely stunning," said a suitably impressed Michael.
"In that case, take me for a fabulous dinner, bring me back safely, remove this dress and make mad passionate love to me, as if your life depended on it; because your future might." She went over, kissed him, putting her hand on his groin
"Hmmm."
"If you carry on doing that, we may not get to

dinner," he said, attempting to undo the clasp at the back of the dress.

"Don't you dare, it took me long enough to slide into it," she laughed. "You'll both have to wait."

They took a taxi to Restaurant *L'Ambroisie*, as recommended by Alain. They dined exceptionally well and Michael remembered why he loved his wife so much. They obviously discussed the future and in passing Michael said, "Radford, the outgoing GM gave me this card," handing it to Juliette, "he spoke to the GM of the Georges Cinq, who is looking for an Assistant Director of Marketing. He thought it may be of interest."

"You don't give up do you?"

"I'll never give up on you, ever."

They leaned forward and gently kissed. They finished their coffee and Cognac and returned to the hotel where Michael attempted to carry out Juliette's demands, which after more than an hour, they both agreed had been achieved.

CHAPTER TWENTY FIVE
Bristol Majestic - Monte Carlo -1925

In June of 1925, Albert Richard Evart Nicol made an appearance in the world. Carolina and Richard were ecstatic, as were the family. Richard's father was chuffed realising that they had given their first born his name and Carla loved the fact that they had given Albert her family name, Evart. There was excitement in the Principality, not at the birth of Albert, but because of Prince Louis II, who was crowned Prince of Monaco in 1922.

He was modernising Monaco and concentrating on Monte Carlo as a tourist venue. In 1924 he oversaw the creation of the Monaco Football Club and business in general was improving, post World War I. The Bristol Majestic was indeed leading the way, along with the Hermitage which was already attracting its fair share of film stars and politicians who appreciated the privacy that such an exclusive resort offered. Work had started on a new luxury hotel that would open in 1929, the Monte Carlo Beach Hotel.

Of course, the casino had been an attraction since the late eighteen hundreds and people came from all over a wealthy Europe and further afield, to try their luck. Cary Grant, Frank Sinatra, Alec Guinness, Fred Astaire and many others enjoyed the Monte Carlo lifestyle.

Richard and his team were preparing their hotel to receive their share of the top visitors. This meant that they had to provide something different and yet familiar.

Health and beauty spas had developed over the years in Monaco, but Richard decided that if he built one in the hotel, then guests wouldn't have to travel which would add to the tranquillity of a spa by just being able to go down in a lift to the basement, where Richard decided to build his project. This was no dark basement; they had skylights in the garden area which would flood the spa with sunlight in the mornings and remain bright all day. He also put in a steam room and a massage room. At the rear of the hotel he built a swimming pool. Food was a very important part of life in Monte Carlo; restaurants were springing up and were becoming fashionable: an important attraction to the World-travelled guests. The Hermitage had a good restaurant but most hotel food did not come up to their standard.

Richard had learned about Le Cordon Bleu cookery school which had opened in Paris in 1895 run by founder Marthe Distel, a journalist who had started a magazine *'Le Cuisinière Cordon Bleu'* the popularity of which prompted her to open a culinary school, which she did with renowned Chef, Henri-Paul Pellaprat. Richard decided that these people would have the contacts to find them a new, exciting Chef for the Majestic's new restaurant, *La Majesté* (The Majesty) so he wrote them a letter.

He was surprised to get a reply together with two recommendations for head chefs that, in their opinion, were ideal for an up-and-coming luxury hotel.

André Marchand arrived at the hotel in a fashionable pair of black trousers and a cotton shirt He was twenty eight, good looking and came with a glowing reference from Pellaprat and the head chef with whom he had been working for the last three years. He told Richard that he was a disciple of both Pellaprat and Escoffier and liked their approach to classic cuisine, but putting his own touches on their dishes. Richard was impressed with his attitude and commitment and decided to give him the job.

A year on in 1926 the Bristol Majestic Hotel launched its *La Majesté* restaurant, The Mayfair Beauty Spa and inaugurated the swimming pool. There was a cocktail reception in the modern Roaring Twenties style, with a live orchestra and the event was attended by local dignitaries and members of the Royal Family, including Prince Louis II. The champagne flowed, canapés were served and the attending guests were asked to officially welcome *La Majesté's* executive chef, André Marchand. The guests were encouraged to wander around the hotel to see the improvements that Richard and his team had made, including the three Presidential Suites on the top floor which had already attracted the attention of Sinatra's people and Winston Churchill. It was not long before the locals and visitors recognised the quality of food and service and facilities that were on offer and the hotel went from strength to strength, much to the delight of Richard's parents and in-laws as well as brother Antoine.

Antoine by now had turned the wine business into an important player in the South of France. They had moved their bottling plant to a highly sophisticated production line and warehouse in Nice. Albert was now at part time nursery school, Carolina was spending more time with Albert than in the hotel, but she still maintained her presence. In fact her department had grown and she had two very experienced and conscientious managers working with her. They had discussed their plan for their little one with the rest of the family and it was decided he would go to a local junior school which meant he would learn Italian and French both standard languages in the Principality. Carolina's mother wanted to send him to Swiss senior school where he would learn German and of course English. The whole family were in agreement although Albert senior wondered why his grandson had to leave the nest to study languages that he didn't need. How wrong was he to be?

In 1929, further excitement surrounded the Principality as the first Monaco Grand Prix took place. It took the co-operation of Prince Louis and the cigarette tycoon Antony Noghès, who had set up the Automobile Club of Monaco with some of his wealthy friends, to make it happen. The Monégasque driver Louis Chiron was also involved and on the fourteenth of April 1929 their plan became a reality as sixteen invited participants took to the circuit of the streets of Monte Carlo with its numerous bends and two hairpins and one hundred laps for a prize of one hundred thousand French Francs. The first winner of what was to become one of the most famous Grand Prix's was William Grover-Williams in a Bugatti T35B in a race dominated by the Italian car manufacturer. Grover-Williams was British and was to be seen all through the weekend at the Bristol Majestic, probably drawn by the name, but he stayed at the Hermitage.

The years passed, the hotel had gone from strength to strength and had become one of the most popular destinations on the coast. In 1930 the family welcomed baby Marc. Albert was by now in junior school and was proving to be a confident young student. Carolina had now left the hotel on a permanent basis but could still be seen as she popped in to see how marketing was going and of course to see how her husband was getting on with his passion project. Giovanni had retired at only sixty, he was still getting his percentage and he and Carla were enjoying their time together. Richard's father Albert had retired, he was 70, leaving Antoine to run the business completely although he could be seen every day during harvest and tastings. After all it was in his blood.
By 1938, Albert had gone to Switzerland to stay with his cousins and was attending a public

school. Carolina missed him very much, but he would come home at the end of each term. However in 1941 Albert wanted to come home permanently. The Second World War had started and both Switzerland and Monaco were neutral although the Italians had tried once to occupy the Principality but were driven back by the Germans. Carolina urged Richard to let him come home and take his *Baccalauréat* in Monaco although Richard was very wary of the situation.

When Albert did return, he told his father that he wanted to work in the hotel, not go on to university which would be the point of taking his *Baccalauréat.*

"What's the point," he would say, "I can be more use working with you, than another profession of which I really have no interest."

Reluctantly his father agreed and was backed up by Carolina who was just so pleased to have her son back.

"You will start as a buttons and work your way up" said Richard, "do you understand?"

"Yes Father, of course, thank you; I will not disappoint."

"I know you won't," he said giving his eldest a hug.

Meanwhile Marc was destined to follow in his eldest brother's footsteps and at the age of nearly twelve also went to Switzerland where he was to stay until the end of the war.

Life was going to change for everyone in November

of 1942 when Italian tanks rolled into Monaco and claimed it. With little resistance they had no problems and started to impose themselves on the country's citizens.

The Italian commander entered the hotel and asked to speak to Richard Nicol. He presented the reluctant hotelier with papers of introduction.

"We will be staying here *Monsieur* and I hope you will co-operate with us and everything can be very pleasant. Please keep a record of all our expenses as this will be paid for by the Italian War Government."

'Fat chance of that,' thought Richard, but he had little choice.

CHAPTER TWENTY SIX
Hotel Paris Majestic
June 1993 – October 1995

"This is pretty smart isn't it'" said Juliette as she wandered into the penthouse suite with Maggie holding her hand.
"Are you pleased you agreed to come then?" asked Michael.
"I didn't go that far," she said. "Don't forget it's summer at the moment and is perfect. I'll let you know in November."
"Best I can hope for then, I suppose."
"Absolutely, now open the champagne; when are you starting?"
"I am going in tomorrow to meet Radford and then he'll introduce me around, then we will do a more detailed tour of the hotel and then he will pass over all information and records to me with his secretary, then we will have dinner and he will leave at the weekend. Chastain I saw last week when he arrived in Nice and I did the changeover. I am happy for him, I think he will do a good job and he's more than ready for it."
"And you?" asked his wife; "Are you?"
"I hope so," he said as he brought over her glass.
"Why? Don't you think I am?"
"Of course *mon chère*. You have been brought up to be ready." She kissed him tenderly on the lips, "I just hope we both are."

Maggie was in nursery school, Juliette had started at the Georges Cinq and Michael was making a name for himself. The hotel restaurant had been awarded its second Michelin Star and Michael phoned Alain to let him know.
"Thanks to you, we got the second."
"Well at least you held on to the first," he laughed.
"And have you held on to mine?" asked Michael.
"Not only have we held on to it, we are on course for our second. How's it going apart from that?" asked Alain "is Juliette enjoying Paris?"
"Yes, I think so; she's working hard at Georges Cinq and I think she finds balancing Maggie and work difficult; and I don't help as I am constantly working, but you know what I am like," said Michael.
"Work Comes First," said Alain repeating the well known mantra.
"Absolutely."
"Well, continued success my friend and call in when you are back in Nice."
"Will do; *au revoir.*"
"*Au revoir mon ami.*"

More than two years had passed and a busy Paris Fashion Week had finished and both Michael and Juliette had spent little time together for the past few weeks. Michael phoned Juliette, "Would you like to go out for dinner this evening?

"I've got to get back for Maggie," said Juliette.
"Well, we could go out about eight and I'll arrange a baby sitter for Maggie."
"OK, I'll see you at home."
He put the phone down; 'she doesn't sound too happy,' thought Michael. 'We haven't been to Nice for a while to see her family, maybe we ought to make the effort.'
When Michael got in, Juliette was in the bedroom lying on the bed. He went over and kissed her.
"You OK?"
"Knackered, thank you," came an exasperated reply.
"Would you rather not go out?"
"No, let's go," she said "I need to be in a different environment for a few hours. All I seem to see is hotel, nursery, home, hotel, home and so on."
"The babysitter is coming at eight, I am going to shower and change."
Michael had booked a table at the renowned Guy Savoy restaurant. To many it would have seemed like a busman's holiday but not only did they love fine dining, he also felt an obligation to know what the other establishments were doing and Guy Savoy had weathered the storm since opening in 1980 and although not having a Michelin Star the rumour mill suggested that he would get one sooner rather than later.
The taxi dropped them at the front and the doorman opened the door. The elegant dining room was welcoming but very formal, as to be

expected.

They dined exceptionally well and enjoyed the wines as recommended by the Sommelier. Michael held her hand on the table sensing that something was wrong. "Are you OK?"

"I'm tired Michael; not so much as in, 'I want to go to sleep', more 'I want to get away'. I thought if it was OK with you, I would take Maggie to Nice next week. I am due holiday and as I haven't spent enough time with Maggie, we could have some Mummy and daughter time together. Maybe you could come down at the weekend?"

"Yes, of course if that's what you want to do."

"It is Michael, I need to re-evaluate things and seeing my mother and father and the sunshine might perk me up a little."

Landing in Nice airport, Juliette could feel a cloud lift and she was suddenly feeling better. They took a taxi to their home, went in, opened the windows and looked out over the park with the sea to their right. It was only small, but it had two bedrooms and it was home. She phoned her parents; "come over for supper," said her mother "and I can see my granddaughter and give my daughter a hug."

"OK, I am just going to get some bits and pieces from the market and then we will be over."

It was good to see them both and they were very happy to see Maggie who they spoilt with gifts and hugs, much to the little girl's excitement. Over a bottle of wine while Maggie had lain on the sofa and collapsed with emotional overload, Juliette started to tell her mother how she felt.

"Have you told Michael how you feel?" asked a concerned mother.

"Not really, we don't have that sort of moment or time. Obviously he is very busy and so am I."

"Would it be better if you were to give up work and have more time for you both, and Maggie of course?"

"God, mother, I would go stir crazy. I don't have many friends in Paris and anyway I would rather spend any spare time I have with Michael and Maggie."

"How are you and Michael getting on?"

That question hit Juliette as she wasn't expecting it. Or was it just that she hadn't dared question their relationship that deeply. "Yes, fine," she replied hesitantly; "I love him very much. He's a great, caring husband and a loving father and brilliant at his job; which I suppose is one of the problems."

"How do you mean?"

"He's there all the time and I feel that we are sort of a second consideration."

"Juliette, that is what a good husband does *ma chérie.*" interrupted her father.

"I know *Papa* but sometimes it's difficult to accept."

"I think your mother and I would agree that you need to sit with Michael and go through everything and work it out. We love Michael and we want you both to be happy; not just for your sakes' but for Maggie's as well."

"I know, thank you both. He's coming down on Friday night for the weekend, we will talk then."

The sun was shining and Juliette and Maggie sat on the *esplanade* letting the warm sun fill them with energy and replenishing their lack of Vitamin D. She was on the way to see her friends and colleagues at Le Negresco.

Michael was flying in tomorrow night and she was determined to have a nice home cooked dinner for him. Not a Michelin dinner but a traditional French family meal. She would do a *Pot-au-Feu. Maggie and she would get the ingredients today.

She heard the key in the door and went to it as her man came in. They hugged and kissed as Maggie ran up calling, "Daddy, Daddy."

He picked her up in his arms and kissed her.

"*Allo mon petit choux*, are you being a good girl for Mummy?"

"*Bien sûr Papa,**"

"Good girl. And has Mummy been a good girl?"

"What do you think?" she said sarcastically.

He smiled and kissed her again.

"I thought we would dine in tonight if that's ok with you?" she continued.

"Whatever you want my darling, it sounds perfect. What are we eating? I am starving, I didn't bother

of course Daddy

with the food on the plane. When will they ever get it right?"

"I have done a *pot-au-feu*?*"

"Ahhh, real food. *Enfin!***"

"I thought you liked fine dining?"

"I do my love, I like looking at Naomi Campbell, but I would rather sleep with you."

"Lying bastard,"

"Truthfully," he said as he put his arms around her and kissed her passionately.

"Later," she said, "if I have the energy or desire."

"Oh dear, sounds ominous," he said somewhat deflated.

She kissed him on the nose, "it's not meant to be. Come on open the wine and let's eat."

It was lovely to all sit together with the evening sun setting with the comforting peace and smells of Nice permeating their apartment There was no doubt about it; Juliette felt at home.

After dinner they cleared up and put a tired Maggie into bed then sat in the lounge with some music playing and drinking a fine after dinner brandy.

"It's nice to be home," said Michael.

"I'm glad you feel that way, as that is how I feel. Michael, I have been giving us, and the situation, a great deal of thought. I want to move back."

Michael was stunned. He looked at her intently.

"On your own?"

"Well, you can't come can you? You have your job

*Rich, French, beef stew with vegetables   ** at last

and career to think about."
"You mean you want to leave me?" he asked.
"No, I don't want to leave you; it's just that I can't stay in Paris any more. I need time with Maggie and I need to be home."
"So you'll remove Maggie from my life?"
"That is not going to happen. Look, you work twelve hours a day minimum. You see her in the morning and then that's it.
She's invariably in bed when you get back. Sometimes so am I. Our sex life has dropped considerably, not that that is the end of the world, but I do miss the intimacy. Maybe the 'absence makes the heart grow fonder' syndrome might work?"
"Or the 'out of sight out of mind' might!" said Michael.
"Well, if that's the way you think."
"No, no it's just that.....I will miss you."
"You may, but you will concentrate on your work and you will look forward to weekends when you can come back here. Maybe not every weekend, but a couple of times a month; and then we can spend school holidays together. Many people work that way Michael and have highly successful work and marriage balance. I have been offered my job back at Le Negresco on a part time basis. Maggie will go to school here, her grandparents get to see her; I am sure it will work out; that is if you want it to?" Michael thought for a moment.
"It will be difficult, but if it's what you want, then

I am happy to give it a go."

She came over to him and sat on his lap.

"Thank you darling, I am sure it will. Now why don't you take me to bed and show me how much you love me."

He picked her up and carried her toward the bedroom and laid her on the bed, "Can you cope with how much I love you?" he said taking off his shirt.

"I'll do my best" she said as she slipped off her jeans.

CHAPTER TWENTY SEVEN
The New Bristol Majestic Hotel
Monte Carlo
Ten Years On — 1955

Much had happened since the re-opening of the family's hotel in 1945. A young inexperienced hotelier had become a strong powerful influence in Monte Carlo's hotel and tourism industry which had received a boost after the end of the war. His brother Marc had joined the business and was doing his stint in all departments to ensure his ability to take control of some of the business in the next couple of years.

Prince Louis II had died on 9 May 1949; he had begun to neglect Monaco, spending most of his time in Paris and lived at his family estate with his wife, Ghislaine Dommanget, whom he married in Monaco in 1946. He did return to Monaco where he died at the Prince's Palace aged seventy eight in 1949. He had an illegitimate daughter Charlotte Louise Juliette, born in 1898 in Algeria. A political crisis loomed for the Prince because without any other heir, the throne of Monaco would pass to his first cousin Wilhelm, the Duke of Urach, a German nobleman who was a son of Prince Albert's aunt, Princess Florestine of Monaco. To ensure this did not happen, in 1911 a law was passed recognizing his illegitimate daughter, Charlotte, as Louis's acknowledged heir, and making her part of the princely family.

This law was later held to be invalid under the 1882 statutes. Thus another law was passed in 1918 modifying the statutes to allow the adoption of an heir, with succession rights. Charlotte was formally adopted by Louis in 1919, and became Charlotte Louise Juliette Grimaldi, Princess of Monaco, and Duchess of Valentinois. Princess Charlotte, who had become the Hereditary Princess of Monaco during her father's reign, had married Count Pierre de Polignac of Hennebont and had two children: Princess Antoinette, born in 1920, and Prince Rainier, born in 1923. In 1944, Princess Charlotte renounced her claim to the throne of Monaco and Prince Rainier became his grandfather's heir. So when Louis died in 1949, Prince Rainier III became the Prince of Monaco. Rainier then took control of building Monaco and Monte Carlo in particular, into a tourist destination surpassing even its popularity pre-war. All the famous faces started to return and Albert and his team had managed to secure bookings from such distinguished guests as Winston Churchill. Royalty came as well, Queen Eugenie of Spain, the Duke and Duchess of Windsor mixed with film stars such as Charlie Chaplin, Cary Grant and Rita Hayworth who were in Monte Carlo for the wedding of Errol Flynn at the Hotel du Paris:

and in 1952 Monte Carlo saw the arrival of Aristotle Onassis, the Greek shipping magnet.

Rainier was promoting international conferences and because of his foresight, hotels developed, new ones were constructed and tourism boomed.

Despite the Monte Carlo Rally being suspended in 1952 as it was a non-championship race it was resurrected in 1955 with great excitement with the title of the 'European Grand Prix'. More importantly, however, was the fact that the Grand Prix of Monaco was the second round in the World Championship, and the first in Europe for 1955. The most important social event of the century for Monaco was the impending marriage of Prince Rainier to Grace Kelly in 1956. Already hotel bookings were going through the roof and Albert and his team were fighting for their fair share — and winning.

By now the thirty year old had not only completed a fairly comprehensive training programme, while still holding down his position as Operations Manager but he had been shadowing his father on day to day management and spending time with heads of department, at the same time ensuring that the hotel maintained its standards and developing new revenue streams. His room service had become the envy of other hotels mainly because of his foresight into putting in floor service kitchens when the hotel was being reformed.

He was particularly enamoured with the art of the

kitchen, like his father. André Marchand had left the hotel to open his own restaurant but had secured his replacement, whose positions had included a stint with one of the greatest chefs of his time, Fernand Point. Jacques Le Fois was a young dynamic chef who had joined the hotel in 1952. Sadly his friend and mentor Point had died this year, too young. But Jacques was determined to improve on where his predecessor left off. Jacques' style of cooking was lighter than that of Marchand's; the influence of Point, who also had other chefs under his wings, like Les Troisgros brothers and Paul Bocuse all of who would go on to great acclaim.

The restaurant *La Majesté* went from strength to strength. Voted one of the top three restaurants in the Principality, the Nicol family were ecstatic. During the coming years they would grow on their reputation.

Albert meanwhile, had met a young woman, Dorothy Wilkins, who was a couple of years younger than him and from the UK. She was in Monte Carlo as her father was a property developer and had come over to discuss building projects with Prince Rainier's team. They had been staying at the hotel and she had become enthralled with the hotel and of course Albert. Despite his workload, they had found some time together. Her father had returned to the UK but Dottie had stayed behind as she was her father's P.A./Representative for Monte Carlo. This had meant that they were able to cement their relationship after a few months of being together, as she had a room in the hotel.

Société des Bains de Mer de Monaco was a company that had been established in the 1800's which owned and controlled businesses in Monte Carlo. Richard had been offered a non-executive position on the board of the SBM, as it was known, with particular focus on the tourist industry and hotel association. Prince Charles III of Monaco (1856-1889) who had the idea of imitating the German and Belgian spa towns, which took advantage of the revenues of gambling houses to ensure a good share of public expenditure and to develop the financial resources of his principality. Prince Charles opened the first **Monegasque** casino in December 14, 1856 which was not that successful but in 1863, he formed the SBM and opened the casino having recruited the French entrepreneur François Blanc who had created the highly successful Bad Homburg casino in Germany. Princess Caroline had been instrumental by persuading Blanc's wife that the area would be beneficial to her health. Charles ceded the area known as *Les Spéluges* (The Caves) for the construction of future glamour projects spurred on by Blanc who suggested that *Les Spéluges* was not a marketing name for the style that they wanted; so, it was renamed Monte Carlo, in Prince Charles' honour. The SBM went on to construct and operate The Hôtel de Paris, the Café de Paris, build luxurious villas and gardens and create the *esplanade* and the *Larvotto* beach. Blanc passed away and his wife Marie continued the work and by the end of the Second World War and later, when Richard had joined, the company had bought *Hôtel* L'Hermitage, opened the Monte Carlo Country Club, was running the Grand Prix and a multitude of other businesses including the Opera House which had been inaugurated in 1879, by Sarah Bernhardt.

Richard called a family meeting between his brother Antoine, wife Carolina, Antoine's wife Claudia, Albert, Marc and Giovanni.
"I want to sell the hotel and open another" said Richard.
They all looked at him with surprise.
"But we are doing so well," said Albert in a bit of a shock.
"Yes, I know; and that is why the hotel is worth a lot more money than it was when we started. We still have a large mortgage on the property, Giovanni needs to relax and know his money is safe."
"It makes no difference to me my son, I am eighty and my only next of kin, since Carla passed, is my daughter, your wife; so my money will remain with you anyway."
"Look," continued Richard, "I have found a property in La Cap de Nice just twenty kilometres

away from here. It is an old hotel that needs re-modernising. It has more rooms than us and has the potential for better services. The profit we make from this will pay off our mortgage, allow us to buy the hotel and leave us the money to renovate. That is if Giovanni was to leave his money in. We would keep the company name."

"This sounds good my brother, but we need a buyer for this hotel," interrupted Antoine.

"That is the point my friends, the *Société des Bains de Mer de Monaco* has agreed to buy the property on the condition that we remain as the management company for a period of three years for which, of course, we will be paid a management fee."

There was silence in the room as the parties all looked at each other.

Albert spoke, "As the youngest member of the family, bar one, I feel a particular empathy with this hotel. But I do understand father's reasoning. While this is a great hotel, of which we should all be very proud, we will never make our fortunes while we have the tie of a mortgage; and yes, Monte Carlo has become an amazing place and we have grown with it, Nice is also a fashionable resort and I can see, in the next twenty years or so, it will become a huge draw, not just from millionaires but top quality tourism from across Europe as travel becomes easier and cheaper. I read the other day that the British have started visiting Spain by car, which is further on than us.

If this deal helps us create a greater presence and a future business, then I am happy to back the decision." He looked at his younger brother.

"I tend to agree," said Marc.

"I am happy," said Giovanni.

"Richard, you haven't been wrong yet, from winery to hotel, so you have my backing" said Antoine.

"In that case family, I will complete discussions with the SBM and inform you as to the outcome; meanwhile, I suggest we go to the bar and celebrate our decision."

They all got up and hugged and shook hands, celebrating their new start.

Marc had gone to school in Switzerland from the age of twelve until sixteen when he returned to France to take his *Baccalauréat*. At the age of nineteen he wanted to return to Switzerland and go to Les Roches Hotel School. At the age of twenty two he returned to Monte Carlo and joined his family in the hotel. Now fluent in German, English and Italian like his brother, he was going to become an integral part of the Nicol family business. Having the advantage of hotel school, he was rushed through the departments in the hotel and soon became the Senior Assistant Manager reporting directly to his father Richard and working closely with his brother. Now he was at the stage in his career when his place at the board table was recognised. His father called him into his office after their family meeting. Antoine was also there. "Your Uncle and I have been discussing the future if we are to sell this hotel. Richard will be going to the new hotel and Albert will be dividing his time between the two until the end of the management contract. This means the day to day running of this hotel will need taking care of. As I still am concentrating on our wine business, we therefore think you should take over as General Manager. What do you think?"

"Of course father, I can think of nothing better."

"And then when the new hotel is ready and you will finish your contract here, you will move to Nice. Is that OK for you?"

"Absolutely," said a stunned but happy Marc.

When Marc had left the room, the two brothers sat down together. "Well, that went according to plan," said Richard

"Yes it will work out well, I think. There is another thing Richard,"

"What's that?"

"I have been thinking about our wine business. I was hoping that one of the boys would be taking over but that would seem unlikely now. And with mother and father passing, there is only me and Claudia, and she has no real interest in it. I have been approached by the *Union des Vignerons des Côtes du Rhône** who want to invest in the vineyard. I thought we could sell them shares in the business and allow them to run it and we will retain a share and a percentage of profits. The sale of the shares can then come back to this company for future development and of course to help with the renovation of Nice. What do you think?"

"Well, *mon frère*, it is your baby, would you be happy to lose control?"

"Depending on the deal, we would still have a say and I would still be on the board."

"I must admit that the idea certainly seems attractive. Why don't you investigate further and at the next board meeting we can go through our options?

"Will do."

Six weeks later, Richard called a meeting of the family once again.

"As you know, the last time we talked, I proposed selling the hotel and buying the one in Nice. I have reached an agreement on the price of the new project and had a firm offer from the SBM. If we all agree we will have to have an Extraordinary General Meeting with our share holders to put it to them. As we are not selling the company their shares will remain. But I intend to make a share issue and instead of paying a dividend to the present shareholders, which we are not obliged to do, through the sale of the hotel, I want them to leave their money in, and issue a share offer to increase our shares and subsequently the money invested. Are we all agreed?"

A show of hands confirmed the agreement. "OK, now I'll pass the floor to Antoine."

"*Merci Richard,* as you all know we have a successful wine business but there is only me left from the family to run it, and with the boys obviously ensconced in the hotel business Richard and I have agreed that we will sell the vast majority of the business to *Union des Vignerons des Côtes du Rhône.* This will still leave us with a share, a percentage of profits and we would have a presence on the board. The money raised will mean that we will buy shares in this company which will boost our reserves and help us with future developments. Are we all agreed?"

Once again there was a consensus of opinion and the two brothers were charged, by the rest, to continue their negotiations.

*a union/co-operative of wine growers and sellers

CHAPTER TWENTY EIGHT
The Paris Majestic Hotel 1997

It had been nearly two years since Michael and Juliette had agreed on their long distance relationship. Over the last Christmas period Michael had managed to spend time with Juliette and Maggie not over the busy weekends, but he got down to Nice during the week between Christmas and New Year. He also managed a weekend every few weeks; they had had a good time, Maggie was so excited and in fairness so was Juliette. Michael also had to admit he had enjoyed the time. The in-laws were also pleased to see them all together. Juliette was doing well at Le Negresco, Maggie was doing well at school. The hotel was also doing well and although the strain of the regular commute often caused arguments between the couple, they were doing their best to make it work, especially for Maggie.

Summer had been good in Paris, business was booming and the city was alive and full of international stars. One of those that were making their mark was Diana Princess of Wales. Her recent liaison with Dodi Fayed, the son of Mohammed Fayed, the owner of the iconic Harrods department store in London, had caused such excitement amongst Parisians as they had been seen on his yacht on the French Riviera and

the shops and restaurants in Paris. At the end of the summer season in August they had returned to
the Hotel Ritz in Rue la Boétie, near the Place de la Concorde not far from the Majestic. The sight of *Paparazzi* was evident everywhere you looked; on their scooters, motorbikes, on foot and in cars.
On the night of the thirtieth of August while Michael was having dinner with a client in the hotel restaurant, Dodi Fayed and Princess Diana were having dinner in their hotel, also owned by Mohammed Fayed. Just before midnight when Michael said goodbye to his client, Dodi and Diana were leaving the Ritz. As Michael was in his penthouse getting ready for bed, the evening tranquillity was rocked by the sound of police sirens everywhere. Michael opened his penthouse curtains overlooking the River Seine in the distance to see, less than four hundred meters away in the distance, the flashing blue lights of police and first responder units near the Pont de L'Alma. 'Another accident by that bloody tunnel' thought Michael as he got into bed hoping that the noise would soon die down.
The next morning he walked into the hotel to find a sombre crowd at reception, among them some British tourists.
*"*Avez-vous entendu les informations monsieur?" asked the head porter.
Before Michael could say no, one of the tourists
Have you heard the news sir?

said, "Princess Di has been killed in a car crash" cried one young woman.

"In your country," called another with venom.

"I am very saddened to hear that," said Michael, "I will try and find out what has happened," as he made his way to his office.

"Alicia," said Michael to his secretary, "have you heard the news?"

"Yes sir, it was all over the radio and TV this morning."

"Do we know what happened?"

"Not really, there has been much speculation but it would appear that the Mercedes they were in crashed into a pillar in the tunnel as the driver was trying to outrun the hordes of *Paparazzi* that were chasing them. The driver, Fayed and the Princess have been killed and her bodyguard is in hospital."

"Jesus, the *Gendarmerie* is going to have their work cut out. Paris won't be universally popular when this news gets out" said Michael. Just then his mobile rang, it was his father.

"What is happening Michael it is all over the British news?"

"You probably know more than I do father as I am sure the British news is giving the incident ample coverage."

"They certainly are. You know what they think of her over here. I trust everything is OK with you? Apparently Prince Charles is flying in later today so there will be more *Paparazzi* and security.

Keep safe."

"I will father, *Merci*.

The mobile went again, "Hi darling, are you OK?" asked Juliette.

"I'm OK, I was in bed when it happened, but it's everywhere at the moment. I haven't looked at the news yet this morning, but Alicia has brought me up to date."

"It's very tragic. It's one of those moments that in the future people will ask, 'do you remember where you were when......? '"

"Yes indeed."

As sad as this event was worldwide, closer to home, this year was to mark a milestone for lesser mortals, such as Michael and Juliette who were to make a decision that was going to have a long term effect on their lives. While things had been going reasonably well over the last couple of years their marriage had met an impasse. They had arranged to have a family get together in November as that was the quietest time for both of them with regard to the hotels. The thought that they could continue their long distance relationship was fading. It wasn't that either had another partner or even a prospective; whether Juliette had slept with someone else or Michael had, didn't really come into the conversation, but both thought it unlikely.

Michael opened the door to the Nice apartment to be greeted by his seven year old daughter.

"Hello Daddy," called out Maggie as she ran toward him.

"*Allo, mon petit choux,* how are you?

"OK Daddy, it's lovely to see you."

"And you *ma chérie*," he said giving her a big hug and a kiss.

"Hello," said a somewhat reserved Juliette. "How are you?"

"All the better for seeing you," he replied, embracing her.

"I have prepared dinner, I thought we would eat in tonight if that's OK with you?"

"Of course, whatever you want."

They sat eating quietly while Maggie sat on the sofa having eaten and was drawing and colouring.

"How have you been?" asked Juliette, "especially after that awful business in August?"

"It didn't really affect us to be honest; I mean as tragic as it was, it didn't take long for Paris to get back to normal."

"It is good to have you home Michael; the first time for a couple of months."

"Yes, I know, but you know what it's like:"

"Sort of, but understandably 'work comes first', I know that, however I have to think about my future — our future," she said looking over to Maggie.

"And mine?" asked a dejected Michael.

"You will always be OK Michael it's inbred in you."

"So what are you trying to say?"

"I think we should get a divorce," said Juliette

looking down at her glass of wine. There was a silence.

Michael leaned over and lifted her chin up. She had tears in her eyes.

"Why? Have you found someone else?" he asked.

"No, of course not, it's just that I can't see a happy ending to this. I mean you are not going to be coming back to Nice are you? God knows where they will send you next; and we need stability — for all of us. And yes it is true that I get lonely and sometimes want the company of someone even just to go out for a drink, but if I do, I feel guilty. I'd probably still feel guilty even if we were divorced; and you have got to move on as well."

"How can I 'move on' as you put it? I have my daughter and I still love my wife."

"And I you Michael and that won't change, certainly not from Maggie's point of view. We will still see each other as and when you want."

"So why change that?" he asked exasperated. "Just so you can go out without guilt?"

"It has a bearing on it, but it isn't the main reason. Look let's have a good few days now you're here and spend valuable family time together. We can talk, we are in no hurry are we?"

"I wasn't in any hurry," he replied somewhat forlornly. She leaned over and kissed him. "Why don't I put Maggie to bed while you pour us a glass of *coñac* and then you can take me to bed and make love to me like you always do."

CHAPTER TWENTY NINE
The Nice Majestic Hotel 1958

Over the last nearly three years, the Nicol family had worked together to create their new flagship. Albert once again asked his new found colleague, Charles-Édouard Jeanneret, *Le Corbusier,* to redesign the hotel and incorporate all the ideas that they had had for Monte Carlo. All rooms had bathrooms, each floor had service kitchens; the reception area was to house one of the first automated reservation systems in France and electronic billing and payments. Each room had air conditioning; there was a gymnasium and beauty salon in the hotel. Albert's intention was to create one of the leading hotels on the Riviera and he was achieving it.

In Monte Carlo, in 1956, Prince Rainier married the American movie star Grace Kelly. After a short courtship of only a year, they were married in a civil ceremony at the palace before the church blessing at the Cathedral of St Nicholas the following day. Over 600 guests were present and the reception at the Hotel de Paris was also attended by nearly three thousand Monégasque citizens. Albert and his father had desperately tried to get the contract but their hotel was just not big enough and if the truth were known, not famous or iconic enough for the event.

Albert had also married Dottie in 1957 and had

had their reception at the Monte Carlo hotel as it held so much for both of them. It was one of the most publicised events in Monte Carlo. So as not to clash with the XV Monaco Grand Prix in May they made their date in June of that year and as to be expected, it was attended by many local dignitaries, including members of the Royal Family. Dottie's proud father, John Wilkins, was there to give his daughter away and Albert's father and John were getting on so well, that they had bought a piece of land behind the hotel on which John was going to build luxury apartments which would be serviced by the hotel: The first arrangement of its kind in the Principality.

So, on the first of August 1958, The Nice Majestic Hotel opened its doors. There was a large reception of dignitaries including old clients and regular visitors to Monte Carlo. The coverage of the event attracted media attention from all corners and the hotel was praised for its modern approach to hospitality.

The year was saddened by the passing of Giovanni in June. He never got to see the finished hotel as he had been ill for a few months and had died peacefully in his sleep with Carolina by his bedside. When Richard got there he had gone. He was buried in Monaco Cemetery next to his darling Carla.

Meanwhile, their contract had finished with the Bristol Majestic in Monte Carlo but a few key staff had made the move to Nice, including their Head Chef, Jacques LeFois. It was Albert's intention to achieve what, at that time, was becoming an important part of the Hotel and Restaurant business in France, the coveted Michelin star. Jacques' mentor would be pleased to see that his followers Les Troigrois brothers had been awarded a Michelin star for their restaurant *Le Bois sans Feuilles in Roanne* in Central France the same year as the Nice Majestic opened its doors and Albert encouraged Jacques to pursue this goal, which he did with great enthusiasm.

Work on the luxury apartments that Albert's father and John Wilkins had built were being sold on long leases, again something that was not that usual on the Riviera, but was very popular in the UK. This meant that whatever happened, the basic freehold would always belong to their company although not being Monégasques, they could never own the land. With forty nine year renewable and saleable leases they were being snapped up by foreign investors from all over. Once again Albert had insisted that there were floor kitchens, wine cellars and housekeeping stations within the development to ensure the five star facilities that he wanted to create would be maintained. Eighteen months work on the Majestic Suites had been completed and once again the project had been welcomed by the city.

However a revenue stream had been removed from the company's portfolio as the apartments would now be catered for by the new operators; this was resolved by Richard and the SBM, when they agreed to pay a rental to Richard's company for the facilities within the apartments, thus allowing the hotel to still service them.

Three important things occurred in 1960, the Nice hotel had more than doubled its profits from the previous year, it received its first Michelin star for its *L'Ambassadeur* restaurant and Dottie gave birth to Michael Albert Richard Nicol. All the family were overjoyed with all three achievements. Albert, at thirty five years of age, reflected on what had happened in less than twenty years and was proud of his and his family's achievements. At the christening Albert sought permission to call his son Nicolson, (son of Nicol) which was granted and after signing the necessary papers, he became Michael Nicolson the future of the family business.

Richard was now sixty but showed no sign of slowing down although he was extremely proud of his sons and their capabilities and progress: Marc was now Deputy General Manager working with his brother who had the General Manager's title while Richard and Antoine were CEO and Managing Director respectively. But Richard and Antoine had fresh ideas. On a visit to Paris they were shocked to see that the famous city had had such a bad recession after the end of the war but it was now battling back. Spurred on by the Paris

Fashion week, the city was alive with foreign visitors and followers of fashion. There were constructions going on in the city and some of the older buildings were being restored. Not far from the Georges Cinq hotel where they were staying, they found a perfect site for a new hotel. It was an old abandoned hotel building and was for sale on a long lease. They arranged a viewing; the perfect site for the Paris Majestic. Over dinner that night the two brothers discussed what they could to with the old building. The old hotel could have 170 rooms, a restaurant, a banqueting suite and a beauty spa. Once again they would get hold of their friend *Le Corbusier* to design the hotel; despite the fact that he was now in his seventies, his enthusiasm knew no bounds. He had built a team of young apprentices to work with him in the hope that they could takeover where he left off. Their next stop was the Bank of France to secure the money necessary for the development. Needless to say the bank needed a lot of information, plus track record and bank references as the Nicols were not that well known in Paris.

On their return to Nice, they called a family meeting, to tell everyone what they were planning. There was a stunned silence until Albert broke in; "Do you think we might be a little ambitious having only been open just over two years here?"

His father replied, "I understand your concern Albert, but it will take us a couple of years to do

the work and providing we get the necessary funding, I think it will be the right time: Your Uncle and I have also decided to sell some of our shares. Obviously Giovanni's shares passed to Carolina and she has agreed we can sell hers. We also agreed that some of the shares should go to you and Marc which will hopefully become worth a great deal as we grow. We would still be majority shareholders but it will give us some working capital without having to rely on this hotel for backing. We will offer the shares to existing shareholders again before a public issue."
Once again everyone agreed that Richard was normally on the right track, so they all gave him the confirmation he wanted; even though he didn't need their permission, they had always taken any action as a family.
Richard sat with Albert and once again said that he thought it would be good if he was to join the development and opening team.
"I also thought we would ask John if he would be prepared to carry out the building work, what do you think?"
"Well, he certainly knows what he's doing and he is family" said Albert.
Albert, Richard, Antoine and John met in Richard's office; they explained the project; "it would mean working with *Le Corbusier* and with a Paris-based architect for the planning permissions, are you interested?"
"Absolutely and, if you would like, I will trade my

costs for shares in the company."

They all looked at each other,

"We will have to have a board meeting, but initially, I can't see a problem with the proposal; if we didn't agree to that, would you still be willing to do the work?"

"Of course, I would love to."

John left and the remaining family looked at each other.

"If he's prepared to do that," said Richard, "it could solve some of our financial requirements and the shares will still stay in the family. What does everyone think?"

Again they all nodded in agreement. They were on their way again.

Work started on the Paris hotel at the end of 1960 after planning permissions had been confirmed and finance had been put in place. *Le Corbusier* had come up with an amazing interior design and once again incorporated all the facilities that Albert had put in the previous hotels. John had gone through his brief with *Le Corbusier*, Richard and Albert. Although November is not the best month to build because of the inclement weather, work went ahead at some pace and they would be working towards an opening date in June 1963.

CHAPTER THIRTY
The Paris Majestic Hotel 1963

Marc had joined the family in Paris for a week or so, and between him and Albert they were to recruit the necessary staff for the opening which was on schedule for June. Among the recruits, was one that caught Marc's eye; she was a blonde girl, Adele, just thirty years of age, who was applying for the head receptionist position. Not only was she very attractive, she was also ideal for the position and after a third interview, this time with Albert present, she got the job. So in April she gave her notice to her previous employer, took a holiday ready to start in June. Aware that he shouldn't, Marc called her one day on the pretence of confirming something about work with her. "On the basis that I will not be running this hotel, my brother and uncle will, I see no conflict if I take you out for dinner, if of course you will allow me."
A slightly embarrassed and wary Adele agreed and that started their relationship which would culminate in marriage at the end of 1963.
The hotel opened on time, everyone was in attendance and it coincided with the Paris Fashion Show where models were in plastic spheres 'floating' around the city. It didn't take long before the hotel was building a reputation among Parisians and the hotel was making its

mark on the international scene as well. Adele and Marc were together as much as possible, although work meant that she was in Paris and Marc was still in Nice; but with less than a two hour flight they would spend their days off in Nice. Everything was going well until, just like his father Richard with Georgina, Adele found out in August, after a short holiday together, she was pregnant. Like before, it wasn't intended, but they had no intention of not going through with it and decided to get married toward the end of the year. They had a small reception for family and friends in Nice in November, and in May, Gabriel was born. They were ecstatic, as were the parents, despite being a little shocked. Much to Albert's annoyance this meant that he was losing one of the most important members of his team. Needless to say that a replacement was found and Adele had moved to Nice permanently before Gabriel was born.

Paris in the sixties was having a boom time. The 'swinging sixties' in general in Europe was creating a feel good factor and Georges Pompidou, Prime Minister under de Gaulle had invigorated the economy which was further boosted when the Anglo French co-operation on the development of Concorde was announced. De Gaulle had been re elected for another seven year term and had been a driving, if not at times preventive, force in the European Economic Community. The hotel was thriving under Richard and Albert's guidance and Marc was doing well in Nice with his new found wife and son.

In 1965 The Paris Majestic was given its five star rating and the restaurant had achieved its first Michelin Star for its fine dining restaurant *L'Ambassadeur du Paris* named obviously after its sister restaurant in Nice. Not surprising as they had brought Jacques LeFois from Nice to head up their kitchen in Paris and his *Sous* chef in Nice, had taken over there.

Richard and Antoine were on a roll: It would appear they couldn't do anything wrong and the family were strong and united.

Richard had resigned his honorary post with the SBM since leaving Monaco but Antoine had continued with his involvement with the *Union des Vignerons des Côtes du Rhône.* Their vineyard had continued success and the group still received an income from that relationship as well access to some good quality wines which were reflected in some of the house wines in the hotels.

By the end of the decade, Paris and Nice had become well established hotels and the brothers were looking to yet again expand; in 1970 they had a visit, one of many, from their colleague John Wilkins. Apart from seeing his daughter and her family and his friends, he had a proposition.

Over a drink in the cocktail bar overlooking the river, he said to Richard, Antoine and Albert, "I have something that may or may not interest you. I am in a position that I may have to take an hotel building in London back in settlement of a bad debt. It's in Battersea, a fairly industrial type of place but is going through a complete reformation and in a few years will be one of the up and coming areas in London. I did huge reform on this particular place earlier in the year and then started on another of one of their projects, when everything went tits for them and they have to go into liquidation. In an attempt to help them, and of course me, I have been negotiating to relieve them of this particular property allowing them to concentrate on the other property that they have that I had started work on. The one I am thinking about, with you in mind, has ninety rooms and four suites: It used to be offices and showrooms which were converted into a hotel several years ago, but the owners wanted a complete refurbishment which I carried out. Learning what I have, working with you guys, I designed it using your standards; things like room service kitchens on each floor — although there are only three, in fairness — it now has a beauty spa and is just on Battersea Square overlooking the park, with manicured gardens around it. I know you haven't probably thought of moving to the UK but I just thought this would be ideal for you. There would obviously be a price to pay, but I am happy to put my debt into the pot as part of it. I can also arrange finance from my UK bank so your investment will be quite minimal to obtain the property and it will also give you a foot into the UK market which will be booming over the next few years."

There was a silence as they took in what their friend was saying.

"Are you saying that you would form a separate company with us, UK based? I wouldn't want to amalgamate the French company; I would want that to remain separate?"

"Yes," replied John, "I would be happy to do that."

"So, we agree to provide the working capital and the management and you will provide the capital investment which as a company we would be responsible for the repayments. Our company will be set up to reflect the shareholdings and at the beginning would be a limited company just between us with no other shareholders? I think that could work. What do you think Antoine?"

"I foresee a few problems. One of us would have to go to the UK for a start. Then who would run it? We have no contacts in the UK apart from John."

"There is a young Englishman at the hotel that was taken on by the owners in an attempt to turn things around. He has done an hotel management degree in Switzerland, has some experience, speaks French but is quite young; about twenty five I think; but he maybe the sort of anchor that you need, I don't know, that would be your territory," said John.

"I suppose the first thing we will have to do, is go

over and look at the property before we do, or discuss, anything further. What do you think?" said Richard.

"Yes, and I think we should talk to the family as well to sound them out!" said Antoine. Once again the family met and Richard set out their plan. Albert and Marc expressed their concerns in much the same way as their Uncle had.

Albert started the conversation, "Well father, you are normally right, but even if any of us has reservations we can't express them until you go over to England and look at the project. But without sounding disrespectful, you are seventy now, do you really want to enter into this venture, which I can see could be fraught with difficulties?"

"Albert, I am not dead yet. Anyway I want to leave you two boys with some challenges when I've gone, so the more problems I levy on you, the stronger you will become." He laughed and followed by saying, "We will not do anything without your approval as you will have to sort it out eventually."

Despite reservations on all sides, it was agreed that the brothers would go to London and meet up with John and the young man, to look at the hotel and its potential.

It was with a certain amount of apprehension and excitement that the two booked their flights to view what could be their next and maybe last, adventure.

CHAPTER THIRTY ONE
London 1970

The taxi pulled up outside the very attractive Victorian building. John was there to meet them;
"Welcome to the Victoria Hotel," said John with almost paternal pride.
The two brothers looked at the impressive building. As John explained it had three floors and well manicured decorative flower beds at the front. They walked up the entrance steps to the ornate front doors and were welcomed by a slim young man in his twenties.
*"*Bienvenue Messieurs, je suis Arthur Radford, enchanté de faire votre connaissance.*"
"*Le plaisir est réciproque,*" said Richard.
The hotel had indeed been reformed beautifully by their friend, John. A circular lobby with a crystal chandelier dominating the entrance, decorated in pale blues with rich gold fabrics and cream furnishings which created a comfortable elegance with an unmistakable scent of leather. They moved into the cocktail bar where the theme of leather and wood continued with comfortable high back chairs and wooden trimmed sofas and mahogany coffee/drinks tables with that familiar scent of leather and essence of cigar smoke.

*Bienvenue Messieurs, je suis Arthur Radford, enchanté de faire votre connaissance: Welcome gentlemen, I am (AR) pleased to meet you.
Le plaisir est réciproque : the pleasure is mutual.

They went in to the elegant restaurant with its dark brown leather seating in curved shapes around tables. Chandeliers adorned the ceilings and the settings were very formal. There was an air of luxury which the brothers loved. They were shown around the rest of the hotel while John explained the work that he had carried out. "All the bedrooms were much the same size, all with bathrooms so it was a question of modernising the bathrooms and redecorating all the rooms. I chose a colour theme for each floor as you can see;" he said opening a couple of rooms on each floor. "And each suite is different," he continued as he opened each one. He showed with pride his room service kitchens and the main kitchen next to the restaurant downstairs and to the banqueting suite which held two hundred: Then into the beauty salon with its entrance to the street.

All three then went to the cocktail bar and ordered coffees.

"So what do you think?" asked John. Richard and Antoine looked at each other. "Most impressive, you have done a lovely job John," said Richard.

"We need to see some figures; would Arthur be able to provide them?"

"Yes, he is a figures man," replied John, calling him to come through to the bar.

"Would you like to give us some background of yourself, the hotel and the turnover?" asked Antoine.

Arthur told them about his background; having passed his A Levels he was going to go to university to take a BA in financial management, but during his summer holiday he took a job in an hotel in reception and fell in love with the life; so he decided to go to hotel school and take his BA there, with a bias towards financial management.

"So, I chose Lucerne; I thoroughly enjoyed it, passed with flying colours and have found my financial training to come in handy working here. I have compiled financial spreadsheets and a profit and loss forecast for the future with the right operators and investments. I will be happy to put them together and post them to you."

"Maybe you could liaise with John when they are ready then he can bring them over when he comes," said Richard.

"Good idea," confirmed John.

"Will do," confirmed Arthur.

"One of the major problems," continued the young man, "was that, when they took on the other premises in London near Park Lane; they over extended themselves. When they bought this building and converted it in the sixties, interest rates were just under four percent, this last year they have more than doubled, which also coincided with the purchase of the other hotel. When Mister Wilkins started the reforms, was when they got into real trouble. When I joined, the damage had already taken its toll and I suppose I was here to reorganise the deckchairs."

The two brothers looked at him and John quizzically.

"I am sorry," said Richard, "I didn't quite get that...."

John interrupted, "It's a reflection on the difficulty of the task ahead, a little like the deck steward on the Titanic that kept trying to organise the deckchairs that kept sliding around as the ship sank."

"*Ah, oui, je comprends,*" said Richard laughing. "A good analogy Arthur; are there many advance bookings?"

"Yes, bookings are looking good. There are a lot of investors around town looking to redevelop the area. Our food and beverage area is not good and only really deals with hotel guests; we are a little old fashioned to be honest, but we had no spare money to invest in a restaurant operation that would have appealed to the general public."

"So, you are running the show at the moment, where are the owners?"

"Fighting fires basically: The company is going to have to go into liquidation unless Mister Wilkins or another investor/operator, comes up with someone to buy this hotel before the liquidators get too involved; I am here to keep it afloat for the time being."

"Are you being paid?" asked Antoine.

Arthur smiled, "Sort of! Will you stay for a light lunch?"

They looked at each other but declined.

"My brother and I have to go back to France and discuss with the family and of course John. If we come to an agreement, we will go through John: One final question Arthur, if we did take over the business would you be prepared to stay on?"

"It would be a pleasure *Messieurs*."

They all shook hands as John and the brothers walked out into the daylight.

"Well, what do you think?" asked John.

Richard and Antoine looked at each other and smiled.

"Come over next week John and we will talk: And thank you."

They got into a taxi to the airport.

"We have a couple of hours until our flight. We need to eat and have a bottle of wine. With the archaic licensing laws here, we are best to eat at the airport. The food will probably be awful, but at least we will be able to have our bottle of wine. We have much to discuss *mon frère*."

CHAPTER THIRTY TWO
Paris and London 1970

John had arrived and they all sat down to go through the figures that Arthur had sent over with him.

"Very impressive," said Richard studying the books.

"Feasible and workable," said Albert. "So, where do we stand on finances?"

"The hotel owes me £150.000," said John. "I have spoken to the owners, they want half a million; they will accept £350.000 after my money is taken into account, but I reckon we can get them down to £300.000 for a quick sale. I have spoken to my bank and it is happy to loan us £200.000 leaving £100.000."

Richard, Antoine and Albert looked at each other for a few minutes.

"Speaking off the top of my head and without prejudice, if we, the French company, put in £100.000 plus £50.000 working capital and the British company signs for the loan, this means that we, the French company and John have put up 50 – 50 of the investment. However, as we are the operating company, profits should be based on a 35/65 split. Net profits, after taxes, would be split in that ratio after including a percentage as a contingency fund. What do you think?"

They all looked at each other.

"I am happy with the arrangement," said John.
"None of us is getting any younger so I think it only right that the company notes that John's share is left to his sons on the condition that they keep their money in. If John passes after the hotel is in profit and the boys want to, we could negotiate a 'buy out'".
"Seems reasonable to me," said John again.
"John would you like to set up the Limited Company, London Majestic Hotels limited, with three of us as directors? I will resign my position as MD when the time comes and place Albert in that position and Marc will take over Antoine's directorship when the time comes. Your boys, John, will have one directorship when you are no longer with us," he said smiling. "Hopefully, not for a long time yet: For any of us."

Six months later Richard, Antoine, Albert and Marc walked in to the rebranded Victoria Majestic Hotel, Battersea. Arthur was there to greet them.
"I think we should have a catch up with how things have been the last few weeks. We also need to check the stock at valuation: Arthur would you do that with Albert please?"
"Certainly Sir,"
"Meanwhile we will have to have a meeting with all the staff. Did you arrange that for today Arthur?"
"Yes sir, two o' clock this afternoon."

"Perfect."

The team had closed the hotel for a week. Arthur had arranged for all bookings to be completed by the end of the previous month allowing time for the rebranding, new signage, stock taking, a deep clean by staff and arrangements made for the reopening at the weekend.

The staff was gathered in the banqueting suite as Richard introduced himself and his family. He confirmed that Arthur was remaining as General Manager. He explained the company's ethos and their plans for the future of the hotel.

At the family's request, Arthur had arranged a drinks party after the meeting so as the staff could mingle with their new bosses and find out more in a relaxed atmosphere.

Later that day, the family sat with Arthur as he went through the state of play. Advanced reservations were good and even banqueting bookings were coming in.

"I have got someone to come in and refresh the restaurant area," said Richard. "The decoration is fine, thanks to John, but we need to modernise the tables and the settings. We have been discussing the menus with our chefs in France but you have been interviewing applicants here, have you not Arthur?"

"Yes sir, I have chosen four for you to see. They are coming tomorrow morning. I asked them to send menus that they would put on if they were to take over the kitchens of the Victoria. I have all the CVs and menus, but I am pretty sure you will be interested in the last one to see you tomorrow. Roger Oakes is a man in his late twenties with some experience before he joined the Roux Brothers at their Gavroche restaurant, which they opened in 1967 and which is taking London by storm."

"Sounds interesting, thank you Arthur."

By the time the hotel was opening for its press party, Roger had joined the team as head chef, alongside Iain Bardwell a Scot who was a Head Waiter at Claridges, but was inspired to join the Victoria as Restaurant Manager, as he was a friend and admirer of Roger.

The young, trendy, Kate Lambard, had been brought in to freshen up the restaurant; including a change of colours for the cloths, in keeping with the existing décor and finishes, and a new style of crockery, glassware and silverware. She even redesigned the menu covers to represent a more modern dining experience; despite the fact that Roger was heavily influenced by his French repertoire, he was adding his flair to classic dishes and the fresh decor reflected that.

Over two hundred people attended the opening with press, local politicians, including Sir Peter Studd, ex cricketer and Lord Mayor of London; a few actors and actresses from theatre and TV, and an army of press.

The Victoria Majestic had arrived and once again the Nicol brothers had made their mark.

Albert was by now being primed to take over from his father and delivered a welcome speech to the assembled guests. It took him back to that day in 1945 at the Bristol Majestic in Monte Carlo at it's re-launch. He had remembered the great feeling of pride that he had then, which he felt now: Their first hotel outside of France.

It was agreed that Richard would attend on a part time basis at the hotel during the first six months but still run the French hotels with Marc, and of course Antoine. Although, they had decided that the two patriarchs of the family would start to slow down and Albert would take the job of Managing Director, meaning he would move to London for the foreseeable future. Arthur would be the resident general manager. This also created the opportunity for Dottie to come back to the UK to see her friends and family, especially as her father was also getting on in age and it would be good for her to spend more time with him. She needed not to worry as he was to live for many more years.

As soon as all the guests had left, Arthur, Richard and Albert convened in Albert's new office to form a battle plan. They decided that the hotel was going to need a public relations and sales manager. Arthur had by then already thought of that and produced some CV's, one of which was the wife of Iain Bardwell who had been assistant director of sales at Claridges. It seemed an obvious choice, as her contacts far exceeded those of Albert and the company. An interview was arranged and Arthur and Albert agreed that she would be perfect. The rest of the senior staff remained and the hotel was now ready to take on London. By the time that Albert's son Michael was to join the hotel in 1985 it was very well established.

CHAPTER THIRTY THREE
The Eighties: The End of an Era

In 1980 Albert and Marc bought two houses next door to each other in a leafy London suburb. Both had houses in Nice, but as Albert and Dottie were spending more time in London than France it seemed a good idea. As the properties were being sold by the same vendor, Albert could see an opportunity to do a really good deal, so offered to buy the two. He told Marc his idea and Marc and Adele came over to look and decided that it was a great idea. As the brothers got older they spent more time in London, especially during the summer months.

The Nicols family had a hard few years in the eighties. Not business wise, that was good, but emotionally. Michael lost his Grandfather Richard in 1984 while he was in Switzerland. He was eighty four and had contracted pneumonia and passed peacefully. Michael flew back to London for the funereal before returning to finish his hotel degree.

His Great Uncle Antoine died two years later at the same age but from cancer. Michael was by then at the Victoria Majestic in Battersea.

Richard's wife Carolina died the year after Richard, some said of a broken heart; Antoine's wife Claudia also passed away in 1988.

John Wilkins also passed away in 1984 from a

heart attack. He had become an integral part of the family and the company. Dottie was distraught as it was so sudden.

But the biggest shock to the family was Marc and Adele's son Gabriel. Although he showed an interest in the hotel industry, he chose a different path and joined cruise liners and worked with Cunard on the QE2. He was also very artistic and Michael always thought his cousin was effeminate but never realised his sexual preferences until he came out as gay to his mother. Being a woman and a mother she was far more accepting than Marc who almost disowned him. But it was to get worse, Gabriel stayed with Cunard for a few more years rising to deputy restaurant manager of the first class section when his chosen lifestyle caught up with him and, at the age of only twenty five, he was diagnosed with HIV/AIDS and died peacefully just before his twenty sixth birthday. There was such a stigma attached to the disease in the eighties and little understanding of it. The family were devastated and it sadly sent Adele into a deep depression. In 1990 she took her own life with an overdose at the age of only fifty seven. This devastated Marc and it took him a while to recover. He had lost his wife and son within six months of each other: But he threw himself into work with his brother.

Michael's father was now sixty five but showed no signs of slowing down. He and his brother were looking forward to expanding, not consolidating or retiring.

The London company had two properties at that time: The Victoria and the apartments that they had bought near Park Lane not long after they had bought the Victoria.

The French company had the Nice and Paris hotels. Richard and Antoine had retired and were back in Nice until they passed. Marc was running France, but would come over regularly and swap with Albert who would then go to Nice. This way, they maintained contact with each other's part of the company.

However, the events of 1984 and 1986 changed the Nicol family, but the show had to go on. Michael had joined the company as a senior trainee manager and his future was being planned by his father and uncle. Michael had also introduced a young woman to the family. They liked Christine although they were concerned that they were a bit young to form a lasting relationship but were not that worried as work and location would have an effect on any long term prospects. Especially with the tried and tested watchword of the family, "Work Comes First."

What seemed the only positive side to the decade was Michael's progression within the company and his marriage to Juliette and of course the birth of Maggie in 1990. In fact, that kicked off another decade of success for the company although tinged with sadness of the events of the eighties. The hotels were doing well and Michael's now almost permanent life in Nice had worked wonders for Juliette and him, but the impending move to Paris was going to cause short term, if not long term, problems.

Albert and Marc were now officially orphans and in Marc's case a widower. But with his brother, they continued their development of the company. The nineties was a good decade for the family business wise and it consolidated their company both in reputation and financially. By the end of the decade, all mortgages had been paid off which meant that the company tax bill was beginning to become eye watering: Time to invest some money.

CHAPTER THIRTY FOUR
The Paris Majestic Hotel 2000

Business for the group was good; the Paris hotel had had its best year ever and the other hotels in the small company were doing exceptionally well; so much so that Albert and Marc had decided that, even at the age when most people would have retired to the South of Spain or France or the Caribbean, that they wanted to build their final venture together. In the sixties, not long after they had bought the Victoria, Richard and Antoine had done a deal with the same owners to buy their other London property which was still in financial difficulties; despite the owner's attempts to turn it into an hotel they had decided to keep it as apartments. The brothers stepped in and bought the unfinished development and let the properties out on 35 year leases. The property was just off Park Lane near 'Hotel Row'; as the leases were becoming free, Albert and Marc had now decided to turn it into an hotel which originally had been the family's long term aim. With accommodation in London growing by an incredible 1700 per cent over the twenty years from 1980, it seemed the right time. Architects, interior designers had been briefed, financing had been agreed; applications for planning permission were then ready to be applied for and their intention was to start construction in June 2000 and to open the hotel in 2004.

Michael had been informed at the end of the previous year that he would be leaving the Paris Majestic so in January 2000 he returned to the UK and joined the pre-opening team to oversee the development of the hotel in conjunction with his father and uncle. Like his father before him, he was to be very involved with the design and functionality of the project which was to be the most exciting project of his life.

He was involved in the original design of the hotel and had the freedom to input ideas and concepts with the architects, from the underground car park — "please ensure there is adequate space between places for cars of the twenty first century" — to the roof garden pool and 'city' club: Michael wanted a place where people would have the advantages of a 'Country Club' but in the heart of the city. There was to be a heated pool, with an electric roof covering for inclement weather, a gastro pub, gymnasium, sauna and steam rooms, driving range (Electronic virtual reality screen into a net) and a cinema room for sports events and other important events. This would cover the whole of the vast expanse of roof punctuated by chimney stacks some of which were obsolete so could be removed. They would build around the ones in use and the soon to be installed extractor units from the kitchens. There was a planned express lift from the foyer direct to the roof with a members platinum card activating the service. As with all the company's hotels there would be room service kitchens on each floor, and in this hotel there would be a butler for the six 'Royal Suites' on the penultimate floor: As well as the banqueting suite, private dining rooms and an eighteen hour brasserie with street access. There would be a 'shopping mall' on the reception level with a florist, a perfume shop, fashion and lingerie, men's bespoke tailors and a book shop. They were going to be on track for work to commence in June.

Sadly the year 2000 was not all excitement and success. Albert's wife Dottie died of cancer having been stricken with the disease for six months; while a blessing in some ways, it still devastated Albert and the family. Michael was glad he was in London to be with his mother and to support his father during the sad time. Despite the need for mourning, Albert ignored this and the father and son team threw themselves into their new project. But sadness was to raise its head again when Juliette and Michael divorced. There was no animosity, they remained friends and as far as Michael knew she had not found anyone and vice versa. Michael was not to learn until sometime later that she had in fact found someone else but by which time it did not matter. The settlement was nothing more than fair. Michael agreed to pay for Maggie's tuitions and allowances until she was at least twenty one or until she had finished her education which he would have done anyway. He would maintain the house in Nice and if Juliette wanted anything she only had to ask. This relationship was to continue for years and the couple remained friends and good parents.

Uncle Marc and Adele had never had a surviving child so the only heir to the company was Michael and it was the brother's intentions to leave it in the best state that they possibly could. To them, the addition of a new hotel was the crowning glory to the group.

The original building was a row of Georgian houses that had been converted over the years and added to as premises became available. It therefore had an extensive façade and only six floors which were to house the two hundred rooms, no two of which, he intended, would be the same. Michael's intention was to give it very much the country house feel. Planning permission for the top floor took some time as planners wanted to ensure that the aspect of the building was not to be out of place. In the end the façade of the top floor was to be finished exactly as the floors below; and even though the glass roof was not visible from the street, care was taken to ensure that the atrium style roof was also in keeping with the Georgian style.

As a gesture of keeping it in the family, Albert wanted his father's old friend and his father in law's company, to handle the refurbishment. Dottie's father John had died in the same year as

Richard in 1984, but his two sons had inherited the business and like Albert they too had reached the golden years, but they, in turn, had made their sons part of the construction business which they now ran. So, J.W. Wilkins and Sons were serious players in modern refurbishments in London, Monaco and Paris. Tim and his cousin Fred ran what was now a multi-million pound company; they were also very pleased to take on the task and their fathers were aware of the importance of the project and maintained a keen involvement.

Work started on schedule and Michael monitored all aspects of the project, especially the financial side along with Arthur Radford. Like his father, Michael also involved himself with the interior design along with the company that they had retained. It was a difficult brief to do all the rooms differently, both from a cost point of view and an artistic one. They decided to take a leaf out of John's book when he did the reform on the Victoria; they would do a different theme on each floor. The six suites would be designed individually; the rest of the rooms on the fifth floor would be junior suites and Michael's suite of rooms. That left three floors where all the rooms on each floor would be stylised.

As the development progressed and they appeared to be on time for their scheduled opening on the first of December 2004, one of the first people that Michael employed was a **Sales** and Marketing Director. He chose a young woman who had been the deputy of Marketing at the Connaught: a hotel that Michael admired and a lot of what he wanted to do with the Majestic was based upon their style: A mix of traditional, opulence and modern innovation. Coleen Brown would be able to capture the same type of market as the Connaught.

One of the most important posts to be filled would be the executive Chef; it had to be someone young, highly experienced in modern cuisine, certainly not a *'primadonna'* and who would, with Michael, come up with creative, practical and satisfying menus for the three outlets within the hotel.

Pierre Dupois was a no nonsense young man, something he obviously inherited from training with Marco Pierre White at Harvey's in 1990 and subsequently with Michel Roux at the Waterside Latterly he worked with Gordon Ramsay and Marcus Wareing. He was perfect for the Majestic. With a French father and English mother, he had spent two years working in France, but wanted to return to the UK.

Greg Wilkins was appointed as Deputy GM and would become the General Manager when Michael took over as MD. Alex Rifkin came from the Grosvenor House Banqueting to take the Banqueting Manager's post. Raymond White and Mavis Gold were the oldest heads of department, both just in their fifties, Raymond as Head Butler who came from the Dorchester to join the team and Mavis had been Head Housekeeper in two of London's five star properties.

The appointments of Angela Clarke and Alan Brooks cemented the front of house. Each head of department was given the brief to employ who they wanted and if that meant getting in touch with their old colleagues, so be it. 'Poaching' staff was frowned upon, but there was something more acceptable when it was old friends that were doing the poaching. They would have to liaise with Richard White the Human Resources Manager who had been with the company for five years and was based at the Victoria Majestic.

So, by the middle of November, all the staff had been employed. There were several staff training days, courses to be taken, health and safety rules and practice and they were ready for a couple of soft openings with invited guests, before the official opening on Wednesday, December the First. At the pre-opening management meeting, Coleen confirmed that the hotel was fully booked for the following weekend and that the press lunch would include five of the top restaurant critics in London as well as the main magazines.

The soft openings went well as did the official opening and press lunch which generated spectacular reviews of the hotel, its facilities and the food.

Michael, an aged Albert and brother Marc, gathered in the cocktail lounge early evening.

Over a bottle of Champagne they celebrated their success.

"Michael you have done a spectacular job and we will write a letter to all the staff to thank them. As you know Marc will be here for a month for no other reason than he wants to have his last fling and adrenaline rush. We will not interfere at all — it is entirely your baby and on Monday the third of January you will become the Managing Director of not only of the two hotels, but of the company, including the French company. But our managing director, your old friend, Alain Chastain will remain as MD of France, but will report to you and I suggest you get over there once a month to keep in touch. He has done exceptionally well as your uncle and I have become a bit too old for it. So apart from praising ourselves I would like to propose a toast to those no longer with us who made this all possible. Giovanni, Carla and Carolina, Richard and Antoine Nicol and John Wilkins, I am sure they are watching over us and will be proud of our achievements; to lost family." They raised their glasses, "To lost family."

CHAPTER THIRTY FIVE
London Majestic Hotel May 2005

It was Sunday May the eighth, the day of the Holocaust Memorial Society London Branch Dinner. Michael went into the banqueting suite with the General Manager Greg Wilkins and Executive Chef Pierre Dupois to survey the room. Michael inspected every table and was happy with what he saw. The flowers were spectacular and last minute touches had been made. Michael's in-house mobile rang, it was his secretary;
"Your father is here Michael."
"I'll be right over."
He went into his office as his father got up and gave him a hug and kissed his cheeks.
"*Comme ça va mon fils,?*"
"*Bien merci Papa.*"
"Is everything ready for tonight?" asked his father.
"Yes, of course," replied a puzzled Michael, "why do you ask?"
Albert took a deep breath, "I am a guest tonight. I have been invited by the Society."
Michael was still not keeping up.
"Why? We are not Jewish are we?" he said laughing gently.
"No my boy, but many years ago things were different. You know just about everything that happened to our families during the war, how we had the Hotel in Monte Carlo, how it was burnt

down as the Germans left and how your grandfather and great uncle and the family rebuilt it and continued to expand until we are where we are today. But what you didn't know and will only find out this evening, is that we were a little more involved than I ever told you."

Albert then related to his son the things that had gone on in Monte Carlo during the occupation and the role that he, his father, had taken.

Michael was a little opened mouthed.

"Why did you never tell me?" he asked.

"I never thought it would ever come up in conversation, but apparently because we did a bit in helping the Jews in Monaco, they have decided on the sixtieth anniversary of the end of the war to recognise a host of people who helped save their compatriots. We did very little. I was just part of a group that formed a resistance."

"You mean you were in the French Resistance?" said a gob smacked Michael.

"Well, not really, the resistance was a huge operation in France, we were just kids; it would be like the difference between being in charge of a five star luxury hotel as opposed to an assistant manager in a bed and breakfast in Brighton," he said laughing.

Michael was still impressed and got up and shook his father's hand; "I am very proud of you father."

"It was nothing special *mon fils*, just what we had to do in a difficult time."

"All the same I still am proud of you all."

"That's nice of you to say so. I am staying tonight and have taken one of the suites some are vacant."

"Of course, no problem; would you like something sent up?"

"Yes, I would actually, I think I'll have a bottle of Champagne."

"Any particular one?" asked his attentive son.

"Bollinger will be fine. Thank you. I'll see you later on," he waved jauntily as he left the office.

Albert sat in his room with a glass of the well chilled Champagne whose bubbles danced on his tongue. He had turned eighty this year. Sixty years ago he never thought he would get to this age, especially without any serious illness; not like dearest Dottie who had died five years earlier of that awful disease, Cancer. His mind went back to that day in Monte Carlo when the Italians came into the hotel. That young boy with no real plan in life except that he knew he was joining the family firm! But he didn't know for how long. He recalled the excitement of the dangerous game they played with the Germans. He tried to recall all the people that they had helped escape the clutches of the Nazis, even the Nazis themselves. 'I wonder what happened to them all?' he thought. And then there was Sarah and her sister and family. But he wouldn't be able to let the day go without remembering his friends and compatriots; René, Claude, Esther, Auguste and his brother and

Franck the barman. Then of course there was young Charles. 'If he had lived, I wonder if he would have reached my age and had a family'. And, there was Sarah; beautiful young Sarah. Tears came to his eyes as he realised the futility of all those that died and those he would never see again. He poured another glass of Champagne and looked out over his adopted city. Would his father be proud of what they had all achieved? Richard had died in 1984 and Antoine in 1986 both at the age of eighty four; 'longevity seems to run in the family,' he thought thankfully. Before his uncle had died he had sold what was left of the wine business and had split it between Albert and his brother Marc. So when he and Marc were gone the company would all belong to Michael and the shareholders. Their personal wealth would also go to Michael. 'He deserves it', thought Albert out loud 'he's worked for it, like most of us did. Work Comes First.'

—⁂—

Michael's phone rang, "Mister Nicolson, I have a Misses Cartwright at reception asking for you."
"Did she say what it was about?"
"She said it was a personal matter, Sir."
"OK, I'll come out."
As Michael walked towards the reception he couldn't mistake the form and the hair. Christine turned around and smiled.
"Hello Boss, *Gisus a job."
Slang: give us / me...

They embraced.
"How are you?" he enquired.
"Good. You?"
"Yes, I think so."
"You don't sound too confident."
"No it's just a shock to see you."
"I'm not interrupting anything am I?"
"No, just the day to day dramas of running an hotel; would you like a drink? or coffee?"
"Coffee would be nice, thank you."
"Claire," he said to the receptionist, "can you get someone to bring me some coffee to the office?"
"Certainly sir," she said picking up the phone.
Michael led the way to his office. She sat down.
"Congratulations on your success. I hear the hotel is doing well."
"I've only been here five months, but yes, it is; and how are you? You are looking fabulous as normal."
"Thank you kind sir, you are looking pretty distinguished yourself."
"Distinguished? Is that another word for 'old'?"
"No, more a posh word for 'hot'," she laughed.
"I'll take that, you have made a distinguished man very happy," he said raising his cup in a toast. She responded.
"So where have you been, what have you been doing? I'm sorry we lost touch; I often think about you."
"I'm sure. It wasn't just you, after all it was obvious that it wasn't going to work while you

were in Nice, then I heard that you had met some 'hottie' and moved on to the Paris hotel and had got married. How is that going, any kids?"
"Yes, a daughter, fifteen now. The marriage is over but we are still friends."
"Is that friends 'with benefits'?"
"None of your business," he laughed, "but no, just friends."
"How was France?"
"Yes, good, I was there a lot longer than I had expected to be. That was really why Juliette and I split up. The hotel business can play havoc with your love life, especially if you keep moving."
"Don't I know that; and, especially with a motto of 'Work Comes First'," she said pointedly.
"Ouch, but yes you are right. Anyway, what happened to you Misses Cartwright?"
"Bit like you, married and divorced. Thought I had found my King Turbot, but instead found a Sprat! Couldn't keep his dick in his pants. It's a man thing you know," she said smiling and taking another mouthful of coffee. "Anyway, I had a few tiddlers on the way. But none that came up to your standard."
"You implying that I was a tiddler?"
"No, more of a Wild Bass I think."
They both laughed.
"I don't know whether you'd like to, but I can be free tomorrow, I could show you around the hotel and then we could go out for lunch. I have a big dinner tonight. My father is going to be here as

well."

"How are your family?"

"Getting old; just like the rest of us I suppose."

"Speak for yourself," she replied, getting up and showing off her perfect legs and slim body.

He smiled, "Maybe you're right. I'll see you here at midday if that's OK and we can really catch up."

"That would be nice," she said kissing him on the cheek.

He walked her to the main entrance. She turned and waved, *"à demain,"* she said as she left with a smile.

'Has she been learning French?' he asked himself: 'I had forgotten how good looking she is. I haven't seen her for nearly twenty years. She has to be forty now. She looks good on it' he thought smiling.

Albert stirred from his siesta and looked at the nearly empty bottle of Champagne. 'That's a good start to the evening' thought the seasoned hotelier as he got up from his chair and headed toward the bedroom to disrobe and take a shower.

He allowed the hot pressure shower to refresh him and set him up for the dinner tonight. He didn't really know what to expect or even why he was invited. His contribution was minimal compared to those that gave their lives. Not that he will know anyone there, so perhaps accept the hospitality, have dinner and make a swift exit.

"à demain, Until tomorrow.

He donned his dinner suit and made his way down to the bar in the banqueting suite.

There was a tall elegant older man greeting guests as they came in. Abraham Lewinburg greeted Albert, "Mister Nicol, good to see you again."

"And you Mister Lewinburg."

"Abe, please."

"Albert" they said shaking hands.

Marc followed his brother in, "this is my brother Marc, this is Abe Lewinburg," said Albert. The two men shook hands.

"The table plan is there," he said pointing to an easel by the bar, "but you are on the top table Albert."

"Oh," replied Albert surprised, "thank you."

Albert and Marc walked to the bar and took a glass of Champagne.

"Top table, eh? Guest of honour?" said Marc.

"It would seem to be," replied the ever reticent Albert.

Abe came over with a man and a woman slightly, he thought, younger than him. "Albert these are your fellow guests this evening, Nanette Blitz Konig, and Lt Colonel, retired obviously, Leonard Berney and Claude Pierre Brossolette. Claude's father was one of the main resistance organisers in Paris and in France in general during the war; and Nanette was a holocaust survivor from Bergen-Belsen which was liberated sixty years ago last April; and Leonard was the commanding officer of the liberating British army."

Albert was taken aback;

"I feel that I am at the wrong dinner," he said humbly as he shook all their hands. "Such distinguished company, I don't know what to say."

"From what we understand, you played more than your part as a young man and you were an associate of one of my father's great friends, René Borghini?"

"I was," replied Albert fondly, "sadly not for long, but I learned a great deal from him, especially about loyalty, friendship and patriotism."

Alex Rifkin had called the guests to order, to inform them that 'Dinner is Served'.

The new found friends talked animatedly as they made their way to their seats.

As people sat down, Albert looked around the room and acknowledged his brother who was sitting on a round table in front of him to the right. He put on his glasses but, as he thought, there was no one there that he could recognise; having said that it was a big room and with nearly four hundred people he probably wouldn't be able to anyway.

Albert was pleased to find himself sitting next to Nanette while Leonard was to her left and Claude was on the other side of Abe and his wife. He was fascinated to listen to her story about the time she was in the concentration camp, her friendship with Anne Frank and the euphoria when Leonard and his team arrived to liberate them.

Not so heart warming was to hear of the dreadful state of everyone there, the stench and the disease. Nanette's message she preaches is that it should never happen again. Albert never did understand 'man's inhumanity to man.'

The meal was served and it pleased Albert very much to hear the compliments that were being bandied about concerning the hotel, the food and the service.

The meal over, Abe stood up to give his welcoming speech and to introduce the guests on the top table. The first speaker was Nanette who spoke about her time in Belsen, the cruelty, the barbaric conditions, her friendship with the legendary Anne Frank — they had been school friends as well as prisoners together — and the feeling of relief and freedom they felt when the British army arrived; yet strangely, although freedom was theirs, no one had rushed out of the gates. Mainly because they had nowhere to go and no way to get there, but in some strange way, many felt comfortable in a place where they had seen and felt so much pain, now that they knew they were safe.

Then Leonard was introduced and the man that had played such an important part in such an historical event was humbling; he talked about the horrendous conditions he found when he and his command arrived. The work he had to do, the clearing of dead bodies and trying to sort out who was who and those that were dead and those that were alive — just.

Then it was Claude's introduction as the son of one of the fathers of the resistance. A banker by profession and a government adviser in the seventies he was born a few years after Albert and was too young to get involved in the resistance, "At least, that was what my father told me" he said, raising a mild laughter among the guests. He told stories of the resistance and made reference to the resistance of Monte Carlo and his father's friend René Borghini. After, once again, tumultuous applause, Abe stood up and said;

"Now ladies and gentlemen and distinguished guests, I would like to introduce you to our most reluctant guest tonight. He is the Chairman of the company that owns and runs this very hotel; he is also from a family that started their business in Monte Carlo in the twenties. His story is interesting because he was in the family business in 1942 when the Italians moved into Monaco and still there when the Germans arrived, which is when he really got involved with the local resistance fighters. We are not sure how many people that Albert Nicol and his colleagues assisted in escaping from the Nazis but it ran into over a hundred in a two year period. Not just Jews were helped, but locals who were being persecuted by the occupying force and even helped some young German soldiers that wanted to escape a move to the Russian front."

'How the hell did he know about that?' Albert

asked himself. 'I'd almost forgotten about those boys. Good God?'

Albert stood up to warm applause.

"Ladies and gentlemen and very distinguished guests, Mister and Misses Lewinburg, I thank you first of all for inviting me and secondly for choosing our hotel as your venue for this very important event. I hope you have enjoyed your evening so far." There was an appreciative round of applause.

"In such distinguished company I am not quite sure why I am here. Compared to what Nanette went through, what Leonard achieved and his part in it and Claude's father, who was the resistance. My contribution, as an eighteen year old, was small compared to people like René, your father's friend, Claude, Auguste and all the brave men that put their lives at risk, not just for our Jewish friends, but anyone who needed our help. In a macabre way it was exciting, but I suppose that was natural for a young man. Also my recollections and achievements pale into insignificance in comparison to my fellow guests. All I do know is we all lost friends and family at the most horrible times in our lives which I, like Nanette, pray that such abhorrent acts never occur again;" another round of applause.

"Before I sit down I am intrigued Abe how you found out about some of our work and the people we helped? Especially the Germans."

"Maybe I can answer that by asking our guests"

said Abe, as Albert took his seat.

Addressing the guests, he said, "Who among our friends and guests know this man on my right?"

There was a shuffle of chairs and then toward the back of the room people started standing up; first a couple, then a woman and a man, then another two and another three. All in all twelve people were on their feet.

"Please come towards us," said Abe. All of them, including the two in wheelchairs, made their way to the top table.

Abe gave the first man, a man in his late fifties, the microphone. In a strong Spanish accent, he said, "My name is Carlos Badeaux Moreno, you and your friends rescued my father, Michel from certain death and made him go to Spain where, as promised, you sent my mother and siblings after the war. If it was not for you, I would never have been born and as the youngest in the family, we will always be grateful."

By now, Albert had moved to the front of the top table, with tears in his eyes.

He embraced Carlos and simply said, *"Le fils de mon ami,"* and kissed him on both cheeks.

Behind him was a woman about the same age as Carlos, "my story is similar to Carlos', you and your friends helped my mother and sister getaway when they were children, my parents died but we made our way to the UK, met someone and fell in love and have four children between us.

*Le fils de mon ami,: the son of my friend

They are called, Albert, Claude, Esther and Pierre."

By now Albert was a wreck. But the last few guests were going to affect him in ways he could never imagine.

A man, a little older than Albert, in a wheelchair with a woman about the same age, approached him. She stepped forward and hugged him. The man spoke, "Hello Albert, you won't remember me, I am one of the four soldiers that you helped avoid the Russian front. My friends and I stayed in touch, I am the only one left, but we all married and had children, if it had not been for your courage and bravery none of us would have had a life like we did and" he said pointing to the man behind him "my son would not have been my son or given me grandchildren."

Another wheelchair, another man; Albert looked at him and the woman by his side; He swore he knew them;

"Hello" she said, approaching him, "it's Rachel Gold."

"*Mon dieu*" said Albert, "how are you? It is so wonderful to see you."

"And this," she pointed to the man, "is my husband, Kurt Schmidt."

Albert grabbed the man's hand and shook it hard.

"*Du bist ein echter Held, danke*"* said Kurt.

"I am so happy to see you safe and well" said Albert now visibly moved, but Abe had kept the

*Du bist ein echter Held,: You are a true hero thank you

best for last.

A woman in her late seventies, but with unmistakeable features, approached him.

"Sarah?" he asked with a shudder in his voice.

"Yes, Albert," she replied hugging him, "and this is my son Ricardo."

"*Encantado Señor*,"* said, the man who appeared to be in his late fifties. "Thank you for saving my mother, without you none of us would be here."

"So, you stayed in Spain?" asked her old friend.

"Yes," she replied, "the best thing that ever happened to us."

"When this is over," said Albert "do you want to meet in the hotel bar for a nightcap?"

"Yes, I would love to, it would be great to catch up."

She went back to her seat. Albert couldn't believe what had happened.

"Now" said Abe, once again on his feet, "is the time for the presentations on behalf of our society. Firstly Nanette, thank you for your continued talks to the public and for keeping the memory of what happened alive so as not to let the truth die." He presented her with a framed certificate. The audience applauded.

"To Claude, in memory of your father and the continued work you do to ensure no one forgets."

He presented Claude with a certificate to more applause.

"And finally, to Albert Nicol whose bravery and

*Encantado Señor. A pleasure to meet you sir.

that of his friends who put their lives at risk to help those more vulnerable. Compassion knows no boundaries of race, religion or creed. Thank you on behalf of all of us."

In tears, Albert accepted his framed plaque and received an embrace from Abe with accompanying applause.

He sat down and saw his brother still on his feet applauding with pride.

CHAPTER THIRTY SIX
Loves Rekindled

Albert walked towards Sarah and her sister. More warm embraces before Rachel and a very frail Kurt left the hotel. Sarah's son Ricardo shook his hand once again and said his goodbyes leaving his mother to talk to her old friend. Over a final glass of Champagne, Sarah said, "It is wonderful to see you Albert, and I was so surprised and proud of the recognition you received today."

"Yes. It was a great surprise for me too. So what happened when you got to Spain with your parents?"

"We were concerned about Rachel until she joined us, once again thanks to you and then even more surprised when Kurt came to our door."

"I can imagine, I was surprised to see him here and Rachel. Obviously he was one of the good ones after all."

"He certainly was and they have been very happily married all this time although I fear he may leave us soon, but he was determined to be here with Rachel today."

"You got married?" asked Albert.

"Yes and you?"

"Yes, after the war we redesigned the Bristol Majestic Hotel as it was burnt down in part when the Germans left. I met a young woman whose father was doing business in Monte Carlo and stayed at the hotel. We got married in 1957 and had Michael in 1960. He is now Managing Director of our small group as my brother Marc and I are on our last outing," he smiled. "It all seems to have gone very quickly."

"It certainly has, and your wife?" asked Sarah.

"We lost her in 2000 from cancer but we had been very happy together: And you? Still married?"

"No, I am afraid it didn't work. He was Spanish and I suppose I was still on a type of rebound and I thought I needed a father for our son and sort of rushed in.............."

There was a stunned silence from Albert as the word 'our' suddenly hit him.

"You mean that Ricardo.............."

"Yes, I'm sorry Albert I didn't mean it to come out like that. Not long after I arrived with my family, I found out I was pregnant. My parents were not happy and generously put it down to the war, 'these things happen in time of fear and despair' my father would say."

"Why didn't you tell me? Does Ricardo know?"

"There was no point in telling you, was there? What would you have done? And no, there was no point in telling Ricardo either. He always thought that Alfonso was his father and in fairness to Alfonso he treated him like his own and did until he died ten years ago."

"But I should have known, I might have been able to help."

"How? Would you have come to Spain? You had a

life and a career in France and I had a new life as a refugee and very happy it was."

"I am glad, but can I help you now. Do you need anything? Do you want something?"

"No Albert, you owe us nothing at all. We are also very comfortable. Alfonso left us very well looked after; and anyway Ricardo is a judge in Barcelona, after having a very successful career as a lawyer, so he's fine. He's married and has three children so I have grandchildren and now great grand children. Life has been good and it's basically all down to you."

"And a lot of others," added Albert. "How long are you staying?"

"Oh, we have a small apartment near Covent Garden which Alfonso bought years ago and put it in Ricardo's name. Ricardo was spending time in London to study British law and qualified so as he could practice in both countries. So when I want to, I can stay there, although I don't travel much these days, it's too much like hard work now, but when I read about today in the Jewish Post, I knew I had to be here. Ricardo was already here, so I knew I would be OK."

Albert laughed, "I know the feeling, I seldom go to France now. In that case, would you like to go for lunch tomorrow?"

"That would be nice, here is my mobile number," said Sarah scribbling on a bar serviette.

Albert gave her his card and said "I'll call you in the morning."

Michael's house phone rang, it was reception; "Misses Cartwright is here for your twelve o'clock meeting Sir,"
"Thank you, I'll come out."
"Hello," he said, walking towards her.
"Hi," they kissed on the cheek.
"Ready for a guided tour?"
"Indeed, impress me," she said with a smile.
He turned to the receptionist; "tell Susan that I am not available for the rest of the day, unless of course it is very important."
"Certainly sir."
As they walked around the ground floor with its boutiques, flower shop, newsagent and such, she asked,
"How did the banquet go last night?"
"Very well; they presented my father with an award for the work that he did during the war in Monte Carlo."
"What work? asked Christine.
"It's a long story," replied Michael, "I'll tell you over lunch."
He took her through to the banqueting suite, showing off the Brasserie, showed her a few rooms and the suites and finally the roof top Club, aptly called The Rooftops City Club.
"Very impressive," she said truthfully. "I love the club idea. Yours I presume?"
"Yes," he said coyly.
"Do you live in?" she asked.

"Yes, I have a suite."
"Are you going to show me?
"If you like"
He opened the door with his card and they walked into a hallway which led into a huge lounge overlooking the park.
"Very nice," she said going to the window admiring the view, "how many bedrooms?"
"Two," he replied walking through to the guest room with its king size double bed, fitted wardrobes and ensuite bathroom and then to his luxury room with a modern four poster queen sized bed, sitting area and self contained dressing room and huge bathroom with walk-in shower, jacuzzi and sauna.
"Bloody hell," exclaimed Christine; "It's a bonking paradise. A few steps up from Nice," she said as she bounced her bum on the bed.
"In keeping with my position," he said light heartedly.
"Which is what?" she asked genuinely interested.
"I am now MD of the company" he replied and when my dear father leaves us I will be the CEO."
"Do I have to curtsy?" she said dipping in mock regality.
"No, just kiss my feet," he laughed.
She walked towards him and said, "I not going that far down — it's an age thing, I'll just do the lips for now," she said brushing her lips against his.
He knew what he was thinking, but was unsure of

her thoughts.

"Ready for lunch?" he asked.

"Hmm, I would be very happy to eat here if that's OK with you. It's such a lovely place. Not in the restaurant, if you agree, I would like the Brasserie if we can, it looks fun and trendy."

"Yes why not and we may not be disturbed there."

They took the lift to reception and walked into the brasserie. They were greeted by the manager of the restaurant, Alison.

"Hello sir, nice to see you in our neck of the woods," she said with a smile.

"I don't eat here enough do I Alison? but then I don't get many opportunities, only with special guests, this is Ms Cartwright," he said introducing Christine.

Alison offered her hand, "Christine," she said to Alison shaking it.

"Can we have a quiet table in the corner Alison?" asked her boss.

"Certainly, this way please," she said picking up two menus and a wine list.

They sat and he ordered a glass of Champagne for himself, "and a Tanqueray and tonic with a slice of cucumber for the lady."

"Certainly sir" said Alison as she left the table.

"Golly, you remember my old habits? Sorry, I should have told you that I have given up alcohol and sex."

"Seriously? what would you like instead?"

"Instead of what, the sex or the alcohol?" she said

smiling.

He looked at her trying to work out her reply.

"You should see the look on your face," she laughed. "Of course I haven't."

"The sex or the alcohol?" he said with a teenage grin.

"I'll have the gin now, the other you will have to wait to see if it's true or not."

'She is definitely in flirt mood like the old days and she's lost none of her sex appeal and still has just the right amount of naughtiness'.

Alison came over with the drinks and said,

"We changed the set menu this morning," and presented a small card to them, "if you are interested."

"I will probably have the menu to try it," said Michael, "but you have whatever you want" he added as he raised his glass to her.

"I think I will go the same way," she replied chinking their Champagne flutes. "Hmm, they have got some of my favourites ingredients on the starters, can we share?" she asked.

"Of course, the *Salmon Wasabi Tartare* and the *Scallops with Black Pudding and Apple*?" he asked.

"You remember," she said impressed.

"Followed by the Wild Sea Bass with Samphire?"

"Very impressive, you have a good memory."

"You are very memorable," he said smoothly.

"I think you said something like that about twenty years ago," she said caustically but with a smile.

They ate and talked animatedly as they had when they first met. They laughed as always. They caught up on their lives, both good and bad. She told him about her 'arsehole of a husband' who was a Food and Beverage Manager she had met when she worked as a Head Receptionist at another hotel in London.

"I wondered where you had gone. I phoned the Victoria and they said you had left to go on leave but had handed your notice in and no one knew where you had gone. Why did you leave?"

"To be honest?" he nodded, listening attentively, "To get away from you. Not in a bad way, but I didn't want to dwell and there were too many good memories around me so I thought a fresh start would be the answer."

"I am sorry," he said hopelessly.

"You've nothing to be sorry about," she said toying with her dessert.

"I could have saved you from a fate worse than death if I had stayed in touch — like marriage."

She laughed, "I don't think a long term *Ménage a trois* would have worked"

"*Touché*," he conceded. "Your French has improved," he said.

"Don't take the piss, it's worse now than when I was at school."

"So, where do you live now?" he asked changing the subject.

"Same place," she replied.

"Really?"

"Yes, but I now own the whole building. My grandmother left it to me when she died a few years ago; which was great as it coincided with me leaving the arsehole and moving back to my flat which my Gran had always kept for me. She had said, with that worldly wise knowledge that only Grans have, 'It won't last you know. So I'll keep your flat for when you need to come back.' Thank God she did."

"I never met your Gran did I?"

"No, sadly, but she was never around much in those days, she spent a lot of time in Barbados. Living off her dead husband's fortune; some people have all the luck. All I got was a fucking tee shirt which said 'I left my husband for love — someone else's."

"I like it!"

"So did I, which is why I had it printed, I ought to have had loads printed."

"You should."

"So what were you going to tell me about your father?" she asked.

Michael related what his father had told him about his time in Monte Carlo and what he had heard at the ceremony the night before.

"It was very emotional for everyone and I think my father was very moved, especially when they brought up loads of people he had helped, to meet him. I also learned this morning that one of the women was his old girlfriend from 1942."

"Good grief," said Christine in amazement, "how

wonderful."

"Yes it is isn't it? And he's having lunch with her today."

"How lovely, obviously the day for remembering."

They finished their coffee and she asked, "Are you taking me for an after lunch drink?"

"Where would you like to go?"

"Not far," she smiled.

"The cocktail lounge?"

"A bit further up from there," she smiled suggestively.

He knew what she meant and agreed. They took the lift to his suite and went in.

"A cocktail?" he asked.

"The only cocktail I want is yours," she said as she approached him and kissed him passionately.

'She has lost none of her directness and honesty' he thought, something he had always liked and admired.

Her hand wandered down to his trousers and caressed him on the outside and she felt him responding. She put her hands over his shoulders inside his jacket and slipped her hands down his sleeves removing it.

"I think you had better remove your suit, we wouldn't want it creased," she said with a smile.

"I have to tell you I have not made love to anyone since Juliette," he said, almost embarrassed.

"Snap! I haven't made love to anyone since you, so it will be, like starting over." She could see his quizzical look as she continued, "I've had a few bonks, which included my marriage, but you," she paused, "were different." They walked into the master bedroom. He threw his coat on to the back of the chair, took off his tie and walked towards her, kissing her again and unclipping the top of her dress and opened the zip which allowed the fabric to slide down over her body revealing that perfect body that had hardly changed. She was as naked and as pert as the last time he had seen her in the bedroom. Once again they kissed and she released his trousers which fell to the ground as she removed his shirt and led him, by his appendage, to the bed where they began to make love. Familiar touches, feelings and sensuality took them back to their younger days and for a minute it seemed that no time had passed, as their coupling produced enormous orgasms that left them locked together as they relaxed.

"*Déjà vu*," she said as she laid there. "Hmm, maybe my French has improved."

It was Wednesday morning, his mind was still on Christine and the wonderful afternoon they had had. It really didn't seem that twenty years had passed, she was just the same. Even more attractive than he remembered, or was that just because he had not felt love and attention for such a long time. Thank God he had had work these last few years to keep him alert. His mobile rang. It was Juliette.

"*Allo ma Cherie*," he said, "how are you?"

"OK, I think. I need to talk to you."
"OK, talk to me."
"No, I mean in person."
"Are you in London?"
"Yes, I have just been in Cheltenham to finalise Maggie's move to college. I have papers you need to sign and I also need to talk to you about something else."
"If you would like to come around about eight tonight we can have a bit of supper."
"I'm not really in 'supper mood' but yes that's fine, I'll see you then."
They put their phones down and Michael thought, 'that doesn't sound like Juliette, I wonder what's wrong?'
That evening his phone rang and he was in his suite. The reception told him that Juliette was here.
"Get one of the boys to show her to my suite please," asked Michael.
The bell rang; Michael went to the door and was greeted by a severe looking Juliette.
"Come in," he said pointing to the hallway.
"This is nice," she said, "why haven't I been here before?"
"I suppose that's because we have always met downstairs," he replied defensively. "Would you like a drink?"
"A glass of wine please."
"Preference?" he asked matter-of-factly.
"I think red is the order of the day" she said

ominously.

"Oh dear," he said opening a bottle of claret, "that sounds depressing."

"It is a little Michael," she said, accepting the glass.

"Is Maggie OK?"

"Oh yes she's fine. Looking forward to going to Cheltenham next year. Hoping she will see more of her Daddy while she's here. You won't let her down will you Michael?"

"Have I ever?" he asked dejectedly.

"No, sorry you haven't, but I am hoping that what I am going to say won't change that.

"What is it Juliette?"

She took a large mouthful of the ruby red wine, and said, "I have met someone else."

There was a moment's silence.

A slightly gob smacked Michael gathered his thoughts and said, "Oh, that's somewhat unexpected. How long have you known him?"

"A very long time," she said realising what this implied.

"So, the last time you were here, you had been seeing him?"

"Yes, but nothing had really happened. It has only been the last months where things have progressed to the point that I feel I have to tell you."

"Very considerate," said Michael sarcastically.

"Come on Michael, it was bound to happen sooner or later. I am stuck in Nice and you are here."

"Your choice," he said adamantly.

"That's not fair," she replied emphatically.

"Maybe not fair, but true." There was a moment of silence as Michael topped up their glasses and sat next to her on the sofa. He held her hand, "Don't get upset. You are right, you are a beautiful woman and things didn't work out the way that we had hoped, but it makes no difference. We have a beautiful daughter, lots of wonderful memories and I would like to think that we are and always will be, the best of friends."

She leant over to him and kissed him, at first affectionately and then with more passion. Neither of them really knew what happened, but they were taken by old love and passion. Their love making went from the sofa to the floor and then to the bedroom. They lay there satiated, holding hands.

"What happened there?" asked Michael.

"I don't know," replied Juliette, "what comes naturally I suppose," somewhat embarrassed.

"Whatever, it was wonderful and it had been a long time. So, who is the man that has stolen my wife?"

"I am not sure that you want to know."

"I may not want to, but I need to know the person who is going to spend time around my daughter."

"I am afraid you know him."

"What? You are kidding. Who is it?"

"Alain Chastain," said Juliette in tears.

"My French MD? and an old colleague? Whatever

were you thinking about?"

"It just sort of happened over time Michael, I obviously knew him before and we are both in Nice. He and Belinda had split up after he came to Nice and we were both on our own and I would talk about you and he, her, and I suppose we just fell into it."

"I bet you did," said Michael sarcastically

"So this was about having one last fuck for old time's sake!"

"That's unfair Michael, that wasn't meant to happen. No matter what happens I will always love you. You were my first real love and you are the father of my daughter. God willing we will always be inextricably linked. I just hope that it will always be as the greatest of friends."

He pulled her toward him and allowed her head to nestle into his shoulder. He caressed her hair and thought back to two days ago. What right had he to question anything?

As for Chastain....

Sarah looked fabulous. Despite the passing of years, Albert felt twenty years old again as she opened the door to her ground floor apartment near Covent Garden.

"I thought we would lunch at *Mon Plaisir* just around the corner. You must have been there."

"No, we keep saying we will go."

"Well now is your chance for a taste of France that you may have missed; one of the oldest

traditional French restaurants in London."
Albert's driver took them straight to the door.
Sitting in one of the romantic booths, Albert ordered two *pastis*. Sally took a taste, "Yuk, I remember I don't like this!"
He laughed, "I am sorry, it is a taste of my past which I don't often drink, shall we have some wine?"
She smiled at the old man in front of her wondering where that young, charismatic, gung ho young man had gone. Then she caught her reflection in the old mirror opposite and knew exactly what had happened. But he still had that young charm and cheeky grin.
Sarah ordered *Moules Marinière* and Albert a dozen *Escargots*, she had *Sea Bass* and he had *Steak Tartare avec Frites*.
They talked about her life and relationship with Alfonso, her son and her sister. Her parents had died some time after they arrived in Spain and could never really settle, but they were so happy to be safe. Father had got involved in the local Synagogue although Rachel and Sarah lapsed which upset her father, but the girls could only see that being Jewish had caused them so much grief, they wanted to put it behind them. Albert told her how his life had been since she left Monte Carlo. How the company had grown, how his brother's son had died and how his wife had taken her own life; and the torment that he himself had suffered watching his wife Dottie die

from that evil cancer. Sarah was saddened, but happy for the success that the family had achieved.

After lunch he took Sarah back to her apartment. "Thank you for a lovely afternoon Albert and it was so lovely to catch up with you."

"It was a pleasure; if you are here for a while, maybe we could meet for lunch again?"

"I would love to." She kissed him on both cheeks and went inside. He sat in the car and cast his mind back to their first date, the cinema, the kisses, the lovemaking; and we thought we had been so careful. 'Why did she never tell me?' Well at least during his last few years he would be able to see her and was happy that her life had worked out so well for her.

CHAPTER THIRTY SEVEN
The Closing Years

After the remarkable events on Sunday, May the eighth, some lives were changed forever. Michael's meeting with Juliette, gave them the last fling of their love story and as requested they divorced amicably and remained friends for the rest of their lives. The beautiful Maggie passed her exams with flying colours and went to Les Roches as planned. In 2015 Maggie joined the company as a Junior Assistant Manager at the Nice Majestic.

Michael's reunion with Christine went better than they could have imagined. Christine and Juliette got on very well and Maggie loved her too. The whole relationship was more than amicable even though Michael was at one stage wary of Alain's involvement. But, Albert and Uncle Marc made him Managing Director of the French company when they retired at the end of 2004, which was under Michael's control. They had been friends for many years and were not letting a relationship break that bond; and anyway they had to work together, so common sense prevailed. In what some considered a strange arrangement, Alain was Michael's best man when he married Christine in 2010: In a quirky reciprocal arrangement, Michael was his best man when he married Juliette some months after. The strange thing about their marriage was that Alain spent most of his time in Paris and divided the time between there and Nice. Much the same as Juliette and Michael had done when they were together. Maybe maturity played a part and then of course the throes of young love may well have calmed down.

After his emotional award and meeting all those people, Albert continued to meet with Sarah and they remained close friends until he died in 2010. Marc passed away in 2012. Thankfully his father and uncle were able to attend Michael and Christine's wedding, but Albert died a few months after and Marc in 2012. Sarah went back to Spain where she passed away in 2011.

Michael had taken over the business in 2010 on the death of his father. He took on a re-modernisation programme throughout the group including the Nice hotel, the Battersea hotel and the London hotel. He also opened the Bristol Majestic in 2015, occupying the site of an old hotel in the Park Street area of that city in a tribute to his father and their heritage; The Bristol Majestic had indeed come home. Under Michael's guidance the company was growing year after year.

In 2020 Maggie was deputy General Manager of the Nice Majestic; by 2023 she was General Manager of the Bristol Majestic and then in 2026, she took over as General Manager of the Paris Majestic.

Despite the tragedy of the pandemic of 2020/21 the company consolidated and came out the other side. At the age of seventy Michael was getting ready to hand over the company to his fabulous daughter. He appointed a Group Operations Director for the UK and one for France — both would report to London Head Office.

Michael and Christine moved out of the hotel on Albert's death and into his house. Juliette and Alain retired at the same time and remained friends with Michael and Juliette until they passed away; the two men in 2040 and their partners in 2044: The end of a dynasty maybe, but one that left its mark and was to continue to do so.

EPILOGUE
The New Royal London Majestic Hotel 2030

Margaret (Maggie) Marie Nicholson Varón adjusted her hair in the mirror, and brushed down her dark blue *haut couture* tailored two piece suit. She stood looking at herself for a minute or so, to ensure everything was in place. With her black hair tied back she epitomised the image of a hardnosed beautiful businesswoman: Stunning features, dark brown eyes and legs that most women would envy. They took after her mother's in shape and length.

She was single, never married but had had her fair share of lovers. Never wanting to be tied down nor wanting to get married and then divorced, the family motto of 'Work Comes First' was embedded into her by her father and his family. She didn't want or need the complication and ties which that life would bring her. The path she had chosen was the one that had seen her to this point without emotional or physical baggage: She had just turned forty years of age; and here she was, in the New Royal London Majestic Hotel, the company's recently reformed flagship. Now, with two hundred and fifty bedrooms, banqueting facilities for up to five hundred and fifty, a health and beauty spa, a three starred Michelin restaurant, twenty four hour brasserie,

Champagne and Caviar bar and an exclusive wine bar and bistro with an entrance from the street, as well as the established roof top 'country club', RoofTops.

After her graduation from Les Roches, she had followed in her father's footsteps and worked her way up the management ladder including spells in Nice and Paris, General Manager of the newly opened Bristol Majestic in Bristol, before taking over the Paris Majestic. She opened the door of the Managing Director's suite of the New Royal London Majestic Hotel and walked out into the top floor hallway as Managing Director of the hotel and subsequently, the group.

"Good morning, Ma'am" said the housekeeper.

"Good morning Mister Clarke," she said looking at his name tag. With nearly three hundred staff, it was going to take some time to get to know all their names and with the transitory nature of the hotel industry she would be unlikely to complete that task. She went into the lift and met a room service waiter wheeling a breakfast trolley to one of the suites on that floor. *"Bonjour Madame,"* said the smartly dressed French waiter.

"Bonjour Charles," said Maggie once again using the name tag as a prompt.

The lift doors opened into the vast, elegant space of the lobby. The smell of luxury permeated throughout as the receptionists were busy booking people out and porters carrying guest's belongings on their familiar electrically driven brass hotel luggage trolleys.

"Good morning Ms Nicolson," said the good looking reception manager around his mid thirties.

"Good morning Andrew," she didn't need the name tag as she had previously been introduced to him, and with his well coiffured hair, sharp features and perfect bum, he was memorable.

Charly Marston, the pretty looking blonde haired woman in her late twenties, the front of house manager, walked towards her and joined her on the walk to Maggie's office. "Morning Ma'am, are we still on for the heads of department meeting at 10.00 am?"

"I see no reason not to Charly; I have got to get to know the team as quickly as possible. Can you ask someone to bring me some coffee and a *croissant*. Also can you let me have the night manager's report? In fact, to get to know the place better, let me have the last two week's reports."

The deputy general manager walked into the office with the night manager's report book. Graham George was the same age as Maggie and was on his last few months here until Maggie had settled in. He had worked with her in Nice and Bristol as her Deputy before moving to the New London Majestic but was now leaving to join the Paris Majestic as General Manager. With his dark looks and swept back black hair, clean shaven, chiselled face and six foot plus with an expensive suit draped over him, he was certainly hot. He

smiled at her as he presented the book, "Good Morning Ms Nicolson, welcome to the hotel."
"Good morning Mister George, how lovely to see you again." She got up and shook his hand, not letting it go easily.
He smiled and reciprocated the grip, "A shame it may not be for long."
"You never know in life what can happen, do you Graham?"
"No, you never know Maggie," smiling the smile that said it all. What had passed and what may yet come.

'The world keeps on turning,
You can't stop it turning,
For love makes the world go round
An old love, a new love,
So long as it's true love,
It's love makes the world go 'round.
D. Furber & L. A. Rose. 'Me and My Girl'

It can start with a dream.
It needs hard work and determination.
It needs love and loyalty to achieve goals.
It is all about family and ethics.
It needs some luck as well as guidance
It can culminate in achievement and success; providing you want it to.
What is 'it'?
'It' — is Life.
'Work Comes First' — should it always?

Printed in Great Britain
by Amazon